G000140873

Amok

ANNA TAN

Published by:
Teaspoon Publishing
Penang, Malaysia.
https://teaspoonpublishing.com.my

This is a work of fiction. Names, characters, places, and incidents either are the product of the author's imagination or are used fictitiously. Any resemblance to actual persons, living or dead, events, or locales is entirely coincidental.

Copyright © 2021 Anna Tan Shuh Ping
Cover image design & layout: Jiwosophy | http://jiwosophy.co

All rights reserved. No part of this book may be reproduced in any form on by an electronic or mechanical means, including information storage and retrieval systems, without permission in writing from the publisher, except by a reviewer who may quote brief passages in a review.

ISBN 978-967-19634-0-1 (paperback)
eISBN 978-967-19634-1-8 (ebook)

Perpustakaan Negara Malaysia   Cataloguing-in-Publication Data
Tan, Anna, 1984-
    Amok / ANNA TAN.
    ISBN 978-967-19634-0-1
    1. English fiction.
    2. Malaysian fiction (English).
    I. Title.
    823.92

CONTENTS

For those who still await the promise.

cg

O Lord God, remember me, I pray You, and strengthen me, I pray You, only this once, O God, and let me have one vengeance upon the Philistines for both my eyes.
—Judges 16:28b

CHAPTER 1

I wait. Of course I wait.

Just that split second before the fight, waiting for Kudus to come through, to finally grant me His supernatural power, the Amok Strength that's supposed to run through my veins.

O *Kudus, Maha Esa, berkatilah hamba-Mu dengan kuasa ajaib-Mu.*

O *God Almighty, grant Your servant Your miraculous strength.*

I push stray hair out of my face as I wait, hoping for that stirring of power, for that gifting Ayahanda has described in multiple ways time and time again: that surety and Presence, the surge of raw power and rage, sparks running through his limbs.

They say Kudus is never changing. He never disappoints. Well, He doesn't disappoint. Nothing happens. No power, no presence. Just the continued silence of the past five years, ever since I started silat training at the age of ten.

Tok Yaakub and I circle each other, bare feet stirring up clouds of dust from the packed dirt of the gelanggang. He slashes at me with his keris and I slash

1

back, dancing backwards and forwards to the warm breeze. There's sweat in my eyes and on my palms, frustration in my soul and in my forms.

This match ends as it always does with his double-edged dagger at my chest. At least this time, I'm not flat on my back. He grunts in disappointment and withdraws his blade. We take a step backwards, bow to each other with our hands clasped in front of our chests, blades facing down. The fight is over and we bear no ill will to each other.

"That was terrible, Putera Mikal," Tok Yaakub says. "What's wrong with you today?"

Everything. It's hot, I'm sticky with sweat, my hair is itchy on my face, I still haven't earned my Amok Strength, there's a delegation from Bayangan no one is talking about, rumour says we're about to go to war, Ayahanda has been distant and busy all week…

"Nothing." I wipe the sweat off my face with the back of my sleeve. It's not that I don't trust him. Besides training me in silat, Tok Yaakub teaches me military tactics and strategies. He's one of the few adults I trust with my life—but he's also one of my father's men and sits on the Majlis as Temenggung, the commander of our military and head of security. Which means I don't trust him with my secrets.

"Come, let us put away the keris and go hand to hand. Get some of that restless energy out of you." He wipes down his keris and lays it on the outer edge of the marked circle.

My keris is about the length of my forearm. I take my time to shine each curve of the iron blade before I sheath it, rubbing away my sweat from the carved, gilded hilt. Then I walk to the opposite end of the circle and place it on the stand. I don't have to. There's no rule that says I should do so. I retie my knee-long hair into a bun so it will stop flying in my face then adjust my belt for the absence of the keris.

I turn to find Tok Yaakub scrutinising me with a worried look. *His* hair is neatly tied at the nape and falls down to his waist. I don't know how he does it. Maybe it's part of the Amok gift that's extended from my father the Sultan to him as Temenggung.

"Are you sure you're not ill?" He crosses the circle towards me and I duck to avoid the arc of his hand that's trying to feel my forehead.

"I said it's nothing, Tok Yaakub. I'm not sick."

He sniffs in disbelief. "It's never nothing with young men like you. Now either you best me or you tell me what's bothering you."

This time I don't wait. I don't bother with protocol that says we have to face each other and bow, that courtesy of making sure he's ready. No one's going to wait for me to be ready in war. He's always ready though, he's always prepared, so I can't break through his defences, no matter how high or how low I strike, arms, legs or elbows.

We break apart and circle each other again.

"Is Terang at war?" I blurt.

A look of caution enters his face, his eyes wary, searching me. "Where did—what do you mean?"

"Where did I hear that? People talk you know, and sometimes I listen."

He grimaces and straightens his stance, dropping his hands. "Do you see any armies? Any fighting?"

I haven't, but Yosua heard it from his father, and Garett's rumours are always right. It may not be here yet, but it's coming. I straighten as well, folding my arms. "Why else are the Bayangans here?" I don't know why I'm saying this—this is Majlis business I'm not supposed to know about—but once I start, there's no stopping the flow.

"They're not here for—"

"Ayahanda doesn't tell me anything. Am I not old enough to be involved in the affairs of the sultanate?"

"Tuanku, your father—"

"I'm next in line to the throne, Tok Yaakub, but I don't know anything that's happening in Terang—or even here in Maha! My personal attendant, my *servant*, knows more than I do!" Yosua has always known more than me through the servant's gossip, but I don't say this. I can't tell Tok Yaakub that almost every bit of news I hear comes from my servant because no one else in the palace tells me anything. "I don't know what's going on and the Majlis thinks I'm stupid and naive. They look at me and say I need to be responsible, that I need to act for the best of the sultanate. Then they look down on me because they think I don't...but the truth is I can't because I don't *know* anything."

My voice cracks and I wince. My eyes are prickling and my face is hot.

I'm fifteen, not five.

I steel myself and glare at the face of my teacher, who looks bemused. It rankles. I am Mikal ayell Simson, only son of Sultan Simson of Maha, the First City of Terang. I am a *prince* not some backwater fool or village champion trying to act smart.

To distract myself, I rush him again, aiming low to bring him down. He turns it against me instead, flipping me to land on my back, his hand pinning my chest on the floor.

"Your time will come, Putera Mikal. It's not that your father doesn't trust you. He's just distracted by this unexpected delegation and Majlis business. He hasn't realised you are old enough to stand by his side and support him. Don't worry. He will remember you. You're still young, Tuanku. There is no rush."

Bitterness spills out of my mouth before I can pull it back. "Maybe you should tell that to the rest of the Majlis. They all look down on me."

"Why do you think that? I've not heard any of them speak badly of you."

"They wouldn't do that in your presence, Tok. They know you teach me. They don't say it to my face either. I just hear their snide remarks in passing, as if I am a child."

Tok Yaakub smiles. He offers me a hand and I use it to pull myself up. "You *are* a child. You haven't even been officially appointed Raja Muda yet."

And I won't be appointed until I gain my Strength. "You know what I mean."

"I do know what you mean. You're a young man with too much energy, chafing at the fact that you have no destiny to fulfil, no war to fight. You think your father has forgotten you and the Majlis snubs you. I assure you, they do not. I will talk to them—"

"No! They will think me even more childish and churlish then, to have come and whined to you."

Tok Yaakub cocks an eyebrow. "Which you have done."

"Yes, but I know you will keep it confidential." I think. I hope. I should never have said anything. Maybe they're right. Maybe I'm not ready enough for this.

"Hmmm." He draws it out and his eyes crinkle and I know he's teasing me now. "And so I will."

We stand there looking at each other until he says, "Are we done?"

"Yes. I'm done."

We make our belated bows. Even though we stopped sparring a while ago, this also signifies the end of our conversation, the battle of our words.

Tok Yaakub lays a hand on my shoulder. "You can confide in me, Tuanku. I'll always keep what you tell me confidential. And not judge you."

"Now I'm worried you will judge me." My laugh sounds stilted and forced even to my ears.

"When have I ever judged you?"

"All the time, Tok. Especially when you disarm me over and over again."

"Ah, but that's only on your ineptitude at silat, not on your capabilities and outstanding qualities as a fine young prince."

The Temple bells toll, a deep and insistent call to the faithful, startling me. We were meant to have finished training half an hour ago. Now I'll have to rush to get ready for the weekly Temple meeting. "Ayahanda will be expecting me at Jemaah."

Tok Yaakub nods. "I will see you there, Tuanku."

I give him another hasty bow, grab my keris, and lope through the long corridors towards my suite.

ɔɜ

Yosua isn't anywhere to be seen when I burst through the door. The suite is dim, light falling on the polished floor in fancy patterns through the carved ventilation vents near the ceiling, but all the wooden shutters are closed and the lamps lie cold.

"Yos?"

It's not like him to be unprepared on Jemaah day—sometimes I think he's more religious than I am. He should be screaming at me and rushing me along right now. I push the nearest two windows open with a clack, letting more light in.

I dodge the sofa piled with pillows—he seems to at least have cleaned and straightened up the living room—and hurry across the open space towards my bedroom. Maybe he's in there, running late. I fling the drapes aside. The large canopy bed is made, mosquito netting tied back. The spot where he usually lays out my clothes is empty.

"Yosua! Where are you?"

The bathroom is cold and dry, lacking the refreshing bath I was looking forward to. This is unacceptable.

"Yosua, why haven't you prepared my bath?" I storm over to the connecting door to his room and pound on it. There's no reply.

"Yos?"

I fling the door open to an empty room. It's not the first time I've seen it, but it strikes me again how small and cramped it is. There's a narrow cot on the left, neatly made, threadbare sheet covering an equally thin mattress. A flat pillow lies at its head and a blanket is folded at its foot. Yosua should ask housekeeping to replace these items. The white walls are bare and stark, cold and impersonal. In the far corner is a single washstand and opposite it, a cupboard. Yosua is a genius to be able to fit all his belongings in that one cupboard and on his bedside table. This doesn't help me find him, though.

I close the door and consider my options. Yos is not here and I'm running out of time. I can't turn up at Jemaah in my training clothes, trailing the sweat and dust of the gelanggang. The priests would not accept it and the council would look down on me even more. I eye the wardrobe, unsure which of the four doors would lead to my Jemaah clothes. The one on the farthest right, I think. With a muttered prayer of thanks, I pull out the first set of baju I see. I'm going to box Yos when I see him next. It's the *one* day of the week I really need clean hair and he's not here to help me.

Washing and combing my hair alone is one of the most annoying experiences of my life. I've done it several times before, but it's always more convenient to have Yosua help me. Most of the time, I feel that the only reason I need a personal attendant is to deal with my hair. I want to cut it, but I can't. Not if I ever hope to inherit the Amok Strength. Not unless I want to give up my vows and my future throne.

By the time I walk through the imposing double doors of the Temple and hurry to the first row of pews, Ayahanda is scowling, lips pressed into a tight line. They can't start Jemaah without me. Right.

"Where have you been?" His voice is as tight as the folds of his turban, as sharp as creases on his trousers.

I haven't bothered with a turban and the wet patch on the back of my trousers is from my still-damp hair. "My training with Tok Yaakub ended late, Ayahanda. Then I was delayed because Yosua had not prepared—"

"You know Jemaah is today. Why were you not ready? No, no more excuses. You must be responsible, Mikal. How can I pass the throne to you if I can't trust you?"

That word again, *responsible*. I'm sick of it. I lower my head and mumble, "It will not happen again, Ayahanda."

"See that it doesn't." He turns away so I follow suit, staring ahead at the priests and trying to calm my thoughts.

I hate it when he makes me feel this way, as if I were a wayward toddler instead of his grown-up heir. His displeasure irks me though, because it really *isn't* my fault. It's not as if I could predict training would run overtime on the same day Yosua failed me. If he'd been where he should have been, this wouldn't have happened. I turn to see if Yosua is anywhere in the crowd.

He isn't. At least, not that I can see. As a Bayangan, he would be way back in the crowd anyway—the first row is reserved for my family and visiting dignitaries, the next block of about four rows for the seven members of the council and their families, followed by another block of six or so rows for the noble families of Maha.

Ayahanda's hand twitches and I focus ahead again. A feeling of unease pervades the Temple and the hairs on my arms stand on edge. Paderi Nur, the second in command of the Temple, stutters in her recital of the liturgy. The serving diaken, her assistant, drops the censer, spilling incense and oil all over the altar. The congregation gasps. Everything comes to a stop.

Uskup Daud, the head of the Temple in Maha, rises to his feet, hands trembling. He steps forward and I expect him to take over the ceremony, or to chastise the offending pair. Instead, he spins to face us and roars one word, "Repent!"

I sense more than see Ayahanda tensing beside me, his hands balling into fists. He's been quarrelling with Uskup Daud for weeks now, ever since he sent the last uskup back to Suci. This isn't going to turn out well.

"The time has come! Terang is far from Me. You must repent or disaster will strike at your borders, and terrors at your very heart. Beginning with you, O Sultan!" He looks straight at Ayahanda.

"Silence!" Ayahanda surges to his feet, face mottling.

No. Ayahanda can't do this. A burst of temper in the Temple might trigger a series of cleansing rituals, guilt offerings, sin offerings—who knew what?—and with a new war looming, no matter what Tok Yaakub says, a formal standoff between Palace and Temple isn't ideal. I try to hold him back, but he shrugs me off.

"Repent! Turn your heart back to Kudus before Terang is destroyed," the uskup bellows.

Repent of what? What has Ayahanda done now?

Ayahanda stalks forward, planting his feet in front of the altar and sneers in the uskup's face. "The Mahan priesthood is deviant. I demand Suci replace you—"

"It is you who brings judgement upon us, O Sultan! Your love has—"

"Silence that blasphemer. Put him in the cells!" Ayahanda turns away and flicks a thumb at Uskup Daud.

Chaos erupts. I watch in horror as royal guards march up to the front of the Temple and lay their hands on the sacred person of the uskup.

Why is he doing this? He's supposed to be protecting this sanctuary, not destroying it!

"Ayahanda?"

Still snarling at the uskup, he doesn't hear me.

The roar of sound builds in the enclosed hall. No one seems to have maintained any decorum. There's yelling and screaming, even from the priests, their usual solemn demeanour stripped away. Groups of frantic diaken—assistants and acolytes in the Temple—swarm around the soldiers only to be swatted away like buzzing flies.

Uskup Daud is dragged out even though he's not struggling. The royal guards aren't armed—no one's allowed to be armed in the Temple—and they don't need to be. Ayahanda's Strength flows through them, fuelled by his rage, and they manhandle the uskup out of the building.

It's Ayahanda who is making the biggest scene, red-faced and screaming. The council members watch us solemnly and I feel the weight of their judgement. I need to do something, say something to calm Ayahanda down. If only my mother were still alive! They say Ibunda used to stop him with a twitch of her eyebrow, the merest glint of her displeasure. I look for support but find none. Tok Yaakub is sitting with his face in his hands.

This isn't the first time Ayahanda has caused trouble with the Temple. Kudus knows he stirred up enough ill will during Ibunda's long illness and her eventual death. He's railed against Kudus, the Uskup Agung in Suci, and the Mahan Temple many times in the intervening years and imprisoned more priests than I can count on both hands. I don't even know what sets him off anymore. But this is the first time he's interrupted Jemaah and arrested the head of the Temple himself in public.

I lay a hand on Ayahanda's shoulder, drawing his attention. He stops mid-rant to glare at me and I want to shrivel up on the spot and die. Before I can say anything, he pulls away and leaves.

CHAPTER 2

There's still no sign of Yosua when I get back to my room and flop down on my bed.

Paderi Nur has assured me the Temple will be alright, reminding me of the priests' Perantaraan gift that allows them to communicate directly to Suci, the holy city where the Uskup Agung is based. Uskup Agung Ikhlas, the ruler of Suci and head of religion in our united sultanate of Terang, will tell them what to do and negotiate with Ayahanda for Uskup Daud's release. Still, I want to find out what Uskup Daud meant—if the guards let me visit him. They'd barred me from visiting the last priest Ayahanda imprisoned.

Though the sun has set and dinner is about to be served, I dawdle, pacing my room as I wait for Yosua. I can't think of any more excuses for him and now I'm beginning to think something must have happened. Has he met with an accident? I finally give in to my hunger and head down to the formal dining room without bothering to change out of my Jemaah clothes. It's not as if Ayahanda will notice anyway.

The troupe has started playing the night's entertainment when I enter the dining room. Several people mutter as I walk past them to my seat at Ayahanda's right. Dinner has been served.

Ayahanda is busy talking to the lady on his left, so whilst I mumble my apologies and sit down, I study her. She has a light cast to her skin, much fairer than the women of Terang, a stark contrast against the deep black of her dress. Her hair is loose, a light brown, almost the same shade as Yosua's. There's a feel of something exotic, something forbidden, and I wonder if she is one of the Bayangan delegation everyone has been avoiding talking about. Ayahanda addresses her as Layla a few times, but doesn't drop any other clues about who she is or what her rank is.

Layla smiles at me. "It's good to meet you, Putera Mikal."

"A pleasure, Tengku." I go for a high title, just short of royalty, just in case. It's better to flatter someone than to insult them, anyway. Ayahanda doesn't reprimand me and neither does Layla, so she must be someone high-ranking.

"Simson tells me you're a very good student," she says. She looks me in the eyes, her hand resting lightly on my father's forearm.

I try not to gawk as I thank her.

"I have nothing but glowing reports from his instructors," Ayahanda says with an indulgent smile. Not at me, at her. A cold hand grips my heart and a shiver runs up my spine.

"I'm sure he's a great asset to you," she replies, returning a bright smile of her own.

I don't know what's more unsettling—the way they're smiling at each other, or the fact that Ayahanda seems so enamoured of this unknown woman. Or maybe the way she casually refers to him by just his name. It's not allowed. Only the other two members of the triumvirate rank high enough to do that. Even *I* don't refer to him by his name, and he's my father! Ayahanda is addressed by his title of Sultan or Tuanku when spoken to in person. When others speak of him, he's referred to as Baginda Paduka.

I ladle a generous portion of chickpea curry on my plate and tear at my roti with my fingers, dipping the warm flat bread into the curry. The rest of the table is filled with council members and nobles, though there is a scattering of unfamiliar faces who must be from the lady's retinue. If this is the Bayangan delegation that's been kept a secret, something significant must have happened today that they are showing their faces in public. Yosua should know something—

Where *is* Yosua? I don't expect to find him in the dining hall—he rarely gets pulled into dinner duty—so it's no great surprise I don't see him anywhere around. I flag down a passing servant to ask, but he hasn't seen Yosua either.

"What's the matter?" Ayahanda asks.

"Nothing important, Ayahanda. I'm just looking for Yosua."

"The Bayangan houseboy?"

That's a strange way to describe Yosua, but I nod.

"A boy from Bayangan?" Layla asks.

Ayahanda is flippant as he replies, "His family is of the line. Been here since the last war, serves in the palace."

"As your slaves."

"No!" Ayahanda bristles. "We don't believe in slaves in Terang, not like you Bayangan."

"Don't you?" Her eyes narrow.

"All our servants are paid. We don't own them or keep them prisoner."

"But they can't return home."

Ayahanda shifts in his chair. "I suppose they could, but they don't want to."

She purses her lips then says, "They don't want to. I see. And how do you know that?"

"Because they don't. None of them have tried to leave."

"What terms did you put on their survival? Death? Torture? Swore them and their families to serve your line?"

Garett has mentioned a pledge before in passing, and I wonder if it's related.

Ayahanda just shrugs. "Nothing they didn't willingly promise to keep the peace. What does that have to do with us now, Tuanku?"

That final formality is the only thing that shows his irritation, and now I know for sure who she is: Permaisuri Layla Regis Ishi, the newly-crowned queen of Bayangan.

Oh.

She pauses, her face thoughtful. "Nothing. I was just surprised to discover that some of my people are here." She turns to me. "What has happened to this servant of yours, Putera Mikal?"

I look up at her, right hand hovering between my plate and my mouth. I put my hand down and answer, "I haven't seen him since breakfast so I'm a little worried if something has happened to him, that's all."

"I'm sure he's fine," Ayahanda says, "He's probably shirking somewhere like they tend to do."

Layla's expression tightens just a little.

"It's not like him, Ayahanda. Yos is always so conscientious. And he never misses Jemaah! Something must have happened."

Ayahanda waves a hand. "Give it a day. He'll turn up tomorrow and grovel."

A hard look flits across Layla's face, disappearing before my father can see it. Her lips part then press into a weird smile. There's an awkward silence between us, masked by the strains of music from the ensemble.

"This troupe is very good," Layla says.

I nod. They're playing one of the founding stories of Terang, a theatre-dance ensemble that features younger performers. I wonder what Layla thinks about the fact that half of them look like they have Bayangan heritage. I'm sure she's just ignoring it out of courtesy.

It's a piece I'm particularly fond of, one that Yos used to perform when we were children, before he'd been assigned to my service. I'd been so jealous I'd begged to be allowed to learn to dance, only to be told that the art was meant for courtesans and servants. Not satisfied, I pestered Yosua into teaching me some of the moves and hand signals in private.

I search for them out of habit: the open left hand, palm down, meaning *wait*; two hands clenched on each other, pulled in to their chests, signalling *trust*. Terang was founded on trusting and waiting on Kudus. The two signals are repeated many times in this piece, though the performers' movements are so fluid it's difficult to pick them out unless you're looking for them. I wonder who selected this piece for tonight. Not Ayahanda, surely. It's not the thing he'd select right after arguing with the Temple. Neither is he paying attention to it. Tok Yaakub is, though, and I wonder if he was the one who requested it. He nods in my direction when he notices me watching him.

I pick at the kuih served for dessert until I can excuse myself from dinner. Ayahanda just grunts his approval, still concentrating on Permaisuri Layla. She gives me a slight smile as I leave.

Since Yosua is not in the dining room, I doubt he'll be in the kitchens, but I check there anyway. Marla, my ex-nursemaid and Yosua's mother, shakes her head and seems surprised.

"I've been busy here all day, Tuanku. I've no energy to chase after wayward sons on Jemaah day. If I see him, I'll help you spank him for causing so much trouble."

"Just send him my way, Marla," I reply in amusement.

"He stopped by during lunchtime, Tuanku," a kitchen help says as she passes by holding a tray full of dirty dishes. "Siti packed him something as he said he was going to do your laundry."

I thank her and hurry off to the laundry rooms. If Yosua had ever been there, he's long gone. If he'd been injured, however, someone would have taken him to the infirmary, so that's where I check next. There's no one there.

An odd thought grips me: maybe he's run away.

CB

I'm still mulling the fact that Yosua might have left Maha, like Permaisuri Layla suggested, when I realise that I'm in the servants' wing heading to Garett's room. Marla may not know where her son is but her husband might—if Yosua had checked in with him before he disappeared. I don't believe it. He would never run away, not without telling me.

The place seems dingier and darker than I remember, the corridors lit with dim oil lamps that look like they haven't been cleaned in months. The walls are blackened with soot from the lamps. It's a far cry from the clean, bright corridors of the main palace. I don't know why none of the servants bother to clean up. It seemed brighter and cheerier the last time I was here. I count the years and am shocked to realise it's been nine years. It doesn't feel that long ago.

I knock on the once-familiar door. There's a scuffling and scraping inside before the door opens and I'm face to face with Yosua himself. His eyes are swollen almost shut, face covered with deep purple-and-red bruises and angry gashes that stand out against his fair skin. Dried blood clings to the cracks of his puffy lips. He's cradling his left arm.

"Yos! What happened?"

Yosua winces and moves to close the door. I stick my foot in the crack and push the door open again.

Yosua stumbles backwards. "Tuan…" *Master.*

"Let him in," Garett's deep voice calls from inside.

Yosua's shoulders slump and he steps aside for me to enter. He shuts and latches the door behind me, then heads back towards his father.

The room hasn't changed much, though it's smaller than I remember. This used to be my refuge from the craziness that descended on the palace after Ibunda's death, the one place where Marla's calm prevailed. Yosua's pallet is still there, next to his parents' double bed; why they keep it, I don't know. It feels like a waste of this cramped space.

Garett has lit a small fire in the grate and is bending over a boiling pot of water. He stands as I approach, his greeting a muttered *Tuanku. Your Highness.* Stacks of bandages line the table alongside a jar of soothing cream. He puts the bowl of warm water down on the table, looks at Yosua, and jerks his head towards the chair. He dips a cloth in the bowl and waits.

Yosua gives me a sidelong glance before he shrugs off his shirt, trying not to move his arm. He lowers himself onto the chair.

"What happened to you, Yos?" I ask. "Why aren't you in the infirmary?"

"Nothing that concerns you, Tuanku, nor the infirmary," Garett says firmly.

Those cuts and bruises look bad. "I'd say it concerns me, Garett. Someone attacked my personal servant. This could be taken as an attack on myself."

"No, no, Tuan. It had nothing to do—" Yosua starts protesting but he's cut off by his father. Yosua's paler than ever, wild-eyed.

They stare at each other, a strange battle of wills I haven't witnessed before. He's usually as compliant to Garett's orders as I am to my father's.

"Would either of you like to tell me what's going on?"

"Tuanku, you know how it is between Terang and Bayangan." Garett has won this round, it seems. He concentrates on treating Yosua's wounds, which look even worse in the light of the flickering candle on the table.

"Do I?"

"Things have been brewing since the delegation arrived last week. Maybe the illustrious Sultan—"

"He tells me nothing," I interrupt. More oblique references to this shadowy delegation. "I hear more from Yos than from him."

Garett apologises, looking up from his work. "I don't know if they bring it up in Majlis, but they surely must be aware…" He trails off at my shrug.

"I'm sure the council knows many things. But as I am not invited to Majlis meetings, it is hard for me to say what they do or do not know."

An uneasy silence falls in the room. Garett ignores me as he continues to apply cream to Yosua's wounds. I stare at the mouldy walls, ignoring Yosua's gaze.

I cannot take it any longer. "Who attacked you? Tell me."

Yosua opens his mouth but shuts it again at Garett's glare.

"It wasn't an attack," Garett says in slow, measured tones. "This was nothing more than a little…racial tension." He ties off a final bandage a little too hard and Yosua winces. Garett's face softens but he doesn't say anything, still not looking at me.

"A little racial tension that has caused my personal attendant pain and has taken him from my service for more than half a day. With no one knowing where he was or what had happened to him."

"I'm sorry, Tuan!" Yosua blurts. He looks close to panic. Good. "I should have returned or informed you—"

"Yes, you should have. You should have let *someone* know or sent a message and I could have helped you. Instead, I have wasted half a day looking and asking after you. Only Kudus knows what everyone thinks of me now!"

Garett and Yosua exchange guilty looks. I can't help but feel victorious, even though it's a petty thing.

"I apologise, Tuanku," Garett says. "That would be my fault. When I found him unconscious, I took him directly back here and didn't think of involving the infirmary or informing you."

"I see. Where did you find him?"

Yosua speaks before his father can stop him. "On the road from the city, Tuan."

O Kudus, had he really been trying to run away? My heart drops. "What were you doing in the city? Who gave you permission?"

"Ampun, Tuan," Yosua apologises in a hoarse whisper. "I just wanted to see the parade. I had finished all my chores, I swear."

My anger has run out and my victory has fizzled and I don't know what else to do but say, "Well, see it doesn't happen again."

I head to the door and am about to leave when I hear Yosua's soft moan. I'm sure he meant to muffle it, but it's loud in my ears. I pause, still holding the door open, but don't look back when I say, "I doubt you'll be much use until you heal, so take the next few days off until your eyes stop swelling, at least. And I want a daily update, Garett."

It's as heartless as I can bear sounding. I walk away, letting the door slam behind me.

CHAPTER 3

I am as restless as the waves so I pace the corridors. I cannot bear the thought of being cooped up in my room right now, no matter how many windows I can open or what winds blow through. With each pass, I study the servants who scuttle by. Their numbers dwindle as activity around the palace slows.

Many of them have a lighter cast of skin and hair like Yosua and his family. They've always been here; I grew up with Yosua as my playmate, his mother as my nursemaid. I don't know what Garett does but he was always out early in the morning and back late in the evening, physically exhausted. I cannot imagine Maha without them, though others older than me can, those who were born before the end of the war, before Ayahanda destroyed the bridge and closed the ports.

The servants look exhausted after dinner, ill-fitting, threadbare clothes stained with grease and dirt. Maybe it's some form of Bayangan frugality—Yosua has berated me often to be less wasteful—but I'm sure the palace coffers are not that empty to be unable to replace some of those rags. The darker-skinned

Mahans are better dressed, smarter, crisper, more confident. Most of those head towards the gates instead of the servants' wing.

Soon enough, there's no one left to study, no one to distract me so I head out to the gelanggang. The sprawling palace complex towers over me, all tall graceful pillars in deep brown, almost black in the moonlight. I slip into the forms, letting their familiarity calm me.

Silat lets me forget about the world. By focusing on my body, on the physicality of movement and control of my self, I can push away the thoughts that buzz in my head, from why the Bayangan permaisuri is flirting with my father to who would dare beat up my servant.

Silat also focuses me on the one thing I lack: my family's Amok gift.

O Kudus, Maha Esa, You created this world, You gave us this power, why do You hide Your face from me? What have I done wrong? Do You not love me enough to give me this one thing? This one thing You have promised? I'm not asking for the world, Kudus. I'm just asking for my inheritance.

I haven't broken my vows—no razor has touched a hair on my head, no matter how much I sometimes itch to shave everything off; no alcoholic drink has passed my lips. I attend Jemaah every first day of the week and have offered my sacrifice every year since I turned twelve as required. I have studied the Firman backwards and forwards and can recite any number of verses, even *chapters*, sometimes better than the diaken. None of the paderi overseeing my religious studies can fault my knowledge or my faithfulness.

Each successive uskup in Maha says to keep waiting, keep waiting on Kudus. They remind me often that everything comes in His time. Maybe I am too impatient and He is punishing me for it. Maybe I have some hidden sin I refuse to confess. Maybe I want it too much, more than I want Kudus himself, which is why He is withholding this gift from me. I must pursue Kudus, the gift-giver and not the gift.

Only Uskup Daud has said the one thing that is raw, honest, and doesn't hurt as much: *Who knows the mind of Kudus? His decisions are not your fault.*

I look up at the stars shimmering in the dark sky, the moon almost at its zenith. I'd meant to visit Uskup Daud earlier, but the prospect of Yosua running away had unsettled me, driving all thoughts of the altercation at the Temple out of my mind. It isn't too late yet. In fact, the timing may even be better—the reduced number of patrols at this time of night would lower my chances of being seen. Prisoners aren't denied visitors as long as they're recorded, but I don't want Ayahanda to find out that I've seen the uskup.

The Mahan jail is a separate building annexed to the palace, mostly empty and sparsely guarded. Ayahanda doesn't believe in long term imprisonment—another reason I should see Uskup Daud as soon as possible. Ayahanda won't execute a member of the priesthood as he does spies and dissidents but he'll exile him in the next few days. If I don't see him now, there's no guarantee he'll still be there tomorrow.

There's no one about as I sneak up to the jail. I pause to listen. Guards parade past at sporadic intervals, but I don't know when the last one passed by to be able to guess when the next one will come. I duck into a nearby recess, the thudding of my heart loud in my ears.

A flickering shadow grows against the wall before the soft thud of soles on the packed dirt registers in my hearing. Sheer luck has kept me hidden. Holding my breath, I press against the wall until the footsteps fade and there are no more moving shadows. I count to fifteen before slipping out of the nook and continuing into the building.

Most of the cells I pass by are empty. Uskup Daud is in one of the cells right in the centre of the building. He's on his knees in the middle of the narrow space, facing north towards Suci, muttering in prayer.

"Uskup Daud!"

His head shoots up, eyes wild. He spins around, searching in all directions before he catches sight of me and sighs in what I hope is relief. His eyes flutter shut for a second as his hand clutches at his chest and he mutters something.

"What are you doing here, Tuanku?" he asks as he approaches me.

"I came to find out how you're doing."

"I'm fine. I will be fine," he amends.

Now that I'm here, I don't really know what I want to ask. Or how to even ask it.

He catches on to my uncertainty. "Does Baginda Paduka know you're here?"

I shake my head. "No, I snuck past the guards. Ayahanda doesn't…I didn't ask him because I didn't think he'd want me to talk to you."

"I see." He massages the bridge of his nose. "What troubles you, my child?"

"Earlier…" I fumble, cheeks burning. Why was I here? Why had I insisted to Tok Yaakub that I was ready for this? "At Jemaah you said—was that a prophecy?"

"What do you consider a prophecy?"

How am I supposed to know? "A foretelling of the future? I mean, what I want to know is if what you said will happen?"

"What was spoken today may or may not come to pass. Whether prophetic or not, it is, at the very least, a warning. A warning that if Maha continues down this road, judgement will come and Terang will be destroyed."

"But then my father…What Ayahanda did wasn't right. If it's truly from Kudus, why did he…" I gesture at the cell and Uskup Daud, unsure how to put things into words.

"Baginda Paduka Sultan Simson doesn't like what Kudus is saying to him, so he punishes the messengers instead."

I look for accusation in his face, but it's neutral, like a statement of fact. "What *is* Kudus saying to him?"

"You were there, Tuanku. Did you not hear the message? Or are you one of the deaf?"

I want him to repeat his message, but he looks at me as if I'm the village idiot.

"Repent?" It's the only thing that stood out in the chaos, the one thing Uskup Daud had repeated over and over, as if he were drumming it into my head. I sag sideways against the bars with a huff. "I don't know. It's all a blur. Repent of his actions, something about him causing destruction to Terang…"

The priest frowns his disapproval. "Judgement is coming, Putera Mikal. If not in this generation, then the next. Instead of dealing with it in the right way, in Kudus' way, Sultan Simson is taking things into his own hands. He seeks alliances and treaties that are not in alignment with the will of Kudus."

His voice rises with each word and I glance around desperately, trying to shush him. He ignores me, speaking as if he is delivering a sermon.

"Has he forgotten that we are not to ally ourselves with the enemy? Yet he entertains the Bayangan permaisuri, gives her parades in the city as an honoured guest, seats her at his own table. I can feel Kudus withdrawing His presence, Tuanku. If your father does not repent, it will go from us altogether, and the fall of Maha and all Terang will come with it."

"Is there no hope? No other way out?"

"You can watch and pray, my child. Prepare your heart—if your father persists in this manner, the mantle will fall on you to bring this city back to the proper worship of Kudus, Maha Esa, Almighty God of Terang."

"I'm just—"

He makes an impatient noise. "You won't always be a child. Do not fool yourself, Putera Mikal. If Maha falls, a penance will be required and the Covenant of Salt will need to be renewed. Whether it falls upon you or upon your children depends on your actions in this time. Kudus' wrath and vengeance can be delayed only for a time."

There's a sound in the corridor and I freeze. It's too soon. The patrols are not usually this frequent. Has someone heard us? I've barely found out anything! Uskup Daud falls silent too, looking past me into the gloom. I strain to listen, but there's nothing else to be heard. False alarm. Perhaps it was some nocturnal animal.

I heave a sigh of relief. "So Ayahanda—"

"Sultan Simson needs to repent. He is departing from the ways of Kudus, which will lead him—and Terang—to destruction. You must stop him."

"But what can I do? Ayahanda doesn't listen to me. No one listens to me. The Majlis—"

Uskup Daud lunges and grips my hands through the bars. "You must tell Baginda Paduka that his past disobedience will catch up with him. The Bayangans in Maha, the alliance with the permaisuri, this Garett—"

"Who's there?" A strident voice rings out from the end of the corridor.

Too late. I snatch my hands away and run. A jutting wall ahead obscures part of the corridor. I scramble towards it, hoping the guard will not think to check past it.

Out of the corner of my eye, I see the guard striding into view and I press back into the shadows, closing my eyes and stilling my breath in the hope that he hasn't seen me. His footsteps are erratic, as if he's pausing to look into each cell. He probably is. I hear shuffling and the sound of mumbling—Uskup Daud has resumed praying.

"Keep it down," the guard says before he stomps away again.

I count to thirty this time, waiting until the only thing I hear is the priest's mumbling. Then I slip out of my hiding place and hurry out of the jail.

This Garett what? It haunts me that I don't know what Uskup Daud was going to say, but I don't dare return to ask. I'd rather live with the question than be hauled up before my father. Worse—I'd be dragged before Tok Yaakub first, as security is under *his* jurisdiction, and I don't know how to justify all this sneaking around to him.

I make it back to my rooms without seeing anyone.

CHAPTER 4

I wake to an insistent knocking on the door.

"Yosua! Yos! Get the door!"

The knocking continues until I remember that Yosua is not here. With a groan, I stumble out of bed.

"Stop it, I'm coming."

The knocking stops. I fling the door open to a messenger who seems startled to see me.

I glare at him through bleary eyes. "What."

"Good morning, Tuanku! Your presence is requested at the Majlis Maha meeting this morning." He holds out an ornate envelope, with Ayahanda's seal on it.

"*What?*"

"This morning, Tuanku." His eyes seem to slide past me to look into my dark room.

I hadn't bothered to open the windows, had forgotten about it rather, since Yosua is the one who takes care of such things.

"In an hour. Should I send up someone to assist you?" He thrusts the envelope at me again.

It takes a while for his words to sink in. "Majlis in an hour?" I stifle a cry, grabbing the letter. "Yes, yes, send someone up. Yosua is, uh, indisposed. And breakfast, thanks."

He nods and leaves. I slam the door behind him and slump against it, holding the envelope in trembling hands. Of all the days to finally be invited to attend Majlis, it has to be the day I'm handicapped by Yosua's absence. I want to rip open the envelope to get to the contents but I know I'll regret it later so I ease it open as gently as I can in my haste.

An *urgent* Majlis Maha meeting with the full Terang triumvirate, which means the leaders of each of Terang's three city-states: Ayahanda as Sultan of Maha and overall leader of Terang, Uskup Agung Ikhlas as religious head of Suci, and Secretkeeper Ramalan as the head of the Justices of Impian. If this is an intervention planned by Tok Yaakub, I'm awed by his efficiency— though, of course, this could already have been organised much earlier. Nothing in the letter indicates *who* has requested my presence or why.

The servant who comes to assist me is slow and frustrating and I want to demand Yosua's return. Yosua knows where everything is, knows exactly what I want without me having explain every single detail, and, most importantly, knows what to say and do to calm my nerves. Instead, I have to direct this servant's every step, from where my clothes are kept to how he's supposed to help me dress. There's only one set of baju I can wear for such an important, formal meeting, so that at least cuts down half my anxiety. Trying to find it raises it again.

"I'm fine, it's done," I snap as the servant hovers, tugging at my shirt and readjusting my samping. The long-sleeved shirt and loose trousers are in the yellow-gold fabric reserved for royalty. Wrapped around my hips is a samping embroidered with gold thread, the symbol of the Mahan Sultanate standing out against its brown weave.

"Ampun, Tuanku."

I wave him off and take a final look in the full-length mirror. My hair is tied up in a turban; the long yellow-gold folds aren't as sharp and precise as Yosua usually does it, but it will have to do.

I'm as ready as I can be.

ॐ

Laksamana Rizal, the head of the Navy, and Tok Yaakub are already in the Majlis room, deep in conversation, when I arrive. Tok Yaakub returns my greeting, but Tok Rizal scowls.

The room is taken up by a large oval mahogany table. At its head is a throne-like chair with ornate carvings and golden trimmings reserved for Ayahanda. Around the table stand seven smaller chairs, each bearing elaborate carvings that corresponds to the ranks of each person in the council. At the end of the room stand two shiny mirrors.

I stand at the foot of the table, not sure what to do. Do I sit? Assume one of the chairs is for me? Send a servant for another chair? Tok Rizal sends another scowl in my direction.

A diaken bustles in and heads straight to the mirror. I wander over, mostly so I don't look so awkward, but also because I'm curious to see how the Perantaraan gift works. She blesses the mirrors with holy water, sprinkling some over the frames then pouring it on the reflective surfaces, marring it with water marks. It seems a strange thing to do.

"Why do you do that?"

She jumps at the question and I apologise.

"Don't disturb the diaken, Tuanku," another voice says, making me jump in turn. Bendahara Ibrahim, Ayahanda's chief advisor, is standing at the doorway, frowning at the setup of the room. "I see you've received your summons."

"Yes, Tok Ibrahim."

Tok Ibrahim calls for a servant and after a short exchange, the servant leaves.

When the servant returns, he rearranges the chairs so that there are four on the right of the table and three on the left. He places the three-legged stool he's brought in at the foot of the table, on the left side.

Tok Ibrahim waves me to the stool before he goes to his place at the head of the table, on my father's right. My cheeks burn as I sit. Didn't Ayahanda use to have a seat in the Majlis when he came of age during my grandfather's reign? Why am I not entitled to use that chair?

One by one, the other members of the Majlis Maha trickle in. Opposite Tok Ibrahim sits Tok Benyamin, the Penghulu Bendahari, who takes care of Maha's finances. He tilts his head when he sees me, as if wondering what I'm doing there. Tok Yaakub and Tok Rizal sit beside them, with the last three chairs filled by the Shahbandars who each take care of one of Maha's districts. The Shahbandars nod at me as they enter, acknowledging my presence, but don't say anything further. I don't know them well enough to engage them in conversation.

This is the Majlis Maha, the council that advises my father and ratifies the decisions he makes. It's a coveted position and outsiders are only allowed into the meetings on rare occasions. I can't believe I'm here. It's only my lack of the gift that prevents my permanent inclusion.

The diaken leaves when Paderi Nur enters. Paderi Nur mutters something over the still-wet mirrors and they start shimmering. We all continue to wait.

The moment Ayahanda enters the room, everyone rises to greet him. Ayahanda takes his seat at the head of the table and gestures for us to sit. He raises his hand towards the mirrors to call a start to the meeting, then pauses when he notices me. He frowns a little as if he's not sure what I'm doing there.

"Ah, you have joined us today, Mikal?"

"Yes, Ayahanda. I received the invitation this morning." My heart pounds in my chest. Has it all been a mistake? Am I not supposed to be here?

Tok Ibrahim leans over and whispers something in his ear and Ayahanda's look of confusion clears.

"That's right." He smiles at me then signals for Paderi Nur to open communications.

Uskup Agung Ikhlas of Suci appears in the mirror on the left, Secretkeeper Ramalan with him. Compared to the rest present, they look ancient. They're at least in their eighties.

What is she *doing in Suci? Shouldn't she be in Impian?*

I hide my surprise as no one else seems to think it strange. The mirror on the right clears and Tun Nadir appears, a bored look on his face. Tun Nadir is not actually part of the triumvirate, but he's the appointed political leader of Impian since the role of the

Secretkeeper is tied to the justice system. In the interest of fairness, she cannot rule Impian.

"Well, let's get this over with, shall we?" Ayahanda says, looking at the Uskup Agung.

"This is no joking matter, Simson," Tun Ikhlas replies sternly.

"As I have said over and over again, this is the best course for Terang—it is the only way to see lasting peace in the sultanate, instead of always having to worry about impending war from Bayangan."

"You would ally with the enemies of Kudus!"

"Well, if Kudus were against them, he can strike them dead and we wouldn't be in this fix of constantly being on the brink of war. Don't you want to end this, Ikhlas? Don't you think the people deserve a chance for permanent peace?"

"Simson, your heart is in the right place, but your actions are wrong. This treaty might offer peace for the short term, but it will only end in disaster," Nek Ramalan says.

Ayahanda grits his teeth. "I've prayed about this and since Kudus hasn't struck me dead, I can only assume I'm not doing anything wrong."

"Do you *want* to be struck dead, Simson?" the Uskup Agung growls. "Kudus has sent His word to the priests both in Maha and in Suci but you have ignored their advice and their warnings! You only listen to your own counsel."

"The Temple itself says each man can approach Kudus on his own and that He speaks to their hearts. My heart says that this is what is right for me and for Terang. Dare you go against your own teachings?" Ayahanda looks like he's trying not to smile. "Besides, the Majlis is in agreement."

The seven men around the table nod. I stare at Tok Yaakub. He has always advised me to obey the Temple. How can he now justify siding with Ayahanda against Suci? Against both the Uskup Agung *and* the Secretkeeper? I try to catch his gaze but he either doesn't notice or he's ignoring me. I'm beginning to suspect the latter.

"We've reworked this treaty over and over again, Ikhlas." Ayahanda sighs heavily. "I've taken into consideration many of the things your priests have demanded, and the many things this Majlis has brought up."

"You haven't listened to the most important one of them all," Tun Ikhlas replies. "You must strike out the marriage alliance!"

Marriage alliance? It's true then? Ayahanda's behaviour with Permaisuri Layla last night seems less odd in the light of this. But after rejecting marriage for so long, why has he suddenly changed his mind? There are so many questions I want to ask, I end up biting my inner lip to keep from interrupting.

"My visions only see dark things if you take this route," Nek Ramalan says. Her face is downcast, her tone low. "I travelled to Suci because these visions are dire, O Sultan. In thirty days—"

Ayahanda bristles and narrows his eyes. "Ramalan, I do not profess to understand the workings of your visions. But I have seen things with my own two eyes and they tell me that this is the best way forward. The people of my city are crying out for help. This treaty will bring jobs, trade, money. It will help everyone from the poor to the rich."

Nek Ramalan scowls and snaps, "Must you marry the girl? Will you not listen—"

Ayahanda's face pinches. "Is that what this is all about? Despite all I have done for the sultanate, all I have sacrificed, you would deny me the right to marry a young woman who is willing?"

"We do not deny you the right to marry anyone, Sultan Simson," Tun Ikhlas holds up a placating hand, "just not her. Not our enemy. Are you lonely? Have we not encouraged you many times to remarry? Pick any of the women of Terang, whether from Maha, Suci, or Impian. We won't oppose it."

Ayahanda shakes his head. "I don't understand you. For all your talk of forgiveness and repentance, you cannot accept when one who was our enemy has repented and is now seeking to be our friend and ally."

Tun Nadir clears his throat. "Fellow rulers, far be it from me to advise any of you, being the youngest of the rulers and only a representative of Impian, but it is our Sultan's right to marry whom he wishes."

"Thank you, Nadir," Ayahanda says as the two from Suci look frustrated.

Tun Ikhlas looks set to start a new argument. "Kudus says—"

Ayahanda doesn't let him complete the sentence. "If I may remind you, Uskup Agung Ikhlas, there are many Bayangans in Maha. All of them believe in Kudus and follow the teachings of the Temple. How can you be prejudiced against them when you preach love towards all? Permaisuri Layla may yet come to know and follow Kudus as we do."

"And has she shown any interest in following our faith?" Nek Ramalan asks sharply. "Or does she merely delay you and tell you it may come to pass one day in the distant future?"

"Permaisuri Layla has visited the Temple in Maha," Ayahanda replies. "I would say she is quite open to listening about Kudus. Belief and faith will come in time."

She was definitely not in Jemaah yesterday, though Ayahanda could have taken her to the Temple at some other point during the week. After all, they'd been keeping the delegation shrouded in secrecy—until dinner last night.

A long silence permeates the room.

"Do you have anything else to say?" Ayahanda asks when a long enough time has passed.

It is Nek Ramalan who says, "It looks like we cannot convince you otherwise."

"No. I have made up my mind, and it is within my rights as the Sultan of Maha and Sovereign of Terang to do so, especially when the Majlis Maha is in agreement."

"One last thing then," Tun Ikhlas says. He looks worn out, as if he's lost a fight.

"What would that be?"

"Will you release my priests? The Temple in Maha has informed me that you have imprisoned Uskup Daud and two Paderi over the last three months. What offense have they made against you?"

I don't recall seeing the two other priests last night, though I had not gone much further past the cell where Uskup Daud had been held. I didn't think they would still be there.

Ayahanda grimaces. "I will release them on the condition that they return to Suci and are replaced with new priests who respect the authority of the Sultan. These priests have spoken out publicly against their Sultan in the middle of Jemaah in an astoundingly rude manner. This is both disruptive and against the rule of law. If they wish to admonish me, or impart their 'words of wisdom', I would advise them to do it in a more courteous manner in private instead of inciting insurrection."

"We will discipline them as necessary," Tun Ikhlas says. "I will recall them today and arrange for their replacements."

"Now, if that is all…?" Ayahanda waits for them to assent before he signals for the priest to break the connection. He leans back in his seat with a big smile. "Thank you for your assistance, Paderi Nur."

Paderi Nur curtsies and packs up her equipment, wiping down the mirrors. The shimmering fades and their reflective surfaces return to normal.

Ayahanda waits for her to leave before he speaks. "I thank the Majlis for your support. I'm glad we have come to an agreement after all these long meetings with my bride-to-be. I know not all of you are happy to be standing against Suci, but as I have said, we must make some sacrifices for peace. I truly believe that with this alliance, we will finally put war behind us."

The seven men murmur in agreement with various degrees of enthusiasm. Tok Yaakub looks the most reluctant of them all.

"I'm also glad that my son is here. It has been brought to my attention that he is nearing the age of manhood—have you gained your Amok Strength yet?"

I blink at the suddenness of being addressed. "Not yet, Ayahanda."

The Majlis looks disapproving.

"Neither have you been tested."

"No, Ayahanda."

"It seems to me that we should test you then. This afternoon, Mikal, we shall spar. I am interested to see how well the Temenggung has trained you."

I open my mouth to protest, only to answer, "Yes, Ayahanda."

"You may go. I will send someone to you with details."

I rise and bow to Ayahanda and the Majlis, sending Tok Yaakub a desperate glance as I leave. He acknowledges me this time with a nod but doesn't say anything.

A test? There has never been a test before, not that I've heard of. Yet most of my ancestors gained their Amok Strength in their thirteenth year, in the midst of war, so there has never been a need for a formal test—the war itself was all the testing they needed.

As my history teachers keep telling me, this has been the longest extended peace in Maha since my father destroyed Bayangan twenty years ago, the first time in many generations that a prince of the sultanate has not been involved in active warfare from the moment he reached puberty. Which goes to say that I'm the oldest in recent history to still not have access to our Amok Strength at the age of fifteen. No one knows what it means or why it is so. Or what to do.

I don't know if I'm blessed for having grown up in peace or cursed for lacking the strongest proof of my legitimacy to the throne. And Ayahanda...I will never live up to his legacy.

I head to the Temple to pray. If I'm going to face Ayahanda in the gelanggang today, I desperately need Kudus on my side.

CHAPTER 5

The prayers don't help. At least, not as much as I hoped they would, especially since I have been praying for the wrong thing. I've been praying not to fail. I should have been praying not to be utterly humiliated.

What Ayahanda spoke of as a private spar, a testing of my abilities, has somehow devolved into a public match with the entire Bayangan delegation, the Majlis, and a crowd of nobility in attendance. I'm not even counting the servants who stop by to gawk—there are too many coming and going for me to even recognise them all.

One I do recognise all too well, though. Yosua is sitting amongst the Bayangan delegation, whispering in Permaisuri Layla's ear. The *traitor*. He's supposed to be on bed rest, not gallivanting about with the enemy.

Ayahanda has already proven his skill in the gelanggang, inviting Permaisuri Layla's guards to fight him ten at a time. Permaisuri Layla's expression changes from sceptical to impressed as he defeats all of them with ease, which I suppose is the point. The current match is against Tok Yaakub, a long, drawn-out battle. Where Tok Yaakub loses out in sheer strength, he makes up with cunning and skill. Even then, Ayahanda emerges the clear winner. He doesn't even look tired. The audience cheer as Ayahanda and Tok Yaakub bow to each other.

And now it's my turn.

O Kudus, Maha Esa, berkatilah hamba-Mu dengan kuasa ajaib-Mu. Please, O Kudus, please.

"Come on, Mikal, you can do it," Ayahanda encourages as he lands blow after blow.

Nothing happens. No power comes over me.

All I feel is the warm wind against my skin, the pain of Ayahanda's blows, the itch of all those eyes locked on Ayahanda and me as we spar. He doesn't hold back his strength, not like Tok Yaakub does. My inadequacies are evident beside him, small and scrawny, not quite grown into my limbs. All too obvious after the Bayangan soldiers and Tok Yaakub. Despite my daily training, I haven't developed the same kind of muscles Ayahanda has, those of an experienced, battle-hardened warrior, who gained his Amok Strength at twelve. How can I compare?

The watching crowd is silent, the familiar air of disdain that envelopes them whenever I am present creeping into the atmosphere. The match ends quickly with me flat on the ground, Ayahanda's thumbs pressing against my neck.

A smattering of polite applause, then the buzz of voices. Ayahanda stands, raising his arms in victory and the cheering starts. I don't move, staring at the clear blue sky and wishing that Kudus would strike me dead right now. It's not as if He has any use for me. Maybe if I lie here until the crowd leaves, they'll forget it's me who has been defeated. It will be just another spar with a faceless opponent, one of many whom Ayahanda has defeated today.

Permaisuri Layla spoils it all. She steps into the gelanggang and congratulates Ayahanda, hugging him as if she is family. The watchers titter. I want to continue ignoring them all, but she looms above me and reaches out her hand. The only thing I can do is take it, allowing her to pull me to my feet.

"Well done, Mikal. You held your own very well."

What does she know? It's not as if she's seen me fight before. I mumble my thanks. No avoiding it now.

Ayahanda and I clasp hands and bow to each other. No ill will, a fair fight. As fair as it can be when he has an additional source of strength I cannot access no matter how hard I try, or how many times I plead. I don't deserve this humiliation. I expect Ayahanda to go into his normal speech about patience and how each man comes into his own at different times and different paces, but all he does is shake his head.

"Yaakub, more training," he says, Permaisuri Layla's arm in his. Then he leaves, holding her hand tenderly.

I clench my teeth to keep from calling after him. Yosua trails after them and I lose it.

"Yosua ayell Garett!"

He spins around to face me. "Tuan?"

"I see you've recovered." His eyes are still puffy, his skin still red and raw.

"Tuan, I—"

"If you're well enough to watch, you're well enough to return to your duties."

He bows. "Yes, Tuan."

"I expect to have a warm bath waiting on my return. Go."

He bobs another bow and scuttles off.

I sink back to the ground, sitting with my head in my hands until there's no one else left in the gelanggang except Tok Yaakub. He reaches out to me but I don't take his hand, pushing myself to my feet instead. I'm done with crutches.

"He didn't mean it that way, you know," Tok Yaakub says.

"Do I? Really. Tell me, Tok Yaakub. What was that spectacle for? To humiliate me? To entertain his new lady love? To show his prowess? Which way did he mean it? This morning, it sounded like a private spar, just my father interested in how his son is doing. What just happened? I don't know what that was supposed to be."

Tok Yaakub searches the ground and the sky and then studies his nails before he says, "Permaisuri Layla was at the next meeting after you were dismissed. Baginda Paduka mentioned the match in passing and she asked if she could watch. His eyes lit up. He wanted so much to show you off to her. He's proud of you, Tuanku, even if you can't see it."

"Proud." I snort. "Of me. If he were truly proud of me, he wouldn't have humiliated me in public."

"Love makes us do strange things." Tok Yaakub tries to lay a hand on my shoulder but I dodge, keeping out of range. He lets his hand drop to his side. "He didn't mean—"

"Maybe she's bewitched him. Used some strange Bayangan witchcraft on him."

"Don't be ridiculous."

"Why else is he so adamant on marrying her? Why else has he left the faith?"

Tok Yaakub sounds exasperated as he says, "You know he hasn't been serious about Kudus ever since your mother passed."

I huff. "Yes, I know. It's just…it's hard."

"Life is hard. Haven't I told you that often enough?"

I don't answer, just fall into the ready stance again. What else is there to say?

Tok Yaakub stares at me.

"Come on." I beckon with my fingers.

"What?"

"Didn't you hear him? More training, he said. So train me."

"No."

"Tok Yaakub—"

"No, Tuanku, you've had enough. You deserve a break. Training now will only hurt you instead of help you."

I drop my hands. "Then what?"

"Then you go take the warm bath you've instructed your servant to prepare for you and relax. It will make you feel better. You're too tense." He shoos me away.

∞

Tok Yaakub is right. A long, warm bath is extremely relaxing. I lie back as Yosua washes my hair. It seems to have stopped growing at my knees for now, and I don't know if it will grow any longer in the future. Sometimes I wonder how long Ayahanda's hair is, having never been cut for over forty years. I've never seen it. He always keeps it in his turban. It has to be longer than mine. In my sillier moments, I wonder if my hair isn't long enough for Kudus to grant me his strength. But it's not as if I can control how long it grows. All I can do is not cut it.

A rose petal drifts too near my mouth and I bat it away, splashing water out of the tub.

"Tuan," Yosua complains. I must have soaked him.

"Sorry." A thought crosses my mind and I twist to look at Yosua. He grumbles at me. "What was this parade you wanted to watch?" He was not the only one who mentioned a parade—Uskup Daud had also brought it up. I didn't think of it at the time, but I don't recall any recent parades.

"Baginda Paduka held a parade in Permaisuri Layla's honour yesterday, Tuan."

"I didn't hear anything about it. I didn't even meet her until after Jemaah."

Yosua ducks his head. "There wasn't any formal announcement, Tuan. The kitchen staff were gossiping about it during lunch; Baginda Paduka had finalised the first tranche of the treaty and he wanted to show off the permaisuri to Maha, and to introduce Maha to her."

Huh. So that's what had brought them out of hiding after a week. "What do you think of the Bayangan delegation? And their permaisuri?"

He looks at me with an unspoken question, taking his eyes off the tangle of my hair in his lap.

"Come on, you must have some thoughts. They're your countrymen, after all."

"I'm more Mahan than Bayangan," Yosua replies. After a pause, he adds, "I don't really think anything of it, Tuan."

"What about this marriage alliance and treaty they're putting together?"

"It's good, I suppose."

"Will you return to Bayangan then? When the port reopens?"

Yosua avoids my gaze, dropping his eyes to my hair, keeping his hands busy.

"Will you?"

"I don't know."

"Why not?"

"I might visit. If I'm allowed. I'm done with your hair, Tuan."

I turn, allowing him access to scrub the rest of my body. I close my eyes and let my mind drift.

By the time Yosua is done, I'm fully relaxed and ready for bed. It's still early so I sit on the sofa, reading. I'm just about to drift off to sleep when there's a knock on the door.

Yosua hurries to answer it, and there's quiet whispering before he comes to tell me that Uskup Daud is requesting an audience.

"Uskup Daud? Ayahanda released him?" I scramble upright, straightening my clothes and rubbing the sleep out of my eyes. "Let him in, Yos, and bring refreshments."

Uskup Daud enters holding a long tube. He's wearing the white jubah paderi of Suci instead of the customary red jubah paderi of Maha.

"Tun Ikhlas has negotiated for my release and they have recalled me to Suci," he explains. "Baginda Paduka has agreed for Paderi Nur to take up the role of Uskup in my place."

I gesture for him to take a seat. "And you have come to take your leave? I assume you have seen my father as well."

"Baginda Paduka will not listen me so I will not waste my time nor risk my freedom for that."

"If you've come to warn me against him again—" I cut off as Uskup Daud shakes his head. "Then?"

"Not against him. But to warn you." He sighs. "The presence of Kudus is departing from Maha. As you are the future sultan, Kudus impressed upon my heart that you should be forewarned. Baginda Paduka's actions will be on his own head, but you may yet be saved."

I frown at him, sitting up straighter. "Saved from what?"

Yosua comes in and sets two glasses of cold rose syrup on the table, as well as a platter of various kuih.

Uskup Daud looks at him as he says, "Treachery and betrayal."

I stare at the priest, mouth hanging open. "From who? What do you know?"

Yosua, hovering by the table, must think I'm asking him because he shakes his head vehemently.

"The Secretkeeper has seen a vision," Uskup Daud continues. "It was important enough, urgent enough, that she travelled to Suci to discuss it with Uskup Agung Ikhlas. They called an urgent meeting with Baginda Paduka and the Majlis, and it was decided that you, as the Raja Muda, should be there and made aware of a vision of such importance."

I don't point out that I'm not *officially* the Raja Muda, though now I know the source of my invitation. "I was there at the Majlis this morning," I say. "They mentioned a vision, but didn't explain…"

"Yes, they told me that Baginda Paduka did not give them the chance to speak of it in full. Which is why I'm here." Uskup Daud glances at Yosua again.

"If you will excuse your servant? The prophecy is for your ears only."

"No." It escapes me before I can think it through properly. I don't need to think it through. "Yosua is my confidant and body servant. What I hear he can hear too."

The priest purses his lips. "Although he is Bayangan?"

I want to strangle the priesthood, especially Uskup Daud and Uskup Agung Ikhlas. What is it with them and the Bayangan? My reply is sharper than I intend. "Yosua is as Mahan as I am. He was born here, as I was. His loyalty is to myself first, then to Maha and Terang. Is that not so, Yosua ayell Garett?"

Yosua kneels before me and takes my hand, lifting it to his lips. "It is as you say, Tuanku."

That's a clear enough signal, that he addresses me in his answer as his *prince* instead of his *master*. "Does that satisfy you?"

Uskup Daud considers us for far too long, his face a blank mask.

"Does that satisfy you, Uskup Daud? Or would you rather I go into this war ignorant?"

He blinks and gives me a wry smile. "I will defer to your judgement in this, Tuanku," he says, holding out the tube he's been gripping with both hands, bowing as he does so.

My heart pounds as I take it.

"The Secretkeeper's vision is inscribed in this scroll word for word. Do not let it fall into the wrong hands. Destroy it if you must. It was only transcribed for your benefit. In summary, what it declares is this:

"'In thirty days, Maha will fall, betrayed by one of her own. The city will be plundered and set to flames.

To save the people, evacuate to Impian. Suci will be attacked within the year, if Maha falls.' There is much more, but this is the main part."

Betrayed? "How can we prevent this?"

"The only way the Secretkeeper saw to prevent it is by refusing the treaty and the marriage alliance. However, Baginda Paduka has already declared his intent. His heart is set on the wedding."

"Is there no other way?"

"Not to prevent it. However, Maha may yet be saved if your father and you keep true to the faith."

"How?"

"The Amok Strength will fall upon you in your time of greatest need." He gestures at another line further down.

Right. The one thing I cannot grasp will miraculously appear when I need it the most. I want to have faith that it will, but I have been disappointed far too many times.

"My father holds the power. I don't have anything. If you were there this afternoon, you would have seen."

His face is kind, almost fatherly, as he says, "I know, Putera Mikal. That power is given by Kudus and He will give it as He wills. I cannot say why you have yet to receive it. I wish I could."

"Why must you priests be so cryptic?"

"I do not mean to be so, Tuanku, but I honestly do not know. All I can say based on my years of serving Kudus is that if you keep true to the faith, no matter what happens, you and your family line will be saved.

"Terrible things are going to happen, Tuanku. Baginda Paduka's actions have set Maha—and all of Terang—on a dangerous trajectory and war *will* come.

Bayangan is a godless country and its leaders seek revenge. Do not fool yourself that you will be safe." The priest rolls his shoulders as he stands. "I'm sorry to be the bearer of bad news, but I could not return to Suci with a clean conscience if you were left unaware of all that is transpiring."

I rise as well, offering him my hand. We should at least separate in peace. "Thank you, Uskup Daud. I bid you safe journey and may Kudus grant we meet again."

He doesn't shake my hand. Instead, he bows and kisses my hand, shaking me to my core. Is he pledging his loyalty to me? What about Ayahanda? Is the priesthood breaking ties with my father?

"Keep the faith, Tuanku. Until we meet again." Then he takes three steps backwards and bows again before he turns to leave.

CHAPTER 6

Let it not be said that I have ever judged Kudus to be unfair. It's not as if I am in a position to *judge* Him. Yet if I have one gripe against the Temple, it is the constant teaching that if you are faithful to Kudus and His worship, He will grant you all the desires of your heart.

He will assuredly not grant you *all* the desires of your heart, and definitely not at the times that you desire them.

Still, as they say, Kudus is inscrutable and His Will is too vast for his mere vassals to understand. I hunger for His approval, yet I do not know what else He requires of me. I have committed to be faithful, however, so I study the Firman diligently, committing it to memory. I have prayed for a way to prove myself worthy of His gift, so this may be the path He has opened for me.

Paderi Nur is elevated to the position of uskup the day after Uskup Daud returns to Suci. I suppose he is just paderi now; I'm not sure if he will keep the title as he is no longer the head of the Mahan Temple.

Uskup Nur is not as patient as Uskup Daud. "I don't see what else there is for you to understand, Tuanku. Just do it." She looks often at the books on her table, as if I am keeping her from some deep reading that's more important than the survival of the sultanate.

"I need more answers, Uskup Nur. How can you expect me to convince Ayahanda when I have nothing to back me up?"

"You have his ear. It is more than we have."

"Ayahanda does not listen—"

"You are his son, are you not? His heir? Find a way."

I stall. The Secretkeeper's vision said thirty days, though I'm not sure exactly *when* she received the vision. Did she receive it in Impian then travel to Suci? If yes, counting the week it takes to travel from Impian to Suci, with the Majlis convening the following day, that leaves us approximately twenty-one days to fix this. If she was already in Suci when she received it, we may still have the full thirty days. If we get past the thirty-day mark without either of the two events taking place, the vision then becomes void. At least, that's how I argue it to myself.

Yosua laughs and says it's too simplistic; that can't be how the vision works.

"Tell me how it works then," I challenge him. "You're the one with all the great plans."

He smirks. "But I can't always be teaching you things, Tuanku. You must figure this out yourself. It's your country, your father."

I send him to his room.

Tok Yaakub is the weakest link in the Majlis right now. He doesn't quite agree with the treaty and the way

Ayahanda is fighting the Temple, so maybe he'll be the first to break. If he removes his support, the treaty and the wedding will be stalled. He's also the only one who will listen to me.

"Another crisis?" Tok Yaakub asks during our next training. "Don't let one setback affect you so much."

It's been two days since my humiliating defeat and Tok Yaakub is kind enough not to have brought it up. Until now. I huff.

"What? Youths, I tell you. So dramatic." He smiles though, and lays his keris down. "Do I need to beat it out of you again?"

I shake my head. "Look, Tok Yaakub, I haven't been able to stop thinking about the Majlis."

"Hmm. That was a good experience, wasn't it?"

"Huh? Yes, it was. But…"

"But?"

I start pacing, trying to frame my words. I'd planned this out the night before, writing out my arguments, wrangling through them with Yosua and memorising them, but now, facing the Temenggung, my brain is blank.

"Terang is divided."

He grunts, folding his arms and squinting at me.

"Suci and Impian are against this alliance."

"Putera Mikal, we are not discussing Majlis matters in the middle of training."

"But you have to listen, Tok!"

"This is not the time, nor the place. And this is above your station."

I stop pacing, glaring at him. "Before this, it's always Tuanku should take more interest in the affairs of the sultanate! Tuanku should learn about politics in

Terang! Tuanku should understand how the Majlis works to bring balance to Maha! But now that I am getting involved, it is not my time nor my place nor my station?"

Tok Yaakub folds his arms. "Tuanku, I merely suggest that this place is too public for such a discussion."

"And who is listening, Tok Yaakub? The birds in the air? The shadows of the trees? The dust of the gelanggang? There is no one about."

Of course, that is when a startled servant scuttles by with a load of produce under his arm, using the gelanggang as a short cut between various buildings of the sprawling palace complex.

Tok Yaakub gives me a meaningful look. He steps up to me and grips my upper arm so hard it hurts. "Tuanku, I have been lenient with you all this while, listening to your complaints, entertaining your fears. You must grow up. Maha needs you, but not in this way. The Majlis has decided, and it will not be swayed. That door is closed."

He leans closer and whispers in my ear. "I know the Temple has put you up to this. Beware of their manipulations as well, Mikal. Just because they claim to serve Kudus doesn't mean all their motives are pure."

He drops my arm and steps away. I stare at him, unsure of what he means.

"Today's session is over." Tok Yaakub picks up his keris and walks away without looking back.

∽

If there is one way to Ayahanda's heart and ears, it is through Ibunda. Yet it is risky. Speaking of my mother may make him soft and weepy, or it may make him hard and angry, then there is no hope of him listening at all. He is already disappointed in me. I do not want to risk worsening his displeasure.

Ayahanda is still preoccupied with the Bayangan delegation, though the frequency of their meetings reduce now that the majority of the treaty has been agreed upon and the delegation is preparing to leave. Permaisuri Layla and her Temenggung, Jeffett, need to return to Bayangan to announce the treaty and prepare for the upcoming wedding. Bayangan doesn't have a council that needs to approve the treaty, not like we do, but they still need to make announcements and issue laws, all kinds of administrative busywork I can't be bothered to understand. With all this, it is hard to catch Ayahanda or to come up with an excuse for a private talk with him.

Over dinner, Ayahanda looks at Permaisuri Layla with a sickeningly sweet smile as they discuss wedding plans. I spend most of dinner trying to ignore them, focusing on the re-enactment of Raja Muda Mahmud's penance, the first time the Covenant of Salt was performed.

It's not a light story—after the Raja Muda fulfilled the covenant, it's not said what happens to him. It's commonly assumed that Raja Muda Mahmud gave up his life on the altar of Suci for the sake of Terang. Noble but also horrifying. The dance only shows a symbolic sacrifice. A new priest-king, the famous Sultan Yosua, whom my servant is named after, ascends the throne with a Secretkeeper wife. It's the first and only time that the leadership of all Terang was concentrated in a ruling pair. There has been one other Covenant-sealing in the history of my forefathers. It all seems very grim. No one except the Uskup Agung and Secretkeeper really understands the requirements and I do not wish to become further acquainted with it.

Which is why we need to stop this impending disaster. Maha must not fall. I do not wish to die.

I'm still lingering over dessert, the kuih sticky on my fingers, when Ayahanda takes his leave.

"So early, Simson?" Permaisuri Layla asks, surprise in her voice.

"I still have final drafts of the treaty to review and approve before our closing meeting tomorrow," he replies.

"Shame. I thought we could spend a night together."

Ayahanda laughs. "In two weeks, sayang, we'll have many nights to spend together." He bends to kiss her cheek, pats me on the shoulder, then leaves.

I gape at his retreating back. It's the first time I've heard him address her by an endearment, but it rolls off his tongue, as if he's used it often. I've run out of time. I have to talk to him tonight.

I wait until I'm sure no one else will come looking for him—not that I've seen anyone since I started stalking the corridor to his office.

"What is it?" Ayahanda calls irritably at my knock. "Who's there?"

"It's me."

His sigh is so loud I can hear it through the door. "Come in, Mikal."

I slip in, letting the door shut with a soft click. "So, it's settled then, Ayahanda? You're going to marry the Bayangan permaisuri?" I can't bring myself to name her, as if doing so will make it more real.

He studies my face for a long time, and I wonder what he sees. Does he truly see me? Or does he see Ibunda? Many have told me that I have my mother's looks, from her large brown eyes and long eyelashes, to her round snub nose and fleshy cheeks. I can't see it. I like to think I look like my father, with his thick brows, firm jaw, sharp eyes, and purposeful air.

"It's settled."

"Why?" It's not what I mean to ask, so I amend it quickly. "What if I don't want a stepmother?" Even though it sounds petulant, it's better than to be seen challenging his authority. I should have come up with a strategy other than *don't offend him*. If I'd asked Yosua, he'd already have a list of ten things to say and another ten of what not to say.

A melancholic look shutters Ayahanda's face. He crosses to the sofa in the corner and slumps into it, beckoning me over. He doesn't speak until I'm sitting next to him, his arm around my shoulder.

"Your Ibunda would have wanted this. Before she died, she told me to find you a new mother so you wouldn't grow up alone."

"It's too late for that now." It's been a decade and I have grown up alone.

"I know. There was just never anyone good enough to replace her." His voice hitches.

And she *is?*

He looks at me for a moment before clearing his throat. "Don't worry, the two of you won't have much to do with each other. After all, you're old enough to look after yourself. Don't you like her? I thought you were getting on fine."

"It…" A hurt I didn't know existed wells up. "It seems a little like you've abandoned Ibunda. The memory of her."

He is silent and I don't dare look up to see if he is angry at me. There's so much I don't know about Ibunda because he doesn't talk about her. I'm always grasping at stories from Marla who served her for seven years, brief mentions by Tok Yaakub, anecdotes from nobles over Jemaah dinner after Ayahanda is out of earshot. Excepting the first, all of these relate to how Ibunda would have reacted in relation to Ayahanda, like she was a puppeteer controlling him. I do not know what she was like as a person or how she would have been as a mother. She is a hole in my being, yet an almost-tangible ghost that hovers just out of my vision.

He shifts away, and the lack of his weight feels like another pointed emphasis of his absence in my life. But then he reaches over and stills my fidgeting fingers, holding my hands in his.

"It does, but Bintang has been dead for ten years. I'm not marrying Layla for her to be your mother. I'm marrying her so that our countries will finally find peace. It's what Bintang would have wanted. I'm just trying to do what's best for Terang."

"But they're our enemies."

Ayahanda's brow furrows. "And now they won't be. Can't you see that?"

I don't know what I see. I see my father in love, straining to pull two water buffaloes under the same yoke. I see the water buffaloes fighting each other, each twist of their head meant to gore and kill with their horns. "Ayahanda, I…I just don't understand. What the Uskup Agung said—"

"Pah, who cares what he thinks? The Temple is not always right." He gets up abruptly and crosses to his table.

"You said that as rulers of Terang, we were beholden to Kudus and Suci."

Ayahanda tilts his head in agreement. "That doesn't mean the priests are always right."

"What happens now that Suci and Impian disagree with your treaty? Are they allowed to? What if it tears Terang apart?"

"They can try, but I am the Sultan of Terang and what I decide is law." His jaw is set, his knuckles white as they grip the edge of his table. "Don't you think I've wrestled through all of this already? The treaty will be binding for Maha alone. None of our new prosperity and trade will go to Suci or Impian, no matter how much they beg later on."

There's an angry glint in his eyes and I know that whatever goodwill I've built up is gone. What did Uskup Nur think would happen? I can't bring up their warnings now, nor the Secretkeeper's vision on the scroll tucked in my samping.

"Was that all? I've got work to do, finalising the treaty."

"Can I see it?"

Ayahanda laughs. "What for? Don't worry, it's nothing that will truly affect you. You'll see it when I'm done. Good night, Mikal."

"Good night, Ayahanda." I lift his right hand to my lips, press it against my forehead, seeking the blessing of his heart.

He smiles, his anger gone as quick as that.

I leave feeling as if I have failed the Temple. I have failed Kudus. Calamity is going to befall us and it will be my fault.

CHAPTER 7

If I thought I'd get a better chance to persuade Ayahanda or the Majlis to halt or slow things down once the Bayangan delegation left, I was mistaken. Things only ramp up in their absence.

My days are filled with wedding preparations and fittings. A new set of baju is commissioned and I'm stuck all over with pins to make sure it fits right. The palace is filled with the sound of music and marching—the pounding of the kompang battles the stomping of feet as dancers and soldiers alike train. I'm talked at and prodded and drilled on protocol. Who sits where? Who stands where? The Majlis will bless the couple, but do I need to as well? I barely see Ayahanda and all my classes, including silat training with Tok Yaakub, are paused.

Since I can't persuade Ayahanda against the alliance, I try instead to convince Tok Yaakub to increase our defences and send the people to safety. The Secretkeeper's scroll is my sole guide, though I don't know if I'm interpreting any of it right. It says to send the people to Impian, so that's what I try to do.

I find Tok Yaakub in his office.

"Tuanku, we are not discussing this again."

"Tok Yaakub, please. Listen to me."

"No. This is getting out of hand. You listen to me. Whatever you think is going to happen *won't*. Stirring up panic and sending people out into the countryside or to Impian is just going to create even more chaos."

"*More* chaos?"

"I have enough to deal with, Tuanku, with the protests in the city. I don't have time to deal with your paranoia as well."

"Protests?" Yosua hasn't mentioned any protests.

"Yes, protests. Riots. Whatever you want to call it—"

We're interrupted by two of his men coming in to report. They hesitate when they see me but Tok Yaakub just waves impatiently for them to continue.

"Three dead, Tok, four injured. The dead are all Bayangans," one says.

Tok Yaakub grimaces. "And the injured?"

"One Bayangan, three Mahan."

"Targeted?"

"We think so. It sounds as if they were cornered, but the Bayangan is scared. He's not giving us any information. The Mahans insist they are innocent."

Tok Yaakub scoffs.

Things start clicking together. Unrest in the city. Protests. Racial tension. Garett's secrecy. He's probably ordered Yosua not to tell me anything. I blurt, "Yosua was attacked too."

Tok Yaakub's eyes drill into me. "When?"

"The other day. When he went missing."

"That was over a week ago!"

"Garett said—"

"Garett knows about this?"

"I don't know! He wouldn't give me any details. He kept insisting it was some kind of racial tension and nothing more."

"Bring him in," Tok Yaakub orders.

"Wait. You can't just—"

"Is he behind this?" Tok Yaakub asks.

I flinch as the door slams. "Why would he beat up his own son?"

"Putera Mikal, you can be abnormally obtuse."

What? Oh, *oh*. "Garett won't retaliate. You know he wouldn't."

Tok Yaakub rubs his cheek, scratching at his neatly trimmed beard. "That doesn't mean he doesn't know who is behind it."

I pace in the Temenggung's office until Garett is marched in by the pair of soldiers, arms held in a vice-like grip. Fear is written on his face and his eyes widen when he sees me. The soldiers push him to his knees.

"There's no need for that," I snap.

They prod him and he performs obeisance. "Ampun, Tuanku. Temenggung," he stutters.

What's he apologising to me for?

"What do you know?" Tok Yaakub folds his arms and leans back against the edge of the table, looking as if he'd like to dissect Garett.

"Temenggung? I…"

"The protests. What do you know about them?"

Garett shakes his head. "Nothing, Temenggung. I'm not involved. I promise. I would never—"

One of the soldiers step closer, pausing when Tok Yaakub holds up a hand. Garett shrinks back.

"You knew about the unrest before anything even started." Tok Yaakub leans forward. "You were predicting *war*. Weren't you?"

"No, no, Temenggung."

"Are you saying that Putera Mikal is lying?"

Garett looks at me as if I have betrayed him.

I protest. "What? No! I never said Garett—"

"What do you know, Garett Regis Baya?" Tok Yaakub lifts him by the collar of his shirt and slams him against the wall.

"Please, I don't...I don't know anything." He chokes as Tok Yaakub twists his collar tighter and I cannot stand it anymore. Garett hasn't done anything wrong. He isn't the one behind any of this.

I reach and touch Tok Yaakub on the shoulder. "Tok?"

He glares at me, but lets go of Garett's collar.

Garett slides to the floor, coughing.

"Let me," I say. I don't know why I say it. What can I say that will make Garett tell us what he doesn't know?

"Go ahead," Tok Yaakub says. He steps aside, keeping his eyes on us. His two men are still barring the door, preventing us—Garett—from leaving.

I kneel beside Garett and lay a hand on his shuddering shoulder. "Are they retaliating for what was done to Yosua?"

Garett shakes his head.

"Speak up, Bayangan," Tok Yaakub orders from behind his desk.

"No, Tuanku. They don't know."

"They don't know who beat him?" I ask.

His head shake is even more frantic. "No, they don't know that my son was beaten."

"But if they knew, they would have retaliated?" Tok Yaakub interrupts again.

Garett freezes and squeezes his eyes shut. Then his head jerks in assent. "But they don't know. I didn't tell them."

"Do you know who is behind this?" I ask. That's the important question.

"I can guess. But we're not the ones instigating it, Tuanku, you have to believe me. It's not us. We're only defending ourselves."

Tok Yaakub grumbles to himself. "What about the war? Ask him about the war."

"I didn't tell him, I promise," I whisper to Garett. Louder, I ask, "Will there be a war?"

Garett clenches and unclenches his hands. He's staring at a spot on the ground as if he's trying to disappear.

"I know who you were, Garett, even if Baginda Paduka has forgotten," Tok Yaakub says. He glares at Garett, leaning forward with his hands pressed flat on the table. "If anyone has any strings to pull, it's you. If the Bayangans create unrest, I know who it's for. So, if anything happens, I know who to look for first. You and your son. And believe me when I say your son won't escape your punishments."

Garett swallows hard. He gets on his knees, pushes his hands flat on the floor, presses his face into the ground. "Tuanku, Temenggung, please. Believe me when I say that I know nothing. There is no war, there are no plans for war. I am not a threat to you, nor to Bayangan. It was just a rumour, one that I quickly stopped. My people were wondering about the presence of the Bayangan delegation in the palace and what it meant. It subsided once we heard about the treaty. This is what we want."

Tok Yaakub narrows his eyes. "And the wedding? Where do you stand on the wedding?"

"I'm not opposed to it."

"But you do not support it."

"The permaisuri will do as she wishes. The marriage alliance will bind my loyalty, but my pledge is to Sultan Simson and to his line alone. My honour demands it and I will not break my word." He kneels up, head bent, lifts his hand to his heart in a salam.

"And don't you forget that." Tok Yaakub rises with a sigh and waves his hand. "You may go, Garett, but be warned. We're watching you."

Garett bows to Tok Yaakub and me before he shuffles towards the door. The soldiers let him go at a signal from the Temenggung, following him out.

I'm floundering in their exchange, drowning in meanings and half-meanings I have no context for, no understanding of. Who is Garett? What does Tok Yaakub know of him that he can hold as a keris to his throat?

Tok Yaakub drums his fingers on the table.

"Tok?"

His fingers stop. "I'm not sure I believe him."

"Why? What has he done? Who is he?" I fold my arms, squinting at my teacher.

"Did you know that Garett and Yosua had a private meeting with Permaisuri Layla?"

"What? When?"

"Isn't that interesting? Did Yosua not tell you about it?" He sits down, elbows on the table, fingers steepled as he narrows his eyes at me.

"No. He didn't mention it." I sit down opposite him, holding his gaze steady. *He was sitting with her during the test.*

"Hmmm, I wonder why."

"Why didn't you ask Garett about it?"

"And show our hand? No. We're watching him. If he's involved, we'll find out soon enough." He rubs a hand across his face and I can see that he's tired. His shoulders slump now we're alone in the room. "I'm sorry you had to see that. It…that's not how I normally do things."

I press my lips together to keep from retorting. I need to figure out if all that was a show to make me stop trusting Yosua and his father, or if it's true that Garett has something to hide. I'm not sure I entirely trust Tok Yaakub anymore, at least not as the fair and impartial Temenggung I had always believed him to be.

cs

The minute I leave Temenggung Yaakub's office, I'm reabsorbed into the wedding madness. The throne room is scrubbed and polished, the thrones regilded so they gleam and sparkle, a large canopy erected for the ceremony. Amidst the yellow-gold of Mahan royalty, peeks the deep blue of Bayangan. There is no denying now the intention of this joining.

I forget to ask Yosua about what he was doing with Permaisuri Layla as I'm hustled from rehearsal to rehearsal where I sit or stand as required, increasingly bored and confused. I try to remember my allocated spots but soon give up, letting the wedding coordinator pull me around. I figure as long as I am near either Tok Ibrahim or Tok Yaakub, I should be in the right place.

Yosua's service is borrowed whenever I can spare him and he runs from kitchens to housekeeping to laundry without pause.

And then it's Jemaah day again, the day Permaisuri Layla is meant to return. The whole palace is barefoot on hot ground, awaiting their arrival. Ayahanda has sent several carriages to the port, along with an honour guard. The entire Majlis and I wait with him on the large, open balcony of the palace that overlooks the city.

Ayahanda paces, grumbling to himself. Tok Ibrahim makes the mistake of asking him to calm down.

"I'm calm," Ayahanda snaps. "What's keeping them?"

"Tuanku, give them time. It's probably the weather."

"The weather looks fine. Do you see anything wrong with the weather?" Ayahanda waves in the direction of the port.

It's a fair, sunny day with a low, warm breeze. The winds look stronger down by the beach though, if the way the coconut trees bend is any indication.

"Tuanku, you can't do any good waiting here. There are things you can still attend to while we wait—"

"I don't care, Ibrahim. It can wait. Everything can wait until after this treaty is properly signed, until after my wedding, after my honeymoon."

"Suci will not be—"

"I don't care one bit about Suci at this point of time. All they do is try to stop me from doing what needs to be done."

Tok Ibrahim backs off. I can see the Majlis exchanging uneasy looks. They gather away from Ayahanda, murmuring amongst themselves.

Ayahanda stops beside me. He looks more haggard than I remember, as if he hasn't been sleeping well. None of us have had adequate sleep for days, with Ayahanda's frantic organising, ordering everyone within earshot to do things that have been done and checked a million times.

"Are you all right, Ayahanda?" I ask. "You look tired."

"Eh?" He looks at me with bloodshot eyes. "I'll be fine." He searches the horizon for the sails of the Bayangan ships.

It is a bewitchment, what she's done to him. I cannot remember my stoic father losing sleep over anything. In all my vague memories of him fretting over Ibunda during her illness, I cannot recall a similar level of agitation.

"Sails, Tuanku! Sails! They're here!" someone shouts and Ayahanda's gaze snaps to the horizon. He watches them pull into port before he chases us all down into the throne room.

Another agonising wait in the throne room. I sit beside my father on the raised dais facing the assembled nobles and try not to fidget. It's a relief when the pounding of the kompang reaches our ears, along with the sweet seruling and other musical instruments. The hall falls silent in anticipation. The doors swing open and the Bayangans are announced.

Permaisuri Layla enters first, dressed in a traditional Mahan baju kebaya. A collective gasp escapes the waiting crowd. The kebaya top is form fitting, in royal yellow-gold, embroidered with fine gold thread. The long sarong she wears is a matching yellow gold, of the finest batik cloth. She is a vision, a beauty befitting the sultan.

A nagging voice in my head questions who has allowed her to wear the royal yellow before the wedding, whether she knows it's a breach of adat that could throw her in jail. Ayahanda won't imprison her though. He is entranced, with eyes for nothing and no one else, even the fact that the Bayangan Temenggung has entered behind her still armed. He doesn't notice the altercation that starts as the guards at the door demand the commander disarm.

Tok Yaakub goes to settle the matter, and when I look back, I see the Bayangan Temenggung approaching with a ceremonial-looking parang still tucked in his samping. *Concessions*. The rest of the ceremonial guards lay down their weapons by the door. The presence of so many Bayangan soldiers—although they are unarmed—makes me queasy. Ayahanda doesn't comment, doesn't do anything except stare at his bride. He rises when she's three steps away from the throne.

Permaisuri Layla drops into a deep bow and Ayahanda steps forward, offering his hand to her. She takes it, bowing forward and kissing its back, then pressing it against her forehead.

Ayahanda's smile widens even more. "Welcome, Permaisuri Layla Regis Ishi of Bayangan. And all of you with her."

"Thank you for your warm hospitality, Sultan Simson of Maha, Sovereign of Terang. May your reign be long and great," Permaisuri Layla replies as she rises. Her eyes are fixed on his.

"We look forward to peace between our countries by the signing of this treaty and the joining of our hands and hearts," Ayahanda says.

"As do we," she replies.

Outside, the Temple bells begin to toll.

"Will you join us for Jemaah?" Ayahanda asks.

Permaisuri Layla dips her head. "Yes, I will."

It's strange having a third person in the front row with us at Jemaah, when it has only been Ayahanda and me for the past decade. I suppose it's something I will eventually get used to. Permaisuri Layla sits quietly, just observing as we go through the motions of the service.

A paderi reads the liturgy, a diaken pours the sacred oil, the scent of incense rising to fill the Temple. Uskup Nur steps forward to deliver her sermon, giving the Bayangan permaisuri no more than a startled look before she begins. Ayahanda sits beside me, Permaisuri Layla on his other side, their fingers intertwined.

I should be happy that Jemaah is peaceful, that nothing untoward happens in this service. No warnings from Kudus, no sudden visions that disrupt the flow, no screaming or chaos.

But the smoke of the incense is rancid, the uskup's words of encouragement hollow and meaningless, the peace that normally comes with Jemaah an oil spill on choppy waves.

CHAPTER 8

"Tuan! Tuan! Wake up, we have to leave," Yosua whispers as he shakes me by the shoulder.

"What? Why?" I groan, rubbing my face into the pillow.

"We have to leave now. The Bayangans are attacking the palace."

I bolt upright, almost crashing into Yosua. "What do you mean attacking? The wedding is tomorrow. Why would they attack?"

"I don't know! All I know is what Ayah told me. He said to get you out now."

"My father? Where is he?"

"I don't know." Yosua dashes about my room, stuffing things into a bag. "Please, Tuan, hurry."

"The scroll. Grab the scroll and destroy it. It cannot fall into their hands."

Yosua nods and grabs it from my desk as I scramble to change out of my night clothes.

"Hurry, Tuan." He keeps looking over his shoulder at the door.

I follow him out. There aren't any signs or sounds of an attack. Everything is quiet and I wonder if Garett is mistaken. We head down the corridor towards the back door of the palace.

"What did he say?" I ask.

"Who?"

"What did Garett say?"

"An attack, Ayah said. He overheard the Bayangans talking about an attack on the palace tonight. He came to tell me—"

I stop him, grabbing his arm. "Has he warned my father?" If Ayahanda is prepared, we have nothing to fear.

"That's where he was heading after he woke me."

Why wake me first? Why lead me away from the centre of the palace, away from the soldiers that guard our living quarters? There are no guards here and it's too quiet. I look around, an uneasy feeling stirring in my gut. Something is wrong. Something has been wrong all evening.

Get the prince, use him as a hostage. Ayahanda will bend to their demands. It's suddenly clear in my mind.

"No." I turn back. I need to get to Ayahanda.

"What?" Yosua clutches at my arm. "Where are you going, Tuan? We have to get out of here!"

"He's using you. He's working with them."

"No! Ayah would never—"

"Thank you, Tuanku. We'll take it from here," a voice booms in the darkness.

Two Bayangan soldiers ahead. I spin to find the corridor behind us blocked by two more Bayangan soldiers. Trapped. Their parangs are drawn and raised, all pointing at me. My hand moves towards my waist but my keris isn't there.

Yosua stands beside me, still clinging to my arm.

"Just as we planned," the same voice says, the tall soldier ahead on my right. "Your assistance is much appreciated, Tuanku. We'll take it from here. Baginda Paduka will reward you greatly."

"*Tuanku?*" I glare at Yosua. They'd been referring to *him*, not me.

"What? I—"

"I trusted you," I hiss at Yosua. My heart twists. *Treachery and betrayal. By one of your own.*

The Secretkeeper had been right. I'd been suspecting members of the Majlis looking to make money, looking askance at the soldiers and servants who seemed a little shady. I hadn't expected to be betrayed by my closest friend.

Yosua stands mute, shaking his head, still hugging the bag he'd packed for me. My keris is sticking out of the top and I try to judge if I can snatch it in time. Had he packed it to keep me disarmed? I can't tell.

"You'll come quietly with us and not make a fuss," the tall soldier says. "Permaisuri Layla wants you alive, but she didn't specify unharmed."

O Kudus, Maha Esa, berkatilah hamba-Mu just this once. Please.

I snatch the keris, shoving Yosua as I do. He falls to the ground. I back against the wall and the four soldiers crowd nearer, their parangs still pointed at me. Their reach is longer; the parang can be as long as their whole arm, some longer. The keris is a short dagger made for close combat, not their cowardly stabbings. Still, it's better than nothing.

A stupid part of me wants to perform the ceremonial bow; the desperate part of me strikes out low as fast as I can. Drop, roll, slash, targeting the open corridor behind them. I bowl down at least one of them judging from his yell. I don't bother to check, sprinting away as fast as my legs can go.

I need supernatural strength, supernatural speed. I need to find Ayahanda.

I make it to the end of the corridor before I'm tackled to the ground. I slash wildly, but there are two muscled soldiers with longer parangs and greater reach and it's all too easy for them to wrestle me into submission. They flip me on my stomach and pull my hands behind my back, tying them tight at the wrists. Then they pull me up by the back of my shirt. Wrenching the rope upwards, they loop it around my neck and tie it like a leash.

Their leader nods and tugs the end of the rope, making me stumble. He then holds it out to Yosua who just stares at him.

The soldier tsks. "Don't be so skittish, Tuanku. It's your right to return to your former master everything he has inflicted on you in your years of slavery to him." He shoves the rope into Yosua's hand.

Yosua takes it without protest. My heart twists again. What did I expect? I guess I still hoped he'd deny it, that he'd fling it back in their faces and say he'd never wanted this. I want him to stand up for me, to remember the way he kissed my hand and swore his loyalty but he doesn't. He just holds the rope and continues staring at the soldier.

The soldier puts an arm around Yosua's shoulders and they walk companionably down the corridor. I can't do anything but follow, the rope tugging at my neck, two soldiers flanking me and the last at our backs.

Where are you, Kudus? My time of greatest need, remember? You said You'd be here, You'd give me Strength in my need. This is my need. Give me Strength.

I strain against the ropes, hoping against hope, begging and pleading for Kudus to come through. I've seen Ayahanda snap rope, even iron chains, like they were toothpicks. Nothing happens. Kudus is silent.

It's unnaturally quiet in the palace. I can't hear anything but the thump of our feet. Where are all our soldiers? Surely they know we've been breached? Surely they have raised the alarm?

And where is Ayahanda? Why is he not leading the charge? If he'd been alerted, he could have gotten out of the palace in time. Maybe he's amassing the army outside and doesn't know I'm missing. It doesn't matter. No matter how many of them come at him, he'll be fine. He'll be able to fight through them with his Amok Strength. As embarrassing as this is, I just have to wait for him to rescue me.

I'm escorted to the jail, where I'm shoved into one of the nearest cells. The door clangs with a strange note of finality.

"Yosua, wait!"

He doesn't turn, doesn't respond, just clutches my bag closer to his chest as he disappears down the corridor.

"Tuanku?"

I turn to see Tok Yaakub huddled on the floor of the cell, cradling his arm. It's bent in an awkward shape. The blood on his clothes doesn't appear to be his.

"O Kudus! Tok Yaakub, what happened to you?"

"Four soldiers. Lots of swords." He grimaces. "No strength."

"What? But you're the Temenggung."

"No *Strength*, Tuanku. Couldn't Amok. It's gone."

He's wild-eyed, gulping in deep breaths of air, or trying to.

"Tok? Tok Yaakub, calm down." I hurry to him. "Say that again."

"Have you seen Baginda Paduka? Have you seen your father?"

"No. No, I haven't seen anyone."

"He must be dead. There's no other explanation. How did they get past my men? How did they kill him?"

"He can't be dead, Tok. No one can kill Ayahanda. He'd overpower them in a second. Even if they manage to defeat his guards, the noise will wake him and he'll be able to defend himself."

Tok Yaakub shakes his head. "I don't know, Tuanku, I don't. But it's gone. There was no Strength! Don't you get it?"

My heart is in my throat. What does he mean *no Strength*? As long as the Sultan is on the throne, his Amok Strength flows to his soldiers according to their faithfulness, rank, and abilities. There's no reason for it to stop. If Ayahanda is dead, then the power should come to me, and the soldiers would still have access to the Strength whether or not *I* personally manifest it. It doesn't matter, I don't matter. As long as a male of my family line is alive, the Strength shouldn't run out. It doesn't make sense.

I try to explain to Tok Yaakub, but he shakes his head, moaning. "Kudus has left us, Tuanku. Kudus has truly left us." He squeezes his eyes shut.

I don't know what to do. There's nothing in the bare cell to set his arm or bind it, not that I can do anything with my arms still tied behind me. I try to cajole him into untying me. He struggles for a short while with one hand before giving up.

A steady trickle of soldiers come and go, shoving prisoners into the other cells. Tok Ibrahim is dumped in the next cell, beaten unconscious. Tok Benyamin bears bruises, limping in with his arms tied behind his back in a similar fashion. I catch a glimpse of the three Shahbandars in a cell further down, but there are too many people between us, nobles, soldiers, and servants alike, for me to get their attention. The only member of the Majlis I'm sure I haven't seen is Tok Rizal and I hope that means he's still free and fighting, defending us from the seas.

No one knows what's happening any more than I do. No one has seen Ayahanda since he retired for the night after Jemaah dinner. Conversation soon falters. There's nothing else to speak about except to ask how this tragedy has befallen us. There are no answers, only more and more speculation, fuelled by Ayahanda's mysterious disappearance.

The words *treachery* and *betrayal* loop in my head as I fall into an uneasy sleep with my back against the wall.

ᦄ

The sun doesn't shine in jail. It's still dark and gloomy, but it has to be morning when the Bayangan soldiers come to get us. They shout at us as they hit the metal bars of our cells with their parangs.

Tok Yaakub is pale. He gets shakily to his feet when the soldiers pull open the door to our cell. I try to push myself to my feet, but it's difficult without the use of my hands and my shoulders are numb. The soldiers don't wait, pulling me up by the arm and shoving me towards the door.

There's a low buzz of worried conversation as we're herded outside. The ones who aren't injured are bound but there's only one soldier to about four of us. We've overcome greater odds before. I'm sure we can overpower them if we coordinate. If I can somehow send a signal. If the Temenggung can issue a call to arms. They'll listen to him. I look for Tok Yaakub but I've lost him in the crowd.

The heat rushes at us as we step out into the sun. It's later than I expected, probably nearing midday by the strength of the heat and the height of the sun. A sudden silence washes over those in the front and the Bayangan soldiers prod them with their parangs to make them move.

"What's happening?" I ask.

No one answers, but they step aside to allow me through. With each step I take, a parang pressed against my back, my heart sinks. What can break our people this badly? What can make our strongest soldiers shake and grow faint? I see it in their eyes, a lost look, as if the world has ended.

I'm pushed through to the front.

Permaisuri Layla sits at the other end of the gelanggang under the shade of a large umbrella. She's flanked by Temenggung Jeffett and Garett. Yosua and Marla stand a few steps behind Garett. Rows and rows of Bayangan soldiers fan out behind them and around the gelanggang, more than I expected.

But that's not what captures my attention.

A man kneels in the middle of the gelanggang. He's dressed in nothing but his sleep pants, his upper body bare. His arms are pulled behind his back, wrapped in thick chains from his elbows to his wrists. His bare feet are hobbled in heavy bands of iron. The sun glints off his bowed head.

It takes two seconds for my brain to catch up with what I'm seeing. When I realise who it is, I fall to my knees with a cry.

O Kudus, save us all.

Permaisuri Layla smiles, but it isn't the sweet smile I've grown used to, the one that proclaims her love for Ayahanda. It's not the demure smile she uses when she murmurs her apologies and blushes, nor is it the bright one that flashes with a witty remark or when she's made a point. No, it's sharp and cruel and twisted.

"Behold your fallen sultan!" she declares.

Now I know why our strength has failed us, why our soldiers are powerless.

Ayahanda's head is bare, shorn of every single strand of hair.

CHAPTER 9

Maha burns.

The smoke is acrid in my nose, the fumes turning the sky grey. What the Bayangans cannot take, they burn. Those they cannot capture, they kill. The soldiers keep us on our knees in the gelanggang. They've traded rope for iron chains, keeping our ankles locked to our neighbours' and our hands tethered to our waists. One of them has treated Tok Yaakub's arm a little, tying it between two rough planks and strapping it around his neck so it's not dangling. They stand guard over us, parangs ready. It's not like anyone will fight back. Kudus left us the moment the blade touched Ayahanda's head.

Who betrayed us? Who let them know our one weakness?

Tok Yaakub grumbles against Garett who walks a step behind the foreign permaisuri everywhere she goes. I wonder at Yosua's protestations of innocence. Ayahanda doesn't say anything. He kneels in defeat, near enough to touch, but unaware of us all.

It is my fault. It is my fault for not pushing enough, not trying hard enough to get him to listen.

My fault for not being strong enough to stand for what I believed was right, for not being able to convince Tok Yaakub to evacuate our people before all this happened. Uskup Daud—no, Uskup Agung Ikhlas himself trusted me, and I have failed them all.

If I had at least done that one thing, more of my people would have been saved. They would be free, on their way to Impian, with the resources to plan our rescue. Now no one will come to save us.

Bayangan soldiers come and go, piling up treasures from the houses they've plundered, bringing in children in chains.

"Why are you doing this?" Ayahanda asks, breaking out of his stupor at the cries of a young girl. "Why do you do this, Layla? Take out your revenge on me. Let the children go."

A soldier strikes him on the mouth. "Show some respect!"

Ayahanda spits out blood.

Permaisuri Layla stands over him. "Why should I let the children go? Did you let our children go? Did you spare any of our people when we cried for mercy? You took our children, our young men and women, leaving us with nothing."

Ayahanda drops his head.

"As you held them to the fire, so we will hold you to the fire. I should kill you and leave your son behind bereft and orphaned like you left me, but I'll not make the same mistake you made. I won't leave behind a child who will come for revenge. By the time I'm done with Maha, it will be nothing but ashes. No one will be left to avenge you."

Then why leave me alive? Why not just kill me?

Garett places a hand on her shoulder. "Layla, please—"

"No, Garett, I will not be placated. I want them *both* to suffer. I will have my revenge for what they have done to me, for what they did to you."

"Layla, nothing good will come of this."

"You weren't there, Garett. You weren't there having to bury our parents, having to bury our brother. You weren't there for the devastation of Bayangan. If it weren't for Jeffett, I wouldn't even be alive. He took me in and raised me as his own—then restored the throne to me. Don't tell me what I can or cannot do, not when you have given up your right to the throne. Not when you're a coward who has tied yourself to this spineless pretender. What is he now? He hides behind his god and his witchcraft and his spirits. Cut off his hair and what do you have left? A shell. Not even a man!"

Garett flushes and looks away. "I did what I had to do to keep our people alive."

"You gave in. You even let him name your child after *them*." She throws a disdainful glance at Yosua, who's watching from a distance.

"*You* changed our family name—"

"To honour Jeffett Ishi, the man who saved me. Who stewarded Bayangan back from the brink. *You* gave up everything."

"What would you have had me do? Sacrifice a name or sacrifice a people? A name is a small price to pay for peace."

"And yet that hypocrite claims to not have kept you here by force," their Temenggung interrupts.

"Jeffett, please—" Garett starts, but the Bayangan doesn't let him continue.

"He vowed you were not slaves, but paid servants who willingly serve and refuse to return to Bayangan. I was there at the dinner table when he justified your subjugation to us. How can you bow your knee to him?"

Garett shakes in anger. "Ask him. *Ask him why.*" He jabs a finger in Ayahanda's direction. "I did what I could with what I had and you will not question me, Jeffett. True, I was not there with you in Bayangan, but you were not here with me either. You do not know how hard I have worked, what I've had to sacrifice, to keep us alive, to give us a semblance of freedom, the ability to even keep our families together."

Both Permaisuri Layla and Temenggung Jeffett start speaking at the same time, but Garett holds up his hands to stop them. He has regained his composure, appearing more like the stoic man I know. During all this, Yosua has crept nearer until he's standing by his father's side.

"What mistakes I have made are mine alone," Garett says, "but every decision I made was for the sake of my people. My honour demands that I uphold them, that I stay true to my word. I have no regrets."

Permaisuri Layla sneers. "And where do your loyalties now lie?"

Garett holds her gaze. "I do not know. When I do, I'll let you know."

At this lull, a soldier comes up and whispers in the Temenggung's ear. Jeffett nods and sends him away.

"The ships are ready. We leave soon. Gather what belongings you have, Garett, if you wish to come with us."

Permaisuri Layla raises an eyebrow. "If? Will you not be coming home, my brother?"

Garett sighs. "I will come. There is nothing left for me here." He gives us an inscrutable look.

"And you, nephew?"

Yosua gulps and looks at his father. "I never thought I'd ever leave Maha…"

"And now you can. You can build a whole new life in Bayangan. Brush the grubby taint of their foul witchcraft and oppressive religion off your soul. Be free to breathe in the fresh air, see the city your ancestors built, what your uncle and I have rebuilt. Your father," Layla grimaces at Garett, "has forfeited his rights but you haven't. You'll be my Raja Muda, Yosua. All the things once denied you will now be in your grasp."

Yosua lusts after it, his lips parting in desire. Beside me, Tok Yaakub swears under his breath. Yosua shoots a glance at me and his father before focusing his gaze on Permaisuri Layla. His body is tense and his hands are clenched before him, right fist resting on his left.

Trust? That's what his hands say, though I do not know who he's speaking to. Surely not to me.

His lips slowly edges upwards as he says, "That sounds wonderful."

Soldiers start shouting orders and I miss the rest of the conversation. They push and prod at us until we're all on our feet.

It's a slow march down to the port. The city is scorched. It's rubble and ash, dead bodies piled up and starting to stink. All in one night. Yesterday, we were eager for the Bayangans to arrive, anticipating a new era of peace. Today, we wish they had never come, mourning what we have lost.

Nothing moves in the city. I wonder if the only living Mahans left are those of us in this long chain snaking its way to hell. It cannot be. There aren't enough of us in this chain to be all that's left of Maha. There must be some who have escaped or are in hiding, some who have managed to flee to the countryside, out of sight and reach. Hopefully, the Temple has been able to get word to Suci and Impian, though they're too far away to rescue us. Maha is the strength of Terang. Neither Suci nor Impian have any significant military presence other than what we provide them. Our divisions have failed us.

I crane my neck. The Temple's spires are missing from the skyline. When our path winds past its shell, my heart breaks to see the spires broken on the ground, the large bell that has always called out to me lying in pieces. The ground glints with the shattered remains of mirrors. The priests lie scattered where they were slaughtered, red jubahs rent apart, revealing wounds that will never heal.

O Kudus.

My hope that our navy is still defending us, that Tok Rizal is somehow still alive, shatters when we reach the port. The Bayangan ships that brought Permaisuri Layla to us yesterday have multiplied, and our ships have been commandeered by them, Bayangan flags flying on Mahan masts. I do not know how they hid from us, how they managed to catch Tok Rizal off-guard and sneak in past our navy.

They take Ayahanda away. The rest of us are split into groups and led to different ships. We are loaded into the holds, our chains secured to great metal hoops in the walls.

By great luck or Kudus' blessing, Tok Yaakub is in the same hold as I.

"You knew," I say. All those secret codes and half-meanings in his office now revealed.

He looks at me blankly. "Knew what?"

"Who Garett is."

Tok Yaakub sighs. "I told your father to be careful."

"Answer me, Tok."

"Yes. Garett is the deposed Raja Muda of Bayangan."

"Permaisuri Layla called him brother." I can't help repeating it. It's a statement my brain keeps rejecting.

"We were supposed to have killed all the remaining royal family of Bayangan. We took Garett hostage, killed his younger brother Brett. We never found his younger sister, but we assumed she was amongst the dead we left behind."

I stiffen. "They're just doing to us what we did to them. What Ayahanda did to them."

"We should have killed them all."

"What?!" We have caused so much death and Tok Yaakub wanted even more?

"Baginda Paduka has never listened to the Temple, not when it came to the Bayangans. He lets his emotions take the reins. It's why we are in this mess," Tok Ibrahim interjects, his voice full of venom. "Look where it has landed us now."

I hadn't realised he was here. Tok Ibrahim crowds against us, a sweaty hand clamped on my shoulder.

"You were first to support the treaty," Tok Yaakub accuses. "You assured me that all would be well."

"It would have gotten him out of our hair! Always harping about the Bayangans years after we defeated them. Let him marry the girl, let him damn himself, whilst the rest of Maha carried on."

"All this wouldn't have happened if he hadn't insisted on taking hostages in the first place. Slaughter them, Suci said. Destroy the city and burn the bridge. We weren't supposed to bring them back as prisoners."

"You agreed to it then too, Yaakub," Tok Ibrahim sneers. "Don't deny your culpability. *Insurance* you called it. You were the one who suggested that holding Garett would be a bargaining chip to ensure Bayangan never attacked us again."

"How was I to know the girl was still alive?" Tok Yaakub gripes.

"It doesn't matter. Simson is out of the picture now. Mikal is who we need." Tok Ibrahim shakes me.

Tok Yaakub stares at him. "How?"

"If Simson is disqualified, who takes his place? The Raja Muda. Putera Mikal. He's still qualified." He grabs at the tail of my braid shoving it under Tok Yaakub's nose.

Tok Yaakub's face becomes calculative.

"It doesn't matter. I've tried," I choke out. "You think I haven't? I still have nothing."

"But you're qualified," Tok Ibrahim insists. "You can inherit. You're our last hope, Tuanku. You're the last of the line, and your vows are still intact. Aren't they?"

They are. But how do I explain that Kudus doesn't listen to me? He doesn't talk to me the way he used to talk to Ayahanda, the way he sends visions to the uskup. I've heard Kudus' presence described in many ways: a comforting presence, a warmth, a voice. But to me, Kudus is a distant, silent figure, has always been silent. I've never been enough for Him.

"Try," Tok Yaakub says. "One more time. Maybe this time things will change, now that your father has disqualified himself. If Kudus blesses you, our Strength will return and we will be saved."

The ship creaks and we hear the shouts of the sailors and soldiers outside. The listing of the ship changes and it feels as if we are moving.

"Hurry, Tuanku. This may be our last chance."

We *are* moving. The ship lurches and sways. We're leaving port.

O Kudus, why? Why me?

What can I do but nod? Not only are Tok Ibrahim's and Tok Yaakub's eyes on me, everyone in the hold who has heard their conversation is looking at me with hope.

The weight of their expectations lie heavy on my shoulders. I shift from my sitting position, dragging and arranging my limbs as best I can around the chains so that I am kneeling on the floor, arms raised as high as I can stretch.

"O Kudus, Maha Esa, berkatilah hamba-Mu dengan kuasa ajaib-Mu."

O God Almighty, grant Your servant Your miraculous strength.

It's the first time I'm uttering this prayer aloud in the presence of strangers. It's always in my head, on my lips, but I don't like praying aloud in public. It feels too exposed, too conspicuous. *What if Kudus doesn't reply?* But they're laying all their hopes and fears on me, their Putera, so I must show them I'm trying.

My feet tingle, there is a warmth in my heart. Fire descends on my forehead; heat flows down from the crown of my head to the tips of my toes.

O Kudus, is this it? You promised to come in my greatest need. I need You now. We need You now. Maha cries out for You. Forgive us O Kudus and save us.

Tears stream down my face. I cannot stop them. Sorrow fills my soul. Kudus is present, but He is silent. He is real but far away. He has promised, but His answer is still *no*.

I pull at the chains, rage at Him, scream in anguish, but it is no use. I have not earned my Strength, and I probably never will now.

CHAPTER 10

It takes a full day to reach the other shore. Faster ships could make it in shorter time, but these are slow ships, full to bursting with men and loot. It's too far to swim, but not too far that a flimsy sampan cannot survive, if you aren't stopped by the Mahan navy or a pirate.

It takes a long time to unload us confused, grieving Mahans and to herd us into something resembling order. We don't seem to have arrived at a proper port, at least not what I'm used to. It looks instead to be the ruins of a port, probably the one that Ayahanda destroyed after the war. With our navy controlling the waters, the Bayangans had retreated from the sea, focusing on trade with other nations by land.

Just past the ruins, the Bayangans have a large camp on a wide, open field. They can't have done that in a couple of hours, so it must have been set up earlier, before Permaisuri Layla and her entourage sailed over. This must have been where the extra soldiers had laid low, waiting until we were busy with Jemaah and pre-wedding feasting before they sailed over under cover of the night.

The tents are arranged in a large circle. It's almost dark by the time we're led into the middle, the tents hemming us in on all sides. The soldiers group us into a large huddle, leaving a large swath of space between us and the tents. In front of me lies a large, heavily-guarded tent which I assume belongs to the permaisuri.

Ayahanda is tethered to a stake driven deep into the ground within the circle of those guards, his face and body bruised in a way that reminds me of Yosua's recent injuries. He's still bound as tightly as he was this morning, no slack in his chains. Passing soldiers kick at him but he doesn't respond, just huddles there with his head hanging.

It's all your fault. Your fault. You should have listened. You should have believed.

The amount of venom that wells up surprises me. Before this, I was panicking because I was not enough, because *I* hadn't tried hard enough, but I see him now, bound and bald, in the light of Tok Ibrahim and Tok Yaakub's squabbling over the past and the truth of it hits me hard.

It *is* Ayahanda's fault. All this is due to his failings, *his* lack of belief, not mine. I turn away.

"No, don't look away, boy." Permaisuri Layla's voice rings out from across the clearing. She walks towards me. Behind me, everyone tries to shuffle out of the way, but there's nowhere to go since we're all chained together. "You should look and see what you may become. You don't want that, do you?"

"No," I grit out.

She stands close, smelling of pungent rose, strong, heady, overwhelming. She reaches over and grasps my chin. "Good. Then listen to me. You obey everything I ask of you and I'll see that you don't become…that. Unlike your father, I do have mercy."

"Didn't he become that because he listened to you? Because he obeyed what you asked of him against the Temple's wishes?" I want to bite back the words the moment I say them.

Permaisuri Layla laughs. "Spirited. But misplaced." She pinches my cheek, as if I'm a toddler. "Terribly misplaced. No, your father's predicament has nothing to do with obedience or disobedience. His crimes have been tallied against him and judged. You, however, still have a clean slate. Relatively." She wiggles her hand. "My nephew likes you. Otherwise, you'd already be dead."

I shiver at her words.

She pats me on the cheek. "Remember what I said, boy. You still have the power to determine your future. Don't waste it." She walks away.

The soldiers pass out hunks of dry bread and skins of water. I drink my fill before passing the skin on but can't do more than nibble at the bread. I haven't eaten since Jemaah dinner and I should be hungry, but my stomach twists inside me and my throat refuses to swallow. Tok Yaakub urges me to eat. I ignore him, hugging my knees as I sit with my back towards Ayahanda.

Some of my people still look at me with hope in their eyes. Not the ones from the ship—those have witnessed my failure, their faces hard and judgemental. There's no hope of slipping away. Even if we can get out of the chains, the soldiers patrol around us, dealing harshly with those they deem troublemakers.

The soldiers aren't too bad. It's the Bayangan servants who stroll by to jeer and spit on us that hurts the most. We've taken them in, given them food, provided them jobs, and now they turn on us. They target the Majlis and the nobles the most, using fists and feet, sticks and stones. Me, they just look at with contempt. I'm not even worth their effort.

It's late when Yosua comes and stands over me.

"Come to do your part?" I ask.

He doesn't say anything.

"Just kick me and be over with it."

"No."

"Then go away." I huddle into myself, hoping he'll take the hint.

He sighs. "I'm sorry."

He's betrayed me and he dares apologise? It's not like he made a simple mistake. He deliberately led me into the hands of those soldiers.

"Why did you do it?" I ask. If he won't go away, he should at least explain himself.

"I didn't—"

"Don't lie." I glare at him. "They knew you would lead me there."

He grinds his teeth. "I didn't know they were there. I was tricked too."

Tok Yaakub snorts.

Yosua scowls at him, then turns back to me. "Look, I don't have time for this."

"Then leave. I'm not keeping you here."

He bends down low, pulling my ear to his lips. "I cannot act like your friend. They're watching me as closely as they watch you. Kudus forgive me, I will have to do things to you that will make you hate me, but it is the only way I can think of to keep you safe. I'm sorry."

What?

Then he twists my ear hard.

I yelp in pain, trying to jerk away. "You crazy—"

"I warned you," he interrupts, still pinching my ear.

I grit my teeth. *How* dare *you! You won't get away with this.*

The soldiers close by chuckle.

"Give him more, Tuanku!" one of them calls.

"I'll have all the time in the world for that," Yosua replies as he straightens. "No need to rush."

"Are you claiming him then?" another asks.

"I suppose. If my aunt allows it."

"I'm sure she will."

This is called keeping me safe? Claiming *me?* Anger surges but I bite it back. What can I do? Flail my elbows at him?

Yosua stands there a moment longer as if waiting for something. His foot taps a rhythm on the ground and I look up at him, confused. Is he expecting me to say something? Then he huffs, rolls his eyes, and leaves.

Tok Yaakub and Tok Ibrahim huddle together, muttering. I glance over at them, but decide to keep to myself. I cannot bear their bickering and their sharp tongues, so full of bile against Ayahanda and me. I'd thought Tok Yaakub to be a friend, to be a kind mentor, but I don't know anymore.

Defeat changes things.

I curl up on the hard ground and try to sleep. Chains clank, as all around me people settle in for the night. There's some tugging and pulling, each trying to claim a space, stretching and curling, huddling together for companionship in the muggy, balmy night. There is someone against my back. I can feel their warmth but I don't turn to see who it is. Who cares? I scrounge up some pity for Ayahanda, knowing that there's no one guarding his back, no one to protect him or warm him. Not anymore.

Nearby, there's a different sound, a click. Then a second. Third. More conferring, Tok Yaakub's voice high and stressed, Tok Ibrahim's a lower grumble. Tok Yaakub shakes me moments later. He holds a finger to his lips. How is he free? I sit up as he squats beside me. Tok Ibrahim sidles over, fumbling at my chains. He has a small blade hidden in his hand that he uses to work at something in the lock until there's another similar click.

"How…?" I whisper.

Tok Ibrahim shakes his head.

Pairs of soldiers still patrol the perimeters of our huddled mass, but the last pair has just passed by without even looking at us.

Tok Yaakub jerks his chin at Ayahanda. Tok Ibrahim frowns and shakes his head. They turn and look at me.

Don't be silly, I want to say. *Save him. He's your sultan.* I just nod.

Tok Yaakub raises an eyebrow, but I can't tell what he's trying to say. Tok Ibrahim's expression is worse. Shock is written over his face. Shock and disgust.

What? I shrug. More meaningful glances I can't decipher. Why is it such a difficult decision to try to rescue your sultan?

Tok Ibrahim shakes his head vehemently. Tok Yaakub just holds out his good hand. There's a long pause, Tok Ibrahim glancing between me and Ayahanda several times before he hands the blade over.

"It's the only way, Ibrahim," Tok Yaakub says in a low whisper. "Tell me I'm wrong."

Tok Ibrahim sighs but doesn't reply. He turns to check on the soldiers. The one stationed down the row notices and starts to take a step towards us, but Tok Ibrahim shuffles away and the soldier stops. He puts his hand on the hilt of his parang as a warning but doesn't do anything. I watch him until he turns away and continues on his route.

When I turn around, Tok Yaakub is gone. Tok Ibrahim's hand tightens around my arm, holding me still. I search the shadows until I see a dark shape sneaking towards Ayahanda. Tok Yaakub stays low, favouring his injured hand. As he nears Ayahanda, instead of bending towards the locks as I expect him to, he rears up.

The blade glints in the moonlight as his hand rises and all of a sudden, I realise my mistake. He isn't planning on freeing Ayahanda.

"No!" The word rips out of my throat before I can stop it.

In an instant, the place swarms with Bayangan soldiers, lights held aloft. Someone—something—flies at Tok Yaakub as he strikes, knocking him off balance.

O Kudus, let that be enough.

Tok Ibrahim pushes me to the ground, clamping his hand on my mouth.

"Stupid, stupid boy," Tok Ibrahim growls as I struggle beneath him.

"Why would he…why would you—"

There is no chance of escape now. One of them pulls Tok Ibrahim off me and we are hauled apart. I struggle, desperate to see what has happened to my father.

"Ayahanda! Ayahanda!" *Please be alive.*

A stinging blow to my stomach takes my breath away, and I hunch over in pain.

"Stay down, boy!" Tok Ibrahim shouts before he too is silenced by rough fists.

By the stake, Ayahanda lies flat on the ground, a soldier standing over him.

Tok Yaakub fights single-handed against two soldiers. He's the best fighter of us all, with or without Amok strength, and now I see why he is our Temenggung. I knew he always held back during our spars, but I had never known by how much until now. He doesn't surrender, fighting with both deadly skill and desperation. It takes both soldiers, ganging up against him and pressing him hard. Another two come to join them, taking over when the first pair falter.

When it is over, Tok Yaakub is dead.

❧

The march into Bayangan continues early the next morning. It's not as if I slept all night. We're given more water and another hunk of bread, which I force down despite my lack of appetite. Tok Yaakub was right. I need my strength.

Why, Tok? Why did you do that? What has Ayahanda done to you that you think he must die?

I can't believe he's gone. Tok Yaakub is gone.

Why?

I don't know where Tok Ibrahim is. I need to find him. He knows why Tok Yaakub did it—he'll have answers. They separated us last night. Maybe he too is dead.

He can't be.

No one talks. What is there to say? I recite to myself the last part of the Secretkeeper's prophecy:

Stay true, stay firm. It is always darkest before dawn. Terrible things will happen and it may seem like your faithfulness is not being rewarded, but do not fret. Kudus sees all. He will honour you in due time. In all things, keep the faith, bowing down to no other powers.

I'm trying to keep the faith, I am. What little I have left. I'm scared that it won't be enough.

Bayangan comes into view in the evening. The walls surrounding the city are still blackened with fire, partially crumbled from the last war. No effort seems to have been made to rebuild them. We pause for water by the gates, where a large party awaits us.

An open carriage, white trimmed with gold, stands ready. The two white horses harnessed to it paw at the ground and toss their manes. Permaisuri Layla takes the hand of a groom and steps up into the carriage, arranging her skirts as she sits down primly. Yosua sits beside her and my anger wells up again.

Ayahanda is brought up behind it. They rearrange his chains so that his hands are bound before him to a bar that runs across the back of the carriage.

Thank Kudus he's alive.

There's a short discussion amongst them, then Temenggung Jeffett mounts a large, black horse. He raises his parang, shouts an instruction, and we set off.

Inside the city walls, rows and rows of shacks have mushroomed in the ruins of old houses. The buildings are haphazard and there's rubble everywhere. The stench of decay and sewage permeates the air.

Is this what Maha will look like in twenty years? I cannot imagine returning to a place like this. I cannot imagine why they haven't rebuilt, why neglect pervades this part of the city when they have money for fancy gilded carriages. Is it the lack of money? Lack of resources? If Bayangan really needed resources, why give up the treaty and the marriage alliance to take us captive? Surely continued trade would help Bayangan more than whatever plunder they've taken from Maha?

The deeper into the city we go, however, the more prosperous it gets. Wood turns to brick and stone. New buildings tower above us. There are some remaining patchworks of blackened stone, but most of the buildings have been rebuilt. We pass a large marketplace where all sorts of wares are on display. It is here that we stop first, where many of my countrymen are led away.

The Bayangan citizens come out to watch, lining the cobbled streets or peeking out of high windows.

"Behold your triumphant Permaisuri!" the soldiers that precede us shout, blowing their trumpets and waving flags.

Trade comes to a temporary stop. The Bayangans cheer for their permaisuri and their army. They jeer at us as we pass, pelting us with rotten fruit. Slowly we proceed through the throng, boxed in on all sides by sharp parangs and ugly, angry faces. The road narrows, inclining upwards. Walls rise again to greet us as we reach the end of our journey.

The Bayangan Castle is tall and narrow, made of scrubbed white stone. There are no large, wide windows for the breeze to flow through, only narrow slits that squint and sneer at us. It is a defensive place, built to repel others, unlike the Mahan Palace, which is gentle, open, and welcoming.

The gates open with loud clanks and the crack of whips, a great maw opening to swallow us whole. There are no open balconies or large gelanggangs, only suspicious turrets and the one crowded courtyard we're being herded into like cows.

The slam of the gates closing behind us is a knell of doom.

CHAPTER 11

I don't have much experience with dungeons, but this hole in Bayangan is the worst place I've ever seen. It's pitch-black and reeks. Things scuttle and squeak in the dark. Food is scarce, tiny crumbs that don't satisfy.

We huddle together for warmth—and because we're chained together so tight we can hardly move. All my limbs ache. My stomach cramps and my throat is dry. There isn't enough water. We've been here for days. Three, I think. I can now tell the difference between shadows, describe their textures and denseness. It's how I guess that it's morning when they next come for us. Not that it makes any difference.

The sunlight blinds me and I stumble on the uneven stones, knocking into the person before me. We're dragged to stand in rows and ordered to strip. Someone protests and there's the sound of fists on skin, so I do as I'm told. Then they throw buckets of cold water at us.

I don't want to enjoy it, but I do. The water pounds hard on my skin, but it's refreshing, and I can almost see the dirt sloughing away.

The soldiers joke about how disgusting we are. I want to ask whose fault *that* is, but I hold my tongue. No point in getting beat up for nothing. I want to brush my hand through my hair to get it clean, but they're snapping at everyone who moves so I don't. Invisibility is good here, no matter how much I hate it, how it irritated me in Maha. There, I lived for attention, tried to be noticed. Here, I decide, my lack of worth is good. It means they won't remember I exist.

Until he appears.

They've been taking prisoners away one by one. I'm near the front of the line when Yosua strolls in, dressed in fine new baju. Dark Bayangan blue. Royal. I stiffen when I see him. He heads straight to the overseer, the one with the whip, and speaks to him.

I'm pulled out of the line and made to stand in a corner. Yosua looks me over without saying anything. *What does he want? What is he going to do to me next?*

The overseer argues, gesturing at me, but Yosua adamantly shakes his head. Is this good or bad? Is Yosua saving me or condemning me? I can't tell.

At last, I'm led into a sweltering room, a furnace burning hot in the corner. They lock an iron collar around my neck. I'm made to kneel before a narrow shelf, held down by strong hands. The blacksmith comes towards me with a long iron bar. The end glows red and orange, fuzzy to my eyes, fresh out of the fire. I panic as he moves behind me, flailing as I feel the heat approaching. I'm pushed down harder, so tense I can hardly breathe. There's a rush of air, a sizzling, the smell of burning flesh. My own screams ring in my ears. They've branded me on my left shoulder, burning through my skin down into my very heart. The pain eclipses everything.

When I regain my senses, Yosua is gone. The soldier throws something at me. A pair of trousers. Thank Kudus. I pull them up, fiddling with the drawstrings so that they won't slip down my hips. He tugs my arm impatiently and I stumble after him.

The corridors of the Bayangan Castle are narrow and uneven. They're made to catch intruders unaware, I think, because I keep stumbling over the stones and stubbing my toes. There's hardly any room to manoeuvre when a contingent of servants troop by laden with plates of food. My stomach grumbles.

Eventually, the corridor widens. Tall columns shoot up along the way. The ceiling gets further and further away. Heavy wooden doors stand open and I'm led into what can only be the throne room.

It's larger than the Mahan throne room, larger than even the Temple's Jemaah hall. The walls are covered with scarred carvings, whether ruined by age or war I cannot tell. Large panels of coloured glass, the first large windows I've seen in this place, line the left side of the hall. The floor is shiny, scrubbed clean and polished. A red swath runs from the door all the way to the end of the hall, ending at the foot of the throne.

We don't walk on the carpet of red hibiscus. I'm shuffled to the side, to join the rows of Mahan prisoners lining the walls. Most of them sport strangely pale heads. There are still more prisoners being brought in. Only a few have been singled out like I have, mostly girls about my age. It doesn't forebode anything good.

The room soon fills with Bayangans, all dressed in fancy clothes and holding their noses when they see us. These are their nobles and their merchants, I guess, come to gloat. When the room is filled to bursting, there is fanfare and an official announcement and the permaisuri herself enters with a large entourage trailing her.

The throne dwarfs Permaisuri Layla when she sits on it, back straight and eyes glinting. To my surprise, Yosua stands beside her. On her other side, Temenggung Jeffett holds out his hand for silence.

"Citizens of Bayangan!" Temenggung Jeffett announces, "behold your victorious permaisuri!"

Cheers fill the room. My throat tightens as he points towards the back of the hall.

"And our vanquished enemy."

The crowd recoils then starts jeering.

I haven't seen Ayahanda since the night Tok Yaakub was killed. He looks terrible. His face is haggard, eyes bloodshot. There's a jagged wound on his upper arm—where Tok Yaakub's strike must have hit him. The clothes he's wearing are encrusted in filth—it looks like the same sleep pants he was wearing when captured. I can smell them from where I stand. He limps in, staggering under the weight of the chains they've wrapped around him. Two guards stand behind him, watching him as if he's still a threat. He's breathing hard as he passes by. I want to reach out and touch him but I can't.

The Bayangans grow even louder as he's led to the bottom of the steps and shoved onto his knees. He shudders then prostrates himself before the permaisuri at a rough jab from the guards.

"For so long, my people, you have been waiting for revenge. For so long, you have been hoping for salvation." Permaisuri Layla rises to her feet. She holds her hands out as if in supplication to the heavens. "I say to you, you need no salvation. We need no foreign god nor deals with evil spirits to save us when we can save ourselves. Bayangan is strong! And we have risen. What use is witchcraft to us? What use is tying ourselves to a crutch that can be so easily taken away when we are deemed unworthy?"

She steps down off the dais to stand over Ayahanda. Bending down, she wrenches his head up and twists him to face us.

"Look long on this face, the face of our nightmares, the scourge that haunted us all our lives. We were terrified of the Mahans for so many years because of their strength. We huddled in fear because they could break our bones with the snap of their fingers. Yet, look now and see what he has become.

"Break your bonds, Simson. Raise your hands and break these chains as you used to do. Do it."

Ayahanda shakes his head feebly.

"Do it."

He struggles to move, pulling at the heavy chains, but he's unable to even lift his hands more than a few centimetres off the ground. Ayahanda closes his eyes. He looks like he's mumbling something under his breath, but he's too far for me to read his lips, his voice too quiet to be audible. Above him, the permaisuri brings a foot down on the back of his neck, grinding his face into the floor.

"We need no gods to make us strong. We need no power that can be snapped the instant we step out of line, the minute our vows are broken. All that stood between us and victory twenty years ago was this." A waiting servant hands her something wrapped in silk. She pulls the cloth aside and holds up a twisted thing, brown and grey that reaches to the ground.

Ayahanda's hair, still in its braids.

My stomach lurches, bile rising up, burning in my throat. I choke it down. Her head snaps up in my direction, eyes boring into me. I shrink back, but there's nowhere to go. I'm pushed forward, fingers and elbows digging into my back.

Permaisuri Layla drops the hair. She turns and climbs the steps again.

"You must be wondering who this handsome young man is, and what he's doing here by my side." She takes Yosua by the arm.

"Maha took our Raja Muda twenty years ago after they slaughtered our Royal parents. They took Garett captive before our very eyes. We thought him dead, that he would be executed in Maha. We were wrong. Amongst the captives we have released and brought home, we found my brother Garett, his wife Marla, and their only son. Garett has given up his rights to the throne, but his son has agreed to stand in his place. Behold your new Raja Muda, Yosett Regis Baya."

There is a long silence in the hall before a slow clapping begins. It builds and builds until the crowd is roaring with adulation. Yosua stands there, watching them, his face the blank mask he assumes when he doesn't want to answer my questions. His gaze cuts through the crowd, skims the prisoners, and alights on me. It gives nothing away, but seems to search me for a long time before he looks away again.

The permaisuri thrusts out her hands for silence. It takes a while before the noise dies down.

"Today, we would like to reward those who have served us, who have in many ways made our victory possible. We cannot give away our biggest prize, of course. Simson belongs to all of Bayangan. But we have an equally great prize. His only son, Mikal."

Soldiers pull me forward, shoving me to my knees beside my father.

"For his assistance in revealing the secret of Simson's vows and in recompense for his years of servitude, we grant to Raja Muda Yosett Regis Baya at his request Mikal, the former Raja Muda of Maha, as his slave."

Heat rushes into my head. My eyes snap up to Yosua. He flinches, shifting where he stands. Permaisuri Layla is still talking but I can't hear anything over the rush of blood in my ears. All this time, wondering who had betrayed our secrets to the permaisuri, who had given the Bayangans power over Ayahanda, and I find it's the same person who betrayed me, who led me into the hands of waiting soldiers.

The memory of the day Uskup Daud came to see me plays in my head; the easy way Yosua had bowed, the earnestness with which he'd kissed my hand and sworn his loyalty makes me sick. The false *Tuanku* that had fallen from his lips, professing a fake allegiance. And I believed him. Even then, he must have known what he was about to do—or maybe had already done.

And he dares stand there smiling at the permaisuri, with his hands telling me to trust him. Again.

Rage fills me, more than the sorrow of betrayal.

My blood pounds in my ears. I cannot make head or tail of what's happening around me any longer. All I know is the anger burning in my veins. Anger and power both, a parang in my gut, a rush of strength.

O Kudus don't fail me now.

I rush at Yosua, too quick for the soldiers to stop me. If I'm fast enough, I'll tear him apart with my bare hands, cut him down with his own keris.

"Mikal! No!"

I ignore Ayahanda's rough yell. He is powerless to stop me. I reach the steps before I'm tackled from behind. Pain erupts throughout my body as I hit the ground. I flip around to wrestle them off me. Feint and dodge, grappling their wrists, twisting away, using every trick Tok Yaakub taught me. I swipe at my waist, reaching for my missing keris out of habit. Someone is laughing, someone else is shouting. I cannot focus on them. My senses are narrowed on the two soldiers still clinging to me, blocking me no matter what I do. I'm hampered by pain, my shoulder still throbbing and weeping from the brand, the metal about my neck weighing me down. Everything fades away when a boot stomps my upper body into the ground.

∞

When my senses return to me, I'm on my stomach, my arms and legs bound behind me.

"All of the Amok rage and none of the strength," Yosua observes from somewhere to my left.

"You have your work cut out for you," Permaisuri Layla says. "You sure you want him? I can give you someone a little more docile."

Yosua chuckles. "What makes you think I don't want the challenge?"

I twist to look, but a nudge to my back with something sharp keeps me pinned to the ground.

"If you're sure," the permaisuri replies.

"I am," Yosua says almost too quickly.

"Do you want to do something about…"

"No, I like it as it is."

"Risky. What if the strength comes back? It would be easier to cut it off, just to be sure."

I can't figure out what they're talking about, with my head still throbbing, my body screaming in pain. I'm hoping they're not thinking of cutting off any of my body parts.

"Maybe, but this way, it will be a reminder to him of all he's lost. I don't think the power is coming back. If it were going to, it would have happened when he attacked me. We've cut off the sultan. That should be enough."

"Fine. But if you notice any resurgence of this dirty witchcraft of theirs, even the faintest signs, chop it off to be safe."

"Yes, Aunt Layla."

Someone snaps their fingers, and the pressure on my back lifts.

"We'll leave you now. I hope you settle in well," the permaisuri says.

There's a shuffling of cloth and sound of footsteps. I cautiously twist, pausing every few seconds in anticipation of a blow, but no one stops me. By the time I've turned far enough, all I see is the backs of three people leaving the room and Yosua staring after them.

The door clicks shut and I'm left alone with Yosua. He sighs and rubs his face.

"What am I going to do with you, Tuan?" he mutters.

CHAPTER 12

Yosua's hands have always been gentle. When he bends over me, I do not know why I flinch. He huffs, then proceeds to cut off the rope that binds me. It is true then, what he said. All the rage but none of the Strength. I do not know why Kudus has deserted me this way, leaving me in the hands of my enemy and my betrayer.

"Come on," he says. He extends a hand to pull me to my feet. I take it and follow him into the bathroom. He makes me undress, then cocks his head to one side as he scrutinises me from head to toe. He circles me, humming to himself, then stops and prods the brand on my left shoulder.

I hiss in pain.

"Sorry." He sighs. He's shaking his head and biting his lower lip when he steps into view again. "You should wash first. You're filthy."

I look from him to the bathing area.

"I'm sure you know how to handle that," he says with a chuckle, then leaves, shutting the door behind him.

I stare at the closed door. What on earth is happening here? Why is he acting this way?

I must have paused for too long because Yosua calls, "Are you alright in there?"

"Yes. Yes, I am!"

I skulk over to the large tank of cold water and pick up the bucket. I'll take what I can get for now and figure it out later. I'm not going to pass up the chance to get clean. It takes a long time and many buckets of water to work out the dirt and the tangles from my matted hair, especially when I can't fully lift one arm and every part of my body is aching. Yosua doesn't seem to mind.

Once I finally feel clean enough, I lay down the bucket and look around. I take the towel that's hanging on the rack, belatedly wondering if it's Yosua's. Well, too late. The trousers have disappeared along with Yosua and I'm not going to go out there naked, so I use the towel to dry myself then wrap it around my waist like a sarong.

I step out and take a moment to examine at the suite for the first time. It's larger than my suite in Maha, with a combined living room and dining area. The sitting area on my left is furnished with plush carpets, four round-bottomed rattan chairs and a low table. Various colourful cushions and rugs are strewn about. A small window set high in the wall is pushed open to let the air in.

On my right is a dining set, made up of a large round, marble-topped table and four chairs. Yosua sits at the table inspecting various bottles of cream. In that moment, he looks so much like Garett, I could have mistaken him for his father.

He glances up at me, then gestures at the chair facing him. "Sit down."

"I don't understand," I say, standing in the doorway and dripping water on his floor.

He raises an eyebrow. "What's there to understand? You're injured."

"Why are you doing this?"

"You don't want your wounds to be treated?"

"Why are you pretending to be nice? After you betrayed us?" My voice cracks on the last two words. "You can take your revenge now. You don't have to patch me up first only to beat me up again."

He presses his lips together, nostrils flaring. "Sit down."

"No."

"You want me to beat you? Is that it? You want me to show the same force Aunt Layla uses against Baginda Paduka?"

"I want to know what you're trying to do. And don't call him that. Not when you don't mean it."

Yosua mumbles something I can't quite make out. "Tuan—" he says, then corrects himself. "Mikal, I assure you I mean you no harm. All I want to do is dress your wounds. Then we can talk. Please?"

I glare at him a moment longer, but there's nowhere for me to go, nothing I can do. I sit. His hands on my body are warm and soothing. I flinch when he presses against sore, tender flesh, but he doesn't apologise this time, just lightens his touch as he rubs the cream into it. It stings first before a cooling sensation spreads across my back. He wraps up the wound from the branding, but there's not much he can do about the rest of the bruises except to rub in the cream.

Once he's done, he hands me the jar.

"For later," he says.

"Thank you."

We sit staring at each other, neither of us knowing what else to say.

Yosua glances at the main door then goes to check that it's locked. He sits back down but doesn't meet my gaze.

"Why?" I ask, when the silence grows too long, too heavy.

He stirs, looking up from his hands.

"Why did you betray us?"

He shakes his head. "I didn't mean to."

"Didn't *mean* to? You betrayed us by *accident*? How does that work?"

"I never betrayed you."

"You still proclaim your innocence?"

Yosua drops to his knees before me. "Upon my honour, I swear to Kudus, I never betrayed you."

"What honour?" It's like a horrible parody. I'm sure he will rise and mock me soon.

"I swear, Tuan, all I've ever done is to try to save you."

"Forgive me if I don't believe you."

"I was tricked, Tuan. She tricked me." His face is turning red. He springs to his feet and starts pacing. "She looked so innocent and scared. She said…she said she was committed to the marriage because it was the only way to save Bayangan. To save the people she loved."

"And that made you reveal all our secrets?"

"She asked what adat she needed to learn to survive in Maha. What would cause offense if she did something unknowingly. So, I told her that…well, I told her a lot of things. All the rules we have to observe in the palace, the things Ayah does to keep the peace.

"Then she asked, but what about the sultan? What can I do to keep the sultan happy? To make him love her? Or what must she not bring up in case it offended him? I told her then that the sultan's hair was sacred but she didn't understand. So…so I explained. I'm sorry. I thought it was something everyone knew. Everyone in Maha knows it! I didn't know it was a secret from the Bayangans. I never thought she would turn it against us." Yosua runs a hand through his hair in distress. "She was going to marry him!"

I want to believe him, I really do. But how do I know if this isn't just an act put on to regain my trust? "But then you led me right into the soldiers' hands."

He shakes his head. "No, I didn't know they were there, I swear! I was supposed to get you out, get you free of the palace. We were supposed to flee to Suci— the Uskup Agung would know what to do. Ayah was going to warn Baginda Paduka but it was too late."

"They knew you would be there."

"I don't know how they knew! Maybe they overhead Ayah. Or they could have guessed." He grips the back of a chair, leaning towards me. "I swear I didn't betray you. I would never."

There are too many coincidences for me to believe that. If Yosua is telling the truth, then someone else tricked him. But how often can he be tricked? He's far from gullible, and his current distress feels real to me. Still, here I am, with a brand on my shoulder and a collar around my neck. "And this?"

I gesture at myself, at the collar, my nakedness.

Yosua winces but doesn't answer, going instead to a door I hadn't noticed earlier. He enters the room and returns quickly with a bundle of cloth. "You should, uh, put this on."

I shake out the pieces to find a singlet and pair of trousers made of rough cotton. They are a light grey, drab and homespun. It reminds me of the threadbare clothes the palace servants used to wear. That Yosua used to wear.

Yosua turns around and goes to stare out the window as I dress myself. The window is just at his eye level. He has to stretch on his toes a little to get a better vantage.

"That wasn't all I meant, you know," I say when I'm done.

"Would you rather go to someone else? Someone you don't know who will abuse you because they can? Just because you're Mahan?"

"You're saying you're not planning on abusing me? You're planning to what, let me lounge around in your rooms?"

Yosua grits his teeth. "Haven't you heard anything I've said so far?"

"I've heard you say a lot of things, but I'm not sure I believe them."

"You're here so I can protect you. At least until we find a way to help you escape."

"We?"

"Ayah and me."

I look at him incredulously. "You expect me to believe that Garett refused the position of Raja Muda, which *you* happily took, but you're both still working together to set us free?"

"It's not like that!"

"Fine, then tell me what it's like."

"Ayah is stubborn. He's holding on to his vows. He's sworn his life to your father and Maha, and forsworn his own crown in doing so. He can't reclaim the Bayangan throne without breaking those vows."

"And you don't have any such qualms."

"I made no such vows."

I stare at him in disbelief. "What do you mean you made no such vows? What was that then when you swore your loyalty to me before Uskup Daud? Playacting? Was that what it was to you? I believed you then. I trusted you."

"I swore my loyalty to you, not my life. My loyalty to you is separate from the issue of a claim to the Bayangan crown."

"I don't see how. You either serve me or you don't."

He slumps back into a chair and slings an arm over his eyes. "You know what, I don't care. I'm doing the best I can and all you do is question my motives and my methods. I don't know how else to help you, Mikal. We're stuck in this situation and I can either pretend to go along with my aunt and keep you close, or I can just forget it and go home. Go back to my father. Let you deal with whatever Aunt Layla or Uncle Jeffett throw at you. Because if I let you go, one of *them* will take you, and I don't think they'll be predisposed to be *kind* to you." He stares at me grumpily and rubs his face. "I can't protect you, not fully. We'll have to pretend you're really my slave in public. Where people can see us. But in here? In private? Do whatever you like. Even if that means being an ungrateful brat."

Yosua storms off into the bedroom, slamming the door behind him.

I look at the door to the exit and wonder if I dare. What would happen if I left? Should I risk it? No, not right now when I'm still injured. I don't know the routines, how many guards patrol the corridors, or how often. I don't know if I'll have another chance, but if Yosua means what he's saying, waiting might be beneficial. I can give him the benefit of the doubt for a few days, until I'm healed. Until I've found something to eat. My stomach growls.

I can't sit still so I pace, even though my body aches with every step. My shoulder is burning again. Looking out the window does me no good. The slight glimpse I get of Bayangan is hateful, its strict lines an eyesore. There's no centricity to it, no focal point that draws your eye, not like how the Temple centred everyone in Maha, or the way the gardens surrounding the Temple served as a hub for community.

There are no families strolling together in the streets, no children running along paths shrieking in delight. Sunlight glints off shiny armour, soldiers marching up and down straight streets like clockwork. Precise. Controlled. No fluidity, the way silat makes its practitioners as graceful as dancers. Everything is in sharp angles, no meandering lanes that lead you to beauty. Here, everything is functional and efficient, still transitioning out of military rule, and Yosua's uncle is in charge of them. Temenggung Jeffett is Marla's brother, Permaisuri Layla is Garett's sister, and Yosua is heir to every single thing in Bayangan. Suddenly, the seriousness of my position strikes me.

He has total power over everything I do. No one would dare stop him, no matter what he did. He is the *Raja Muda*, and they'd let him do anything short of killing me. No, they would let him kill me, if he wished to. And I'd just argued with him like a fool.

O Kudus, I really am an idiot.

I've been treating him like I used to, as if *I* were the prince. But now the tables have turned and I've been too dumb to realise it. And he's been too kind to do anything about it. It's no wonder the Majlis thought I was too young, too immature.

"Have you turned into stone then?"

His voice from the door startles me and I yelp in surprise.

A short, bitter chuckle. "No, I suppose not."

I should apologise but the words stick in my throat. I don't know what to do and it paralyses me. He sighs again.

"Look, I know this is hard for you. It's hard for me too." He moves over to the living area and sits on one of the rattan chairs. "Uh, you can, you know, sit." He gestures at the chairs and my brain finally catches up enough to take a seat.

"I don't know what to expect, Mikal. I'm speaking the truth when I say that I'm on your side. Aunt Layla expects me to be cruel to you on principle. For revenge. We'll have to figure out a balance based on how others act. Will you be all right with that? Or should I just keep you in here?"

"How long can you keep me in this room?" He knows I'm too restless to just *stay*.

"Not for long. They'll ask why I'm not using you and sending you on errands. You'll eventually have to do that, and I won't be able to protect you then."

I nod. This isn't what I expected. I don't know *what* I expected, but this isn't it, sitting down and discussing with my former servant how I'm supposed to serve him, how he's going to treat me.

He groans and buries his face in his hands.

"Hey, hey, Yos. We'll be fine. I'll..." I swallow hard. "I'll try. I mean, I can't promise..."

"You shouldn't call me Yos. At least, not out there."

Of course, idiot. I don't realise I'm chewing on the end of my braid until Yosua tugs it away. It's a bad habit I had as a child that I thought I'd gotten rid of.

"Mikal..."

"Tuan," I say in a small whisper.

Yosua freezes.

"That's what I have to call you, don't I?"

He looks away.

"You don't have to coddle me. I'm not a child."

He gives me a sidelong glance. Then his face shutters. "Right, you're not a child. And yes, you should address me as Tuan."

I drop the end of my braid, flushing.

"I know you don't believe me, but I can't afford to have you given away to someone else and lose track of where you are. If there is one thing that you understand, understand this. Both my father and I are committed to returning Sultan Simson and you to the throne of Maha. Even if we can't agree on how we'll do it."

I nod. I'll take that, for now. "Do you..."

He waits.

Courage is a slippery fish, constantly slipping out of my fingers. Permaisuri Layla said that Ayahanda belongs to Bayangan, but I don't know what that means. If she had explained, I missed it once the rage had over taken me.

"What's going to happen to Ayahanda?"

Yosua nods. "He's been sentenced to work in the fields. It's hard labour, and he'll be under very close guard."

"Is there any chance I'll be able to see him?"

"I don't know. I don't have any reason to go out there. But if I know Aunt Layla, she'll be showing him off at every official function. Maybe you'll be able to see him then." He stands and looks at the door. "Well, I don't know about you, but I'm hungry. Come along."

I take a deep breath and whisper the words that will become my expected response. "Yes, Tuan."

CHAPTER 13

It doesn't take me long to run afoul of the permaisuri. I attempt to copy the behaviour of the slaves that scurry through the castle, but it's like learning a silat move without proper instruction. I'm always a step behind, a move too late, earning myself stinging blows. I try to remember how the servants in Maha behaved, but it's not good enough. The adat here is completely different and I begin to empathise with Yosua's claim that Permaisuri Layla was worried about fitting in to Mahan court life.

I try to follow Yosua's orders, but it's impossible. My first impulse is always to answer back, to order *him* around, leaving both of us red-faced and frustrated.

Permaisuri Layla's summons comes like a lightning bolt. Yosua doesn't protest, just waves me to go with the messenger, whom I recognise as the leader of the soldiers who captured me in Maha. He drags me along by the arm.

"Let go," I protest, trying to pull my arm away. "I'm not going to run."

He scowls at me. His fingers dig deeper into my arm and he shakes me. "Hold your tongue."

"Or what?"

He shoves me against the wall and punches me in the mouth. I groan and he cocks his hand for another punch. I clamp my mouth shut and he nods. Then he resumes dragging me down the corridor.

Permaisuri Layla is waiting for me in her office. She raises an eyebrow at my dishevelled state and the bruise developing around my mouth.

"I should have warned you that Captain Karett isn't a very patient man."

He grunts. A swipe at my knees from behind sends me sprawling forward.

"Look, Mikal. I'm doing this for your benefit and for Yosett's."

The name throws me, until I remember the new Bayangan name she has given Yosua according to their royal naming conventions. I raise my head to look up at her, but a hand shoves it down.

"I can't blame Yosett. He's kind-hearted and he's so…Mahan. Garett has taught him nothing about Bayangan or our adat. He will learn, eventually. You knowing your place and acting appropriately will help him. Do you understand me?"

I nod.

"Let me hear you, Mikal. I'm giving you chances because I know you don't know your role either. But I won't be lenient forever."

"Yes, I understand."

"Yes *what?*"

I think hard, stammering out a "Yes, Tuanku?" just as Captain Karett raises a hand to strike me.

She chuckles. "Smart boy. See, you can learn."

I open my mouth to retort but clamp it shut at the captain's movements, fuming in silence instead.

Permaisuri Layla leans down and tilts my chin up to look at her. "The Captain will be providing you a very thorough training in a short while. Before he does, I want to make several things clear to you.

"Firstly, what I said on the journey here still stands. If you obey me and my nephew, you'll have a good life here in the castle. You'll have food to eat, a place to sleep, work to do. If you don't, I'll remove you from Yosett's care and destroy you." She seems to wait for something. "Do you understand?"

"I understand. Tuanku."

"Secondly, don't even think of escape. There will be no escape for you. You will live and die here in Bayangan. If you try to escape, your father will suffer for it. As shall you suffer if he tries the same. In fact, I'll follow your father's wonderful example. The price of your disobedience will be taken out on not just you, but all the Mahans in Bayangan.

"And if you harm my nephew in any way, I will cut you to pieces and throw you to the dogs. I will break you, Mikal, for all the wrongs your father has done to me."

She straightens and nods to the captain. He drags me out to the courtyard and my torture begins.

∽

Yosua is as changeable as the wind, as unpredictable as the storms. For all that we grew up together, virtually brothers, I do not know him anymore. Maybe I never knew him, deluding myself that our proximity, our closeness had meant friendship, brotherhood, and loyalty.

Is this what he felt for me all these years? This resentment and anger and fear? I remember the way I used to send him all over the palace, for even the simplest of things that I was too lazy to do myself. I'd listened to his concerns and complaints every once in a while, but disregarded them at my whim. I'd scold him for petty things, just because I was feeling out of sorts, or because someone else had reprimanded me. He is a stronger person than I to have stood up to my moods and argued so freely with me.

There are days when he is mean and difficult, free with his fists and his fingers, causing pain for the smallest infraction, the tiniest of faults. He pulls my hair then, winds it around his arm to yank my head backwards, and mocks me for it.

"What good are your vows, Mikal? Do you still imagine that this rat's nest will grant you the magical strength you always dream of? Should I cut it off, shave you bald like your father? But no, this is better. This is your shame, hanging around your neck. The mark of the ex-prince who could never measure up."

His words pierce my heart, my every vulnerability once shared with him in private now aired in front of his new friends in this new court. They snicker, pulling at my hair and using it to yank me around. Yosua doesn't let me bun it, doesn't let me hide it in a turban, makes me leave it loose or sometimes braided in a long tail that's easy to grab. I wish he would just shave it off.

Oh, how that word slides off my tongue now. *Tuan. Master.* It makes me shudder though I'd accepted it with ease from his lips all those years. How he must have hated me all that time without me realising it.

Today, I'm kneeling at his feet in the dining hall. It's habit now to slip to my knees at the flick of his finger. Captain Karett spent two weeks beating that into me. Sometimes I still hesitate, recalling myself, who I used to be. Yosua's face will grow sorrowful, as if it pains him as much as it hurts me when he kicks at my knees.

"You coddle him too much," Permaisuri Layla comments from the high table.

I look up from where I'm scraping my bowl with a spoon to see Yosua flush. The gruel is thin and tasteless, but it's all I'll get today.

"He gets restless cooped up in the room all day," he replies.

"So? Set him to proper work."

"Then I'll never see him."

She cocks an eyebrow. "Coddling." She smiles indulgently.

A sharp blow to the back of my head stuns me. "Don't look up at your betters," a low voice growls. I nod and stare down at the floor, fixing my gaze on the empty bowl.

"Thanks, Captain, but I'll ask you to refrain from touching my slave without permission," Yosua snaps.

"I apologise, Tuanku. It won't happen again."

It will happen again, when Yosua is not around to stop them, when he sends me out on the same errands he used to run for me. Laundry, messages, cleaning, dusting, polishing, getting food from the kitchens when he's hungry. And classes, endless lessons, where I'm both his scribe and his whipping boy. Constantly making sure his suite is clean and tidy. I used to wonder how he kept his tiny closet-room neat. Now I know how—he hadn't owned enough to scatter things around the way I used to.

At least he had a room. I have a pallet at the foot of his bed. Or a cupboard he threatens to lock me in when he's upset, though he hasn't done so yet.

There is a scattering of other Mahans in the castle. I've seen Tok Ibrahim a few times along with several of the daughters from noble families Ayahanda used to bring up as potential matches. There are others I don't recognise. We never talk. We don't have time and what is there to say?

"Focus, Mikal," Yosua says in an annoyed tone, pinching my ear.

"Sorry, Tuan."

"I don't want to, you know."

I hang my head, fighting back bile.

Like you really care.

"Mikal, oh Mikal, what will I do with you?"

I don't even know what it is I've done wrong this time. There must be something wrong about the way I look, or the manner in which I kneel, or some kind of reaction I've had, but I don't know what it is. The slap isn't hard. It's just humiliating to be corrected in public where everyone can see. Tok Ibrahim looks away, embarrassed.

Permaisuri Layla sounds amused as she says, "I could send him for more training with the good captain. You'll find his behaviour much improved."

"That's all right, Aunt Layla. I don't like the thought of other hands on him. It's no matter for me to discipline him myself."

"If that's what you want."

Yosua leans down. "I asked if you're still hungry."

Oh, that's what I missed. I am hungry. I'm always hungry, but I shake my head. "No, Tuan. Thank you for your provision."

He gets up and I follow after him, two paces behind, to his left, eyes on the ground.

I never did this to you, I want to scream at him. Ayahanda was right, we didn't believe in slaves, we didn't treat our servants as if they were less than human, as if their existence was a punishment. But he was also wrong. The Bayangans in Maha were never fully free either, tied to us by their promises and their words, and the provisions and rights we denied them if they stepped out of line. I realise that now. Yosua takes his revenge for those years of humiliation in public.

Yet at night, with the windows shuttered and the doors locked, he holds me close and weeps into my hair, murmuring his apologies over and over again.

"I cannot help it," he claims. "It is what they wish to see."

He searches my eyes for understanding, forgiveness, but I do not know that I can give it to him. I cannot make myself trust his words any longer.

"I cannot cut this," he says, stroking my hair. "I have to believe that as long as your vows are kept, Kudus may yet come through."

I don't tell him that Kudus will never come through for me. He never has. I don't think He ever will.

Yosua keeps up the pretence though. He holds Jemaah every week, or a parody of it, in his suite. We sit facing Suci, or the closest approximation towards Suci he can work out, and he recites the prayers from memory. He doesn't have oil or incense, so he lights sandalwood sticks and scented candles, begging Kudus accept them as a suitable substitute.

"Don't lose hope," he tells me over and over again. "Ayah is finding a way. He'll find a way. A ship. Something. You'll be restored to your throne."

As if.

There's no uskup or paderi to preach over us, so he reads from a copy of the Firman he hides deep in his drawers in fear that someone will find it. The Bayangans don't believe in Kudus. They call our gifts witchcraft, say that we dabble with spirits and dark powers. As Permaisuri Layla proclaimed, they believe in their strength alone. Sometimes I wonder if they're right.

"Why?" I ask.

"Why what?"

"Why would you do this? Why would you restore us when we haven't treated you as well as we should have? When we've made you and your people bondservants in Maha?"

"Because despite whatever has been done to us, we swore to serve you of our own free will in front of Kudus and the Temple. We do not take our honour lightly, Tuanku. And neither should you."

What use is believing in Kudus if He doesn't save us when we need it? What use is keeping my vow when Kudus hasn't kept His? Yet my body is not my own and Yosua refuses to let me cut my hair.

To keep me pure, he says.

To taunt me, I think.

He watches what I eat and drink, saying he wants to make sure that I keep away from alcohol. He's keeping my vows for me, now that I am powerless to keep them myself.

"What can I do to convince you?" Yosua pleads.

Nothing. It's a trick question. One meant to make me vulnerable to him again, to open up my heart for further betrayal and humiliation. I shake my head.

"You don't call me Yos anymore."

I've finally grown smart enough not to after the many beatings I have suffered for addressing him as such. If I only think of him as Tuan, I won't slip up.

"It is not allowed, Tuan. I have learnt my lesson."

He cries harder.

If only I knew earlier what a great actor he was, I wouldn't have been surprised at his betrayal.

Kudus, if You truly are real, save us. Please.

CHAPTER 14

Three months pass before Tuan decides to bring me on a visit to his father. Garett lives in a small house in the outer rim of Bayangan, as far away from the city as he can get without being in that awkward haphazard zone of decay. I'm familiar with it, having dropped off and picked up various packages, but I've never been inside. Garett is always nice and polite if we meet on the front porch, but he doesn't encourage conversation.

As I step into the house after my master, I can feel Garett scrutinising me.

Marla sees me and exclaims, "Yosua, how could you?"

"What?"

"Have you been starving him? He's all bones."

"He always says he's had enough!" Tuan protests.

"As if he wouldn't, the poor thing," Marla says. She comes forward and enfolds me in a hug. "Oh, Tuanku, I've been so worried for you."

I freeze for a moment, uncertain who she's talking to. "I'm...I'm fine, Mem."

"O Kudus, you don't have to call me that."

I cast a fearful glance at Tuan.

"If he makes you, I'll slap him silly. In this house, his rules don't matter. Now come." She pulls me into the kitchen. "We'll let them argue whilst I get some good food into you."

Marla's kitchen smells like home. She has fresh roti warming on the pan, and thick curry bubbling away. She pushes me to sit in a chair and ladles generous portions onto a plate.

"Go on, eat."

I thank her and tuck in.

"How are you, Tuanku? Really?"

"Please, Me—Marla, don't call me that."

She shakes her head and lays a warm hand on my forearm. "You'll always be my Putera, Tuanku."

"I don't deserve to be. Even Kudus Himself has proclaimed so."

"Mikal, I was there at your birth, I pulled you from your mother's body, held you even before she held you in her arms. I've watched you grow. You were born of Sultan Simson and Permaisuri Bintang, the heir of Maha. Don't tell me what you do or don't deserve to be."

I wish I could believe her. "Maha is no more."

"Does Yosua tell you nothing? It was so hard to get him to keep secrets from you back then."

I don't know how to answer her. This house feels out of time and place, like I'm six and sulking in Garett's room and nothing has changed. I just eat in silence.

The sound of Garett and Tuan quarrelling reaches our ears.

"Look, Ayah. I don't care what you swore in the past. Maha has fallen, Simson is no longer sultan. You aren't bound to his service any longer."

"We swore an oath of fealty. That doesn't change on a whim."

"*You* swore an oath, not *we*. And it isn't a whim. It's a fact. A truth. Why would you continue to have fealty to a man who is now below you?"

"I taught you better than that, Yosua ayell Garett."

"What? To lie down and roll over? To sign away our rights forever to no purpose?"

"The honour of your family—"

"Don't speak to me of honour when you won't even honour your name. MY name."

The thump of flesh on wood makes me jump. "As you wish, Tuanku Yosett Regis Baya."

There is a long silence. There are too many secrets in my father's and Garett's pasts, secrets that they still hold and still affect us now. I don't want to stir up ghosts, but I need to ask, I need to understand.

"What did Ayahanda do? What did he threaten you with?"

Marla's smile wavers. "The past should remain in the past, child. It's gone and over with. Nothing good will do from airing them now. Not anymore."

"Tok Yaakub said they weren't supposed to bring captives back to Maha."

"Did he?" Garett says from the doorway. "Yet Simson took many prisoners from Bayangan, most from the families of rich merchants. He reckoned to break Bayangan's spirit. Remove the heirs and break the cycle of wealth and leadership, and where do you leave a country?"

"I'm sorry," I say. "I—"

"Almost every merchant lost a child or two, whether young or old, male or female. He didn't count on our pride. In that first year, we started insurrection after insurrection. Some escaped but not many. None of them made it back home."

I turn to face him. Garett leans against the door post, face hard. He looks like a battle-worn soldier, not the tired servant he's been masquerading as all the years I've known him. I can see Tuan in the space behind him, leaning against the wall, arms folded and a sullen look on his face.

"Finally, Simson had enough. Four of my soldiers and I had fought free the week before. He rounded up the women, the children, those who were injured or otherwise unable to fight, then issued his ultimatum: surrender and swear fealty, or they would all be burnt to death."

Marla goes over and takes Garett's shaking hands in hers. He squeezes back then pulls his hands away, putting an arm around her waist before continuing:

"Simson chained the hostages in the public square, eighty or so of them. Then he had stakes erected, building a large wooden pyre. He released one of the wounded to carry his message, knowing we'd find him, not caring if we didn't. He gave us three days to surrender before all of them died. Twenty-five soldiers standing guard on eight-hour shifts, sharp and fresh, to my five hungry, bedraggled men.

"We fought, damn it, we fought. We killed ten and lost three, then Simson shows up, burning with that infernal power, holding a keris to Marla's neck. What was I to do, *Yosett*? What would you have done? Let them all die? Tell me!" He spins to face his son, hands held out in both question and accusation.

"They lit the pyre then. Put their filthy hands on the youngest children. He demanded that I kiss the keris. My fealty for their lives. My obedience for their survival. Otherwise, he would burn them from the youngest up, and Marla he would bleed out slowly."

"That's all over, Ayah. You are back in Bayangan. Your sister is on the throne. He has no more hold over you, except what you let him have."

Garett looks his son up and down. "When you agreed to be Raja Muda, you told me you would find a way to keep Mikal safe. You promised you would find a way to help him escape."

Tuan's face turns moody. "I'm trying."

Garett asks the question I want to ask. "Are you really?"

How can Tuan reconcile his promises of escape with his argument that they are no longer under fealty to Ayahanda? I doubt he will try to free us of his own good heart. No one is that pure, no matter what he babbles in his prayers.

"Then why won't you agree to help us?" Two strangers step into view, a man and a woman. They look, well, not Mahan, but at least from Terang. It's the woman who spoke. Tuan shies away from her, backing into the kitchen.

"It's not that I don't want to," Tuan stammers. "It's too risky. I'm watched everywhere I go. It's— there are many things I have to do because it's expected of me," he sends me a guilty look, "not because I want to. Right now, they humour me because they think I'm just a soft-hearted child. If I get involved in an *actual* rebellion, and Aunt Layla or Uncle Jeffett find out, I'm dead."

So you'd rather have me dead instead.

"As are all of us," the man replies. "What makes you so special?"

Tuan shakes his head. "Not special."

"Or are you hiding something?" the woman says. She says it like a simple question, but Tuan treats it like an accusation.

"I've told you everything I know," he protests.

She turns to face me. She looks at me and it feels as if she is seeing right into my soul. Her dark brown eyes are sharp and piercing, wise and knowing. If I step closer, she will tell me everything I've ever done and everything I've ever thought. Then she will judge me for it and find me wanting.

"It's not our place to judge you, Tuanku," she says as if in response. She makes a low bow. "I am glad to find you well. As well as can be."

I look from her to the man. He too steps forward and bows.

"Suci sent us," the man states, "to coordinate the rescue of the Mahan captives in Bayangan. Refugees are being provided for at Impian and the Impian army is getting ready to take back the city."

"Our mission is to rescue as many Mahans as we can and bring them back to Terang. However, our top priority is the freedom of Baginda Paduka, Tuanku, and the Majlis," the woman adds.

Now? Why now? Why not a month ago when I still had the strength to care?

They look at me expectantly. I don't know what to say. It's impossible. It's like the ship again, all their hopes and dreams weighing on my shoulders. Their faces blur. Their words are like babbling underwater. The ground sways.

ᘓ

"Tuanku?" Marla's voice is soft in my ear.

I'm lying on the sofa. I don't know how long has passed. I rub my eyes with the palms of my hands. My head is light, floating. Nothing seems real, but everything seems sharper, more defined than ever, like a veil has been stripped from my eyes. They've done something, cast some spell, but I don't know what it is.

Marla helps me sit up. Four of them—the unknown man and woman, Garett, Yosua—are sitting around the table, watching me. Marla kneels at my side, holding a wet cloth. She's been dabbing my face with it.

"You'll be fine, Tuanku. Just a dizzy spell."

"Thank you, Marla."

She nods and sits beside me.

"I would like to repeat that I do not agree to anything as yet," Yosua says.

"Point noted," the man replies.

"Who are you?" I ask. It feels rude. I want to take it back.

"I apologise. We should have introduced ourselves first," the woman replies. "My name is Rahsia of Impian. This is my colleague, Mahmud of Suci."

I nod as if any of this makes sense.

"As I said, we have been sent to rescue you," Mahmud says.

"Nek Ramalan believes Terang may yet be saved if you are restored to the throne," Rahsia says.

"Nek Ramalan?" The name is familiar but I cannot seem to remember.

"The Secretkeeper."

Ah. No, that's not good. The vision. I've forgotten all about the vision, about the prophecy. "The scroll."

"Scroll?" Rahsia looks puzzled.

"There was a scroll—Uskup Daud, before he left. He gave it to me. I don't know what happened to it." I look towards Yosua, disoriented, fighting my instinct to look down, look away. *Don't look him in the eye.*

"You asked me to destroy it."

"Did you?" *Too accusatory.* My heart pounds. I drop my gaze, take a deep breath.

"Yes," he says simply, but he looks away.

It must be somewhere in the suite. Somewhere safe, I hope.

"Will you join us?" Mahmud asks.

I look from him to Yosua. "What do you require?" There's not much I can do if Yosua doesn't allow it, my obedience enforced by the constant oversight of the soldiers and overseers in the castle. I don't know why I even ask. It's not as if *he* would allow it.

"We need you to spread the word amongst the Mahans in the castle. Ask them to prepare. Our first wave will target the Mahans out here in the city and the fields, but our second wave will be those in the castle, including you. They must be prepared to fight. It won't be easy. We're planning to hit as fast as we can so that by the time anyone realises the first group of Mahans has escaped, we'll already be getting the second group out. But it's risky—that's why you need to prepare to defend yourselves."

I don't know if it will work. I don't think it will work. Yosua—*Tuan*—sits there, scowling.

"They will follow you, Tuanku. They will rally around you," Mahmud says.

That's when I know that all their plans are a dream. "No one will follow me."

"Why not?"

"Kudus has deserted my family and my line. There is no more Strength in Maha." There will never be any more Strength in Maha.

"But your vo—"

I wave my braid at them. "This means nothing anymore. It's nothing but a symbol of my shame. You'll have to find someone else."

"There is no one else."

"Tok Ibrahim is in the castle. If you can get to him." The people will follow the Bendahara. He's recognisable as the second-in-command of Maha, Ayahanda's trusted right-hand man. Everyone knows who he is.

Rahsia and Mahmud exchange looks.

"It has to be you, Tuanku," Mahmud says. "*You* are the Raja Muda."

"Aren't you afraid the knowledge will betray your presence? Servants talk. They talk too much in the wrong places. It's too easy to be exposed. Then all your plans will fail," I say to deflect the conversation. If they haven't heard of my failure, I'm not going to be the one to bring it up. Let them hear some other way. Let Tok Ibrahim himself expose my failures.

"We'll take the risk."

"I won't," Yosua says. "I forbid you, Mikal. You can't do this. It's too dangerous."

"Tuan...Yos—"

"I shouldn't have brought you here."

"Yosua!" Garett reprimands him. "Remember the prophecy. Mikal must return to the throne."

Me? Return? Hah. Ayahanda must return, you mean.

"We're going." Yosua stands.

"As you see, I am not my own man," I say bitterly, as I rise to follow him.

The veil is falling again. This past hour has been nothing but an empty dream, raising hopes only to dash them. Whatever lightness has been infusing me dims, and I fight the veil of despair descending upon me.

Garett rises as well, his hands clenched. Father and son stare at each other in challenge. It's Yosua who breaks first, who turns away and heads to the door. Garett holds out a hand to stop me.

"*Now*, Mikal," Tuan calls, his voice sharp and impatient.

"Yes, Tuan," I reply as I hurry after him. "Sorry," I mouth to the group as I leave. I don't wait for a reply.

CHAPTER 15

Everything seems worse after that brief moment of hope. I hadn't realised how far I'd fallen into despair until now. Yet now that I know rescue is coming, I feel even more helpless and impotent. There is nothing I can do without Tuan's approval, and his orders feel even more restrictive than usual. I want to tell Tok Ibrahim about the rebellion, even if I have no details to tell him, nothing concrete to share, but I don't have the opportunity.

Tuan keeps me close. Except when he goes to visit Garett, which suddenly increases in frequency from hardly ever to every three days.

Why are you keeping me from them? Was everything you ever promised me fake? You lied to me, Yosua. You said you were trying to set me free. It feels like you're trying to keep me captive instead.

He forbids me from leaving the suite during these visits. I would leave, but I don't dare. I don't know where or how to find Tok Ibrahim, and even if I manage to lie convincingly to anyone who finds me skulking around, I'm in trouble if anyone tries to verify it. It's stupid. I should be able to go, but fear keeps me back.

Stupid Karett. Stupid training.

I rearrange the cushions on the floor facing the window and flop down on them. Outside, birds wing their way across blue skies. I wish I were out there with them.

I just need a little more time to gather my courage.

The door swings open with a creak.

"Look who's back," I say without thinking.

A cold silence greets me, followed by the sound of a throat clearing. My heart sinks. It's not Tuan.

I jump to my feet to face the intruder. I can feel the blood draining out of my face at the sight of Captain Karett. I fall to my knees, prostrating myself before him as I beg for forgiveness.

"Good to know you still remember *some* manners," the captain says gruffly.

"How can I serve you, Captain? My master is not in."

"I gathered. I'll wait." He takes a seat on one of the rattan chairs.

I don't know what to do now. Do I get up? Remain where I am? Serve him something? In all the time we have been here, no one has come into the suite uninvited. No, no one else has come into the suite at all. Tuan doesn't entertain guests. If he has to meet others, he does it somewhere else. This is his haven and mine, and now it's ruined.

"Would you like any refreshments, Captain?" I ask, just in case.

"Hmm."

What does that mean? I suppose a drink shouldn't matter. I pour a glass of cold water and place it on the low table near his hand. He doesn't acknowledge it, but neither does he correct me, so I suppose it's the right thing to do. I can't keep hovering here, so I make a stab at the best protocol, all the things he'd beaten into me months ago. I kneel near the door, as far away as I can get from him without being too obvious, and pray desperately for Tuan to return quickly. I hate that I'm depending on him, but what else can I do? Who else will protect me?

What seems like hours later, the door opens and I almost heave a sigh of relief to see Tuan. He stops in surprise when he sees me.

"What—"

Captain Karett rises from the chair, drawing his attention.

"Oh, I didn't see you there, Captain Karett."

"I do apologise for dropping in unannounced, Tuanku," he says with a short bow.

"How can I help you? Did you wait long?"

"No matter." The captain waves it away. "It's just a routine inspection."

"An inspection?" He glances at me. I duck my head. I've never heard of an inspection either.

"To maintain a high quality of service in the castle, we perform random checks on all slaves to see if their behaviour is up to par."

"I see."

"Would you like to know what your slave is up to when you're away?"

Tuan eyes me, gesturing for the captain to continue. "I wonder…"

My heart starts pounding, cold sweat forming. *O Kudus, no.*

"Lounging about on your cushions and being exceptionally rude." The captain points at my abandoned nest. I cringe.

"What am I going to do with you, Mikal?" Tuan stares at it then rubs at his forehead, as if he has a headache.

"Sorry, Tuan," I mumble, pressing my face into the floor.

He grabs my hair, pulling my face up to look at him. "Do you really want me to punish you?"

"No, Tuan, please. I won't do it again." I hate the whine that creeps into my voice, but it only makes the captain chuckle.

"Thanks for telling me, Captain. I'll deal with it."

Captain Karett just stands there, though, looking at us with speculation. "I'm sorry, Tuanku, but *I* will have to deal with it."

I gulp.

Tuan gapes at him. "Excuse me?"

"As this happened during an official inspection, the punishment is to be decided by the reporting officer. Which is me."

"I see."

"I have noticed that you continue to have trouble with disciplining your slave. I don't want to fault your kind heart, but it's not good for him or for you. I would like to request that I take over the discipline of your slave for you. If you would compile a report of his infractions on a weekly basis, I will ensure he is appropriately disciplined."

No, please. Tuan, for the sake of...of whatever we shared...

"I'm sure it's fine. I don't want to trouble you." Tuan's voice is still steady, but his hand is twisting in my hair. I wince as he pulls.

"It's no trouble at all, Tuanku. In fact, it's part of my duties as the new disciplinary captain in the castle." He smiles. It's a hungry, predatory smile. I shudder.

"I see."

"Baginda Paduka is concerned for you. She believes that this slave, as your former master, still has a hold over you. Which is why I decided to step in."

"Uh, thank you."

"Now, for this instance of laziness and insubordination, I would suggest a public whipping."

O Kudus, save me. I cringe where I'm kneeling, trying to beg Tuan with my eyes.

"It has been more than three months, after all. He should know better by now."

Tuan swallows hard, but doesn't show any other expression on his face. Instead of protesting, he asks, "Will there be permanent damage? I don't want to ruin his beautiful skin."

"Not if you do it right. I can raise maximum pain without breaking the skin."

The captain has threatened this before, in that first week, but he hasn't done it. I've seen slaves whipped in public and hurried by, praying fervently it won't happen to me.

Tuan nods slowly. "I suppose I can't say no."

Captain Karett's smile is cold and menacing. "Not really. It's under my purview. I'm just giving you the courtesy of getting your agreement."

"Yes, yes. I agree."

"Come along then, slave. Let's not drag this out."

Sorry, Tuan mouths when the captain turns.

I follow on their heels.

In the courtyard, I'm made to strip. My hands are chained above my head to the whipping post. I'm sharply aware of all the people around us, who stop to stare. I close my eyes to shut them out, but they still reside in my mind, jeering at me.

"Twenty strokes, Tuanku?" Captain Karett asks.

I suppose Tuan nods because I don't hear any audible reply. There's the swish of the whip somewhere behind me and I tense.

"Don't tense. It'll make it worse," the captain says.

I try to relax, but it's impossible. One by one, the strokes rain down on my back. By the time the captain finishes, I'm unaware of anything but the pain flaring in my back and my buttocks.

"I hope this has taught you a lesson," Captain Karett says.

"Yes, Tuan," I reply through my sobs. "Sorry, Tuan. Ampun."

He releases my hands and I crumple to the ground. "I will check on your behaviour very frequently, boy, and you had better show improvement or this won't be the worst you'll experience."

I nod.

"Get up." He thrusts my clothes into my hands.

I push myself up on shaky legs.

"Should we—does he need medical care?" Tuan asks.

"No. He'll be fine."

"Great. Well, I have to go. Come along now, Mikal." He turns on his heel and heads towards his suite, not waiting to see if I'm following.

"Well?" Captain Karett jerks his head in Tuan's direction. "What are you waiting for?"

I flee after him as fast as I can manage.

"Damn it, Mikal," Tuan growls as he slams the door shut after me.

What do you mean damn me*? This is all* your *fault. You left me alone!*

"I thought it was you, Tuan. He didn't knock! Who enters someone else's room without knocking?" It's all I can do to not shout at him, to keep my voice low. My fists clench anyway.

Stop it Mikal, you're in enough trouble today, I berate myself, trying to grab hold of the hurt and bitterness and rage—

"I told you they were watching us. I told you— they were waiting for you to do something wrong." He paces. I watch him, chest heaving, biting down on my lip. "They waited until I left without you, waited until you relaxed. They timed it perfectly to catch you out."

And you still left me behind anyway. "Tuan—"

"Go clean up."

I glare at him. He jabs a finger at the bathroom, giving me a shove. I stumble over, Tuan right behind me. The cold water on my back is soothing, as is the cream he rubs into it. I'm sure Captain Karett will frown in disapproval at my master rubbing cream into the red lines he so carefully marked me with, but he's not here and Tuan is fretting.

As if you have anything to really fret about. I'm the one bearing the brunt of your mistakes.

"I can't protect you forever. You're going to slip up and the Captain will see—or worse, Aunt Layla or Uncle Jeffett will see, then where will we be? You'll be beaten until your bones are broken and they'll give you away. I can't have that!"

"It's always about you, isn't it?" I blurt.

"Mikal!" He looks at me, hurt. "That's not true. I promise."

But it's true. He refuses to work with Garett and the Terangites because he says it will endanger *him*. He refuses to let me help them for my own benefit because it puts *his* position in danger. And now I need to act the proper slave, despite his promises to the contrary, so that *he* can keep me close to him. For what?

"Ampun, Tuanku," I bite out, "But everything you've promised me has been a lie."

✂

"If...if we work with Ayah and those two spies from Terang..."

It's early morning and I'm still half-asleep. Not that it matters to Tuan nowadays.

"I know you don't believe me, but I do want to help you escape."

Then why are you stalling?

When I don't reply, Tuan leans over the edge of the bed to look at me. He never can take the hint to just leave me alone.

"Working with them could mean death," he continues.

I shrug. Death is better than this hell. Ever since the whipping, Tuan has been acting even more strangely than usual.

In public, he's harsher than ever, especially with Captain Karett's constant hovering. The captain doesn't punish me directly, but Tuan follows his lead. It feels like no hour goes by that I'm not being corrected in some way or another. My body is a canvas of bruises and cuts. This means that in private, Tuan is even more weepy, caressing me softly and tenderly as if to balance it out. I don't dare push him away, so I just close my eyes and wait for it to end. He gives up faster if I don't respond, looking at me as if I've betrayed him.

I want to run away, but I don't know where else I can go. He's still the best option. *I'll remove you from Yosett's care and destroy you,* Permaisuri Layla's threat echoes in my mind.

"I've been talking to them, the spies. If we help them, you need to be in the first wave, not Simson. The prophecies all mention you, not your father."

I disagree. What I remember of the prophecy seems to refer in general to the Mahan royal family. Tuan interprets it to mean me, since he doesn't recognise Ayahanda's rule any longer. I believe that Ayahanda can still be restored. He should be. I don't think I have enough faith to hold Maha together, let alone Terang.

"Come, we should pray about it," Tuan says.

I sigh. *Must you keep up this pretence? Who are you trying to fool that you're still faithful? Me or Kudus?* A tiny sliver of guilt rises in my throat. Tuan is at least trying. I'm just going through the motions at his command.

I follow him into the living area. He locks the door as I fetch the candles. The candles are not in their usual place in the front of the drawer, so I reach in and dig through the contents with my fingers. They land upon a long cylinder. Tuan is still setting up the room, dragging the rattan chairs away so that we have an open space on the carpet, so I pull it out.

It's the scroll.

This wasn't here yesterday. I know. I just cleaned out this drawer. I'm sure I'd put the candles back in the front as well, so where have they gone?

O Kudus, hopefully it's just Tuan and not some other visitor.

"Mikal?"

I shove it back into the drawer, as deep as I can. "Coming, Tuan."

A second rummage reveals a couple of candles and I grab them, along with the flint. My hands shake as I light the candles and place them in the holders. I knew he hadn't destroyed the scroll, but I hadn't expected him to leave it around so carelessly, where anyone could just stumble upon it.

Tuan waits until I am kneeling beside him before he starts.

"O Kudus, Maha Esa—"

My mind supplies the words once so familiar on my mind and my lip. *Berkatilah hamba-Mu dengan kuasa ajaib-Mu.* But he's saying something else.

"Guide us. Reveal to us Your will in this. We believe You hold the world in Your hands and everything that has happened to us is in accordance to Your will. We beg forgiveness for our sins and our disbelief and we pray, O Kudus, that You would cleanse us again. Bring us back to Terang, to Your holy land, that we may sacrifice to You again. Save us, O Kudus."

His prayer is good and hopeful, but my brain runs counterpoint to it.

I'm sorry. I don't know any longer. I don't know how to trust You. I don't know how to trust him. Nothing makes sense. I'm sorry. Forgive my unbelief. But I can't.

Trust Me.

I spin to look at Tuan, but he's still praying, eyes closed, hands raised. He hasn't heard it.

I can't. I can't. I don't know You.

You can. You do.

I'm hallucinating. This tension has gotten to me, this dual personality of Tuan's is creating one in me as well. I scramble backwards. The smoke from the candles coalesce into a cloud, forming the shape of hand, palm down, fingers raised.

"Mikal? Are you alright?"

I shake my head, still staring at the cloud. *Wait.* Tuan turns, but he doesn't see it.

"What's going on?" he asks.

Wait on Me.

"Mikal?"

"Sorry, Tuan, I—"

I put out the candles. The cloud dissipates and I heave a sigh of relief.

"What's going on?"

I can't explain it. I don't know how to put it into words. I don't even know how to explain it to myself. Is this what the voice of Kudus sounds like? Or have I truly broken and am now hearing things?

A knock on the door breaks me out of my shock. Tuan looks at it with wide eyes.

"Quick," he whispers.

I grab the candles and throw them into the trash. There's no time to rearrange the furniture, so Tuan just throws the rugs and cushions back into the middle of the empty space and drapes himself across it. He nods at me and I go to open the door.

Captain Karett is standing there, hand poised to knock again.

"How can we help you, Captain?" Tuan calls from where he is.

The captain goggles at him. I look back and gape to see that Tuan has rucked up his shirt and messed up his hair. The captain turns to me and smirks. I drop my eyes, realising that I look just as dishevelled, and he must have all sorts of wrong ideas running through his mind.

"Your presence is requested in the court, Tuanku. We've caught a spy from Terang."

CHAPTER 16

They've caught Mahmud.

Permaisuri Layla has summoned all citizens into the large building that stands on the edge of the market square. I've passed it often enough and wondered what it was for, but never had the opportunity to ask. Now I know. It's their court of justice, where the permaisuri pronounces judgement on the guilty. I've never been in a Court House before. It is Impian that decides guilt and innocence for Terang, the mindreading Justices there who assess memories and proclaim justice on criminals.

Permaisuri Layla sits on an elevated throne looking down on the assembled people. Across from her is a long wooden block, stained and pitted. Below her is a cage of metal where the accused stands. Rows of chairs fill the rest of the hall where the rich merchant class of Bayangan sit, their slaves kneeling at their feet. The common citizens stand farther back, crowded together and craning for a better view. Each household is required to send at least one member to each sentencing, their attendance enforced by the soldiers that march the streets and now guard all the entrances and exits. Yosua sits on a smaller throne on the right of the permaisuri. I kneel beside him, as much on display as the criminal in the cage. Even more so, because I face them whilst all they see of Mahmud is his back.

Mahmud grips the bars as he stands facing us, his head held high. His face and posture declare his defiance. I search the crowd as best I can and find Garett sitting in the third row of merchants, Marla by his side. Moments later, I spy Rahsia in the middle of the crowd of citizens towards the back of the hall. Relief floods through me. All is not lost.

Ayahanda is led in to stand beside the cage. He's lost weight, muscles gone stringy and bones showing through his skin. His hair has grown, a short mess that covers the tips of his ears. He keeps his head down.

My heart sinks. *Ayahanda, what have they done to you?*

"What do you have to say for yourself?" Permaisuri Layla demands.

"Your time is coming, O Permaisuri of Bayangan. Do you still dare set yourself against Kudus, the Almighty God of Terang?" Mahmud declares.

Whispers spread across the congregated Bayangans.

The permaisuri's face darkens. "You implicate yourself further, spy."

"Listen, O Mahans! Your salvation is at hand!"

A soldier strikes Mahmud through the bars.

He must be a priest—no other Terangite would dare speak on Kudus' behalf. Belatedly, I remember that he is from Suci and curse myself silently. If he is a paderi, I could have spoken to the Uskup Agung himself back in Garett's house. If they'd wanted to convince me—and Yosua—they should have used his Perantaraan gift to open a mirror to the Uskup Agung or to the Secretkeeper. Why hadn't they offered? Or had they done that for Yosua and he'd still refused?

And if Rahsia is from Impian, what are the chances that she has Mindreading powers? Suci wouldn't send their weakest members. They would send those with power enough to help, power enough to make change. She *has* to be a Justice. Is that why Tuan is so scared of her? A realisation strikes me—that sudden clarity of mind must have been her doing. Had she reached into my mind and done…whatever it is her gift does? I'm not quite sure what it entails.

I miss what has been going on before me, lost in thought, until Permaisuri Layla steps forward, sceptre in hand.

"For the crime of using forbidden witchcraft in Bayangan, practice of an outlawed religion, and for treason against the throne, I sentence Mahmud to death."

The execution is immediate. There's barely a pause from the end of her sentence before Mahmud is dragged out of his cage and onto the executioner's block. They force him down, position his neck on the block. A parang glints in the sunlight as it rises. Everything is moving in slow motion and yet too quick to be stopped. It falls to a haze of red and to complete silence in the court.

Defiance dies. I'm left, mouth agape, my mind spinning and yet frozen.

No. No, Mahmud was supposed to set us free. No, Kudus, how has it come to this? Have You truly left us? Are You not mighty? Could You not have stayed her hand? Why?

The permaisuri holds out a hand, calling for order before the crowd can disperse. "We are not done yet."

Not done? How is this not done? Mahmud has been executed. Surely, we are done! Who else must you murder?

Unless they've also caught on to Rahsia? But no, Rahsia is still in the crowd, face pale and grim. Her eyes are closed. There aren't any soldiers near her nor is anyone looking at her, so she is safe for now. A murmur spreads through the crowd.

"You think we didn't see you, Simson?" Permaisuri Layla sneers. "Simson was caught talking to the spy."

My heart drops.

"Please, Tuanku, I—" Ayahanda stammers.

"I know it wasn't your fault. I know that you denied him."

"Yes, Tuanku! I denied him!"

"But you still listened."

Ayahanda opens his mouth to protest, but she silences him with a gesture.

No Kudus, not Ayahanda. Your prophecy. You're supposed to save him. He's supposed to lead us home.

"We are not without mercy. But we must still make you an example. Let this be a warning to all of you, Mahans. If you think we have been harsh with you, we can be a thousand times worse. There will be no rebellion! Remember your place and thank your masters for the provision they give you."

She glares at me. I can't help but shrink back. Tuan's hand on my collar stops me.

"Remember your place," she snarls. "For the crime of attempted treason, Simson's eyes will be put out."

Ayahanda gives a great cry and falls to his knees. Two soldiers grab him by the arms and drag him over to the bloody block. They kick Mahmud's body out of the way and heft Ayahanda onto it, holding him down on his back. He struggles weakly as hot iron comes down twice on his face.

"No." My heart twists in my chest. A deep pit opens up in my stomach. "No, Ayahanda."

Permaisuri Layla turns to me. "We are watching you too, boy. You'd better watch your step."

Tuan's hand freezes on my collar, holding me in place. I don't know if I was moving to run, or if I was going to attack her. He holds me as I flail. "Stop it, Mikal."

The thump of his hand on the back of my head doesn't help. It makes my head even more jumbled, my body trying to react to too many things at one time. I collapse in a heap.

Ayahanda is still bellowing his pain somewhere in front of me. I don't open my eyes. I cannot bear to see him. He cannot see me.

The Court House isn't silent any longer. The people are leaving, now their entertainment for the day is over. They laugh as they chatter, as if nothing important has happened, as if this cruelty is a normal and expected part of their lives. I lie there until Tuan tugs on my collar for me to rise.

I get up and follow him out. He locks me in his suite and doesn't return for hours.

❦

In thirty days, Maha will fall, betrayed by one of her own. The city will be plundered and set to flames. To save the people, evacuate the city to Impian. Suci will be attacked within the year of Maha's fall, triggering the Covenant of Salt. The Firstborn of the Sultan must fulfil the covenant for Terang to be restored.

Repent, O Sultan, and you may yet be saved. Maha depends on your faithfulness, Terang on your loyalty when darkness descends upon you. When vision fails you, call upon Kudus, Maha Esa and He will incline His ear to you in your desperation.

Listen carefully, O Strength of Maha. The Amok Strength will fall upon you in your time of greatest need.

Stay true, stay firm, O Firstborn. Terrible things will happen and it may seem like your faithfulness is not being rewarded, but do not fret. Kudus sees all. He will honour you in due time.

In all things, keep the faith, bowing down to no other powers.

I put the scroll away, shoving it as deep into the drawer as I can. I should destroy it. I know I should. But I can't. I keep myself busy by cleaning the suite, putting back the furniture to their original positions. I make the bed, clean the bathroom. Tuan—Yosua still doesn't return. It's getting dark outside. I am weary, beyond weary, but so restless.

I've missed my chance to talk to Suci. I want to blame Yosua, but I can't. I had the opportunity, but I let it slip through my fingers, falling back into creeping despair. Now it's too late.

No. Rahsia is still here, is still active. It's not too late. Even if there's no paderi to work their Perantaraan gift, she can at least keep us safe, can lead us home. That must be how she escaped detection. She must have read the approach of the soldiers with her mindreading powers but was unable to warn Mahmud or Ayahanda in time.

Who do I trust? If I have to trust someone, it would be Garett. I don't know enough about Rahsia, except that if she is sent by Suci, surely she can be trusted. *If* she is. Who's to say she isn't here for reasons of her own? I hate how distrustful I have become. I don't know about Yosua. I trusted him once, but he's too tainted by Bayangan, too influenced by the permaisuri and this castle, his new friends, that I hesitate. His fluctuating behaviour is manipulative, like his aunt's. I don't trust him, but I need him. I need his support, because he's the only one who can protect me.

Why won't he return?

I sit on the ground, hugging my knees.

O Kudus, what do I do?

The memory of the voice in my head grips me. I cannot allow myself to slip into despair again. With Ayahanda so maimed, responsibility for our people now falls upon me. Maybe I was wrong. Maybe the prophecies refer to me as Yosua believes. There is no one left. I cannot keep hoping that Ayahanda will rise up and save us all. No matter how far I've fallen, I need to return to Kudus and faith again.

I've asked for it long enough. It's time I claimed it in faith.

If He will speak to me.

I don't know if I can believe again. Not when Kudus has never answered me, has held back his promises from my life.

Have I?

Fine, he's not so silent now. Still, he answers questions with questions, leaving me blind and confused. Blinder than Ayahanda. I don't know where to put my next step.

O Kudus, Maha Esa, berkatilah hamba-Mu dengan kuasa ajaib-Mu.

The words slip into my mind like a fish into a net. It flops there and won't go away, trapped. I am agitated, caught in this web of intrigue, locked in this room with no escape. I fall into the once-familiar forms.

Silat takes me out of my head, puts me back into my body, centres me once again. But this time, instead of pointing out my lack, a Presence envelopes me, a warmth enfolds my soul. It grieves with me the loss of Tok Yaakub. It rages with me against the destruction of Maha. It comforts the pain of Yosua's betrayal, soothes the fear of what may come with the loss of Ayahanda's eyes.

There is no return. No return.

Trust Me.

The voices war in my head until I don't know which is mine and which is Kudus' and which is the spirit of fear and despair that claws at me. I focus on my body, letting the forms take over. I may not have the Amok Strength, but at least now I have His presence.

Forgive me. I will try. I will trust You.

In a tiny corner of my heart, there is a core of certainty. *It is time. It's my time to rise above. Maha will be saved.*

The sound of the lock turning in the door spurs me to spin, landing with a thud on my knees.

Yosua locks the door behind him, a startled look on his face.

I rise.

"Mikal?"

"I have to return to Maha." *If you were ever truly loyal to me…*

He fidgets.

I look up into his golden-brown eyes. His brows furrow. The conflict is evident on his face.

I swallow hard. "Yosua, I need to speak to Rahsia."

"It's not safe."

"I know. But we will never be safe until we are home."

"And where is home?"

"I don't know about you, but home for me is Maha."

He walks over to the window. A smattering of stars glint in the dark sky, but the moon is hiding.

"You'll have to decide, Yos, but I have made my decision. I cannot hide behind Ayahanda any longer. Not with what has happened today. Even if…" I falter. What if he forbids me? What if he has turned against me and decides to punish me for this treason?

O Kudus, give me strength. And wisdom. And courage.

"I'm not asking for your permission. I'm telling you what I'm going to do, whether you agree with me or not. If there is a chance of us escaping to Maha, I have to be a part of it."

He doesn't move. He stands there, head hanging.

"Yosua?"

His eyes glisten when he turns to me again.

Fear grips me. "What happened? Is Garett all right? Is Marla?"

"I don't know if I can do this."

"What—*Yosua.*"

"No, listen, Mikal. It's not that I don't want to let you. I'm afraid. I'm *terrified*. I don't want you to die."

I snort. "You would rather I stay safe here as your slave forever?"

"No! That's not what I—" His voice hitches and he takes a deep breath. Exhales slowly. "You're right. I've been selfish. It's what you need to do. What we need to work towards. I've talked to Rahsia. That's where I was, at Ayah's house. I told her we'd help. *I'd* help. In any way I can. We have to get you out before it's too late."

Doubt falls upon me again. "What if it *is* too late?" *And how can I tell if this mysterious voice is truly Kudus?*

But you can know, the voice whispers. **Seek Me and you will find Me. I speak to all those who follow Me.**

Is that You? Is that You, Kudus?

How am I to know? How am I to be sure? I hate this constant battle of thoughts, flipping between faith to doubt in a second.

My children recognise my voice.

They're familiar words, phrases from the Firman that the priests proclaim boldly, that Yosua reads aloud in a shaky voice. Now they resound in my head.

"It's not," Yosua says, but his voice is weak, unsure.

The tide turns yet again. My courage and my faith surge with it, whilst Yosua's recedes.

"Have you ever been sure of anything?" It's supposed to be funny, rhetorical, a joke, but it's too barbed, too raw in light of our moods right now.

"No," he says. "Even when I thought I heard Kudus speak, it was as if He were behind glass, under water. I did the best I could."

"You've heard Kudus speak?"

Yosua nods. "Once. When I told you I couldn't act like your friend."

"Outside Bayangan?"

"Yes." He drops his eyes. "I'd been praying, asking Kudus what I should do, and He told me to keep you close at all costs. It broke my heart, Mikal. I didn't want to treat you the way I did, but if I hadn't, Aunt Layla would have given you to someone else. Who knows where you'd be and what state you'd be in right now?"

Broke your heart? If it truly broke your heart, you wouldn't have gone through with it so thoroughly.

And yet he's right. If I'd been given to anyone other than Yosua, I would be broken, instead of sitting here sullen and insufferable, but still fighting.

I thought I was grown back in Maha, been resentful that none of the Majlis thought I was ready, upset that Ayahanda hadn't trusted me, but they'd been right. I was a child. I am still a child. Now I need to think ahead, to devise a way to return to Maha and save the sultanate, rather than gripe about how everything has been taken away from me.

"We have to escape."

"They're revising their plans," Yosua says.

We've lost Mahmud, but we still have Rahsia. "I need to meet them again."

"Tomorrow," he promises.

CHAPTER 17

"May Kudus provide clarity and inform our steps to come, keeping us all safe." Garett raises his voice and hands in prayer.

There are eight of us around the table—Garett, Marla, Yosua and myself along with Rahsia and three other Mahans I have yet to be introduced to. We all bow our heads as Garett continues praying.

"O Kudus, ruler of the heavens, Sovereign over Terang and the true Sultan of Maha, we acknowledge that You are greater than all the powers in the world, all the forces that exist on this physical plane. We do not understand why You have brought us here, or what Your plans are, but we pray that You reveal them to us.

"Speak to us and give us wisdom even as we seek to restore Maha and the rule of Your chosen ones, Sultan Simson and his son Mikal, to Maha and seek to reunite Terang under Your name again.

"Keep us safe from the wiles of Permaisuri Layla and Temenggung Jeffett who seek to destroy all that You love. Help us to trust in You, no matter what may happen, no matter how dark this journey may seem.

We believe that You are sovereign over all and that You love us. As we plan to fight against the Bayangans we pray that You show us Your way, Your plans, that Your name may be great in all the nations.

"You alone are great, You alone are worthy."

A peace falls upon my heart. I don't understand it. Whilst I'm still worried and anxious, it's as if the atmosphere has changed. It's like an outpouring of strength and serenity. Whatever comes against me, I can face it.

Garett introduces the three men to me as Hakim, Iskandar, and Ali before Rahsia takes over.

"Thank you for coming," Rahsia says. "With the loss of Mahmud, we have no way of communicating with Suci or the rescue team. Whatever plans we have made to meet the Impian forces can no longer be changed. We have two days, three at the most, before they arrive. Then we must strike, first the city then the castle."

"Raja Muda Mikal must be our priority," Yosua interjects. "I told you that yesterday."

I frown. *What's he been telling them that he won't tell me?*

"People will rally around Sultan Simson. They don't know *Putera* Mikal enough."

I hate the way she emphasises Putera, reminding us that whilst I am son of the sultan, I have not been appointed as the heir to the throne. It's a small matter, but a legal technicality which means that my status hasn't been confirmed. By blood, I have the right to inherit if Ayahanda dies without appointing anyone as his heir. Yet if Ayahanda wanted to, he could name anyone else of pure Mahan blood to be his heir and they would inherit the Amok Strength the same as if they had been of his blood line. It has happened before in the past, when the sultan had no living sons. I'm not sure what will happen in the case where there are sons of the line. I imagine the Strength will shift from me to be passed to the new heir.

"Didn't Mahmud say that you needed Mikal because people will rally around him?" Yosua reminds her.

"That was Mahmud's opinion, one which I didn't quite share," she snaps. She softens in the next second, looking a little guilty. "Unfortunately, we have lost him and we have no means of getting any further advice from Suci."

"The people know who Raja Muda Mikal is," Yosua insists.

"They know how much of a failure he is," Hakim sneers.

I tense. I do not recognise Hakim, but he must have been one of the people on the ship. It had been dark and I never got a good look at anyone. Especially since I was busy hiding from the shame.

"What do you mean?" Garett asks.

"Heard it told that the Bendahara and Temenggung tried to get him to invoke the Strength, but he couldn't," Hakim says. The other two men nod.

"No one could, not after the sultan's hair was cut." Garett's voice is steady, but I can see him clenching his jaw.

"They said he should have. He's the heir after all."

"They were wrong," Rahsia says.

She's the last person I'd expect to come to my defence after her frosty reception. Everyone looks to her for explanation.

"As long as Sultan Simson is alive, the Amok Strength resides with him—which is why we need to secure his release as quickly as possible. Once he renews his vows, the rest of the soldiers will receive their share again. It's only with his freedom and the return of his Amok Strength that we can win this war."

Tok Yaakub's last words come back to me. *It's the only way, Ibrahim.* So *that* was why he attempted to kill Ayahanda! He'd known this. He'd known this and still asked me to try invoking the Strength whilst in the ship. What had he expected? That with Ayahanda disqualified I'd somehow magically be deemed worthy by Kudus? I dig my nails into my thigh, trying to tamp down my boiling anger.

Damn you, Tok Yaakub.

"All this is a pointless distraction," Rahsia continues, giving me a curious glance. "We need to get back on track. Without the sultan, there is no point to anything we do."

It shouldn't hurt that Rahsia hadn't really been defending me, but it does. I shove it aside and try to concentrate on the discussion.

"Do you know where he is being held?" I ask.

"Yes. We've got eyes on him and his guards. He's even more heavily guarded now so it's not going to be easy to get him out. We'll also need to assign someone to guide him now that he's been blinded."

They pull out maps and spread them across the table, discussing various approaches and how best to disarm the guards. I don't have any insights to share so I just listen. It's strange to see Bayangan laid out on several pieces of paper. Even though I am becoming familiar with the layout of the city, especially their major landmarks, there are many places I've never seen. The narrow roads and squished together buildings make it seem like the city is small and confined, but the reality is that it's quite large and sprawling. The areas near the castle are crowded with people whilst the areas further out, like Garett's house here, are sparsely populated.

Ayahanda is held in one of the inner areas, which makes it difficult to break him out. There are soldiers at every junction and the frequency of patrols don't reduce in the night. Every morning, a squad of four marches him out to the fields where he works all day without break. A different squad marches him back in the evening. The best place and time to try to break him out is whilst he's at work in the fields or in transit. There are too many soldiers, though, and too many other slaves, both Mahan and Bayangan, who might get killed in the fighting. The men are sure the Mahans will join in the fighting once they know it's to secure their release, but no one knows how the Bayangan slaves will react. Would they support us? Or would they run back to their masters and report us? Garett wants to spend more time infiltrating the field slaves to see how many will support the rebellion.

Rahsia's shoulders slump. "I can't, Garett. There are too many of them for me to read all their minds. Not alone, and not across such a vast area. If there were ten of us, maybe. But I can't. I may be powerful, but not *that* powerful."

I was right, then. She *is* a Justice.

"I'm not even sure it's allowed," she adds.

"What do you mean?" Marla asks.

"We are supposed to ask permission before we read minds, except in cases of emergency. It's not something that we do for the fun of it."

Marla frowns as she asks, "You can turn your gift on and off?"

Rahsia rubs at her forehead. "Not on and off. I am always aware of the presence of minds around me, but I don't press further. I do not attempt to read their thoughts except by invitation, and I actively try not to listen to those who project too much." She winces and turns to me, "You, Tuanku, project entirely too much. You're giving me a headache trying to tune you out."

"Project?" I ask. I don't know what she means. I'm just sitting here keeping my thoughts to myself.

"Your thoughts are too loud, like you're shouting. It's like trying not to eavesdrop when the person is screaming at the top of their lungs."

"Sorry. I don't know how to control the, uh, volume of my thoughts." I want to dig a hole and bury myself. I'd been angry at her and she knew it. This is not the way to make allies and convince my subjects that I'm fit to rule. No wonder she's so insistent on Ayahanda's release!

"It's not your fault. I'll...It's fine." She sighs and leans back in her chair.

"We need to break this meeting up soon," Garett says. "The men need to get ready for work."

Rahsia nods. "Back to your point, we don't have the time to screen everyone. When the Impianans arrive, we need to break Sultan Simson out and try not to get him killed in the process. We have to take our chances and hope the rest of the Mahans don't mess it up. I would try to slip messages to them, but that's too risky now. The castle though..." She looks speculatively at me.

I look away.

Yosua has been silent all this while, but now he leans towards Rahsia earnestly. "Don't you think that breaking out Sultan Simson first is going to spoil the surprise and ruin the rest of your plans? Right now, Aunt Layla thinks she has the upper hand, having caught Mahmud. If Sultan Simson escapes, she'll know she has missed something."

"Explain," Garett orders with a frown.

"You're showing your hand. You attack and you release that first group, but then what? If you're not ready to strike the castle straight away, it's too late. Aunt Layla will clamp down on the rest of the Mahan slaves. Nobody," he nods at the three men, "will have any freedom left to move about on their own. All the masters will lock up their slaves in an instant. The patrols will increase, and that's going to leave everyone else in the city vulnerable."

"Putera Mikal will be fine with you in the castle," Rahsia says frostily.

"I'm not just referring to Mikal." Yosua tosses his head and grips the table. "I'm referring to every single Mahan in Bayangan who isn't released at the same time as Sultan Simson. I'm talking about the fact that Aunt Layla could announce the slaughter of every single Mahan, no matter who or where they are, if Simson were to be found missing and his guards killed. Is that what you want?"

Rahsia looks to Garett. "Do you think…"

Garrett is pacing before she even finishes the question, fingers worrying at his chin. "It's possible," he says. "Layla hasn't been very rational in anything related to Maha. I'm sorry." He glances at Marla. "Jeffett has nursed her desire for revenge to such an extent that she can be quite unpredictable."

"Uncle Jeffett won't be able to stop her. He's…well, he's balanced, but Aunt Layla holds the power now."

Rahsia glares at Yosua. "What else do you know? Do they invite you to their meetings?"

There had been a few in the earlier months, that I remember amidst a haze of fear and terror, before Yosua got distracted—serious meetings aren't as exciting as the parties his group of peers put on. His attendance wasn't required, so once he'd missed a few, they'd assumed he wasn't interested and stopped notifying him about them. After all, most of the decisions were made between Layla and Jeffett; the meetings were more to update the nobles than to get their input.

"I haven't heard much." Yosua gulps. "It was just the one meeting I was at."

"Try to attend more," Garett says. "Whatever information you can gain is vital at this stage."

Yosua looks at me. "But—"

"You don't have to keep protecting me, Yos," I say. "I'll be fine on my own."

"No, you won't, not with Captain Karett keeping an eye on you."

"Lock the door and keep the key."

"You could bring him with you," Marla interrupts. "No, listen, it's expected," she says when Rahsia starts to protest. "As long as Mikal keeps his head down and does what he's told, no one will question his presence. Jeffett is traditional. Extremely traditional. He won't question a slave kneeling at his master's feet. He probably won't even notice that the slave is there. You remember what it was like, Garett."

"Aunt Layla might notice," Yosua mumbles. "I don't even know when they usually meet, let alone how to request to be there."

"Look, as interesting as this discussion is getting, we have to go," Hakim says. He seems to be the spokesperson for them.

Garett nods. "Stay safe, Hakim."

Hakim nods in return and the three men leave.

CHAPTER 18

As easy as it is for Marla to say that we should attend their meetings, it's not so simple for Yosua to get himself invited to one on short notice, especially when we only have a couple of days to work with until the Impianans arrive. Yosua is unhappy with the decision. I agree with his argument to some extent, yet I also agree with Rahsia's reasoning.

If they can get Ayahanda to Suci and they can somehow plead for Kudus' forgiveness and restore his Strength, then the rest of us still trapped in Bayangan will have the ability to fight for our own freedom. If they fail, we're trapped here forever. Of course, it may already be too late for those of us in the city if Permaisuri Layla decides to go on a murder spree. *When*. She *has* threatened to take out her revenge on the Mahans if Ayahanda and I attempt to escape. What's best for Terang needs to be considered and, for now, Ayahanda is still our best chance.

I try not to entertain the idea that Ayahanda must die for me to inherit his power. There's something wrong with *that* conclusion somewhere—since

Ayahanda had grown into his powers *and* fought in many battles even before my grandfather had been slain in battle. They'd *both* had the power then. I cannot figure out why we cannot share the power now. I'm missing something and Rahsia isn't inclined to discuss it.

Only now that I'm looking for ways to approach the other Mahan slaves do I realise how difficult—and easy—it is. The castle is filled with soldiers, both on duty and off. Yosua is right—there is someone trailing him all the while, but he doesn't pay attention to me as long as I act as I'm supposed to. Which is subservient and terrified. It's not difficult. I *am* terrified.

When I notice Tok Ibrahim head towards the kitchens after breakfast, I nudge at Yosua's foot. He looks down without saying anything.

"Please, Tuan, would you like anything else to eat?"

He frowns at me then follows my line of sight. "Fine. But be quick about it."

"Yes, Tuan."

I hurry after Tok Ibrahim.

"I have news," I whisper to him when I've caught up.

"Have you." His tone is low and disinterested.

The corridor is empty, so I risk a glance. He isn't looking at me, his eyes fixed on a point ahead.

"Rahsia—"

His eyes snap up and he shushes me. "Not here."

Ugh, it's just like Tok Ibrahim to be so difficult. Still, he's right. People can overhear us here, or one of the Bayangans could decide to discipline us if we stand about in the corridor whispering. I say the first thing that comes to mind. "Please send regards to your master and convey my master's well wishes. Raja Muda Yosett would like to invite your master for tea in his rooms at eleven."

A frown furrows his brow, as if he's trying to figure out what I want. "Both of us?"

"I'd prefer only you, but if your master must come then so be it." Even I wince at the stupidity of my statement. Subterfuge is not my strong point.

"Mistress," he corrects. "Che Carla Tuah would love to accept, I believe. I will ask her and inform you of her decision shortly."

We split as I arrive at the kitchens, where I request a random selection of pastries to be sent to Yosua's suite along with tea at the specified time.

Yosua raises an eyebrow when I return to him empty-handed. "Were the kitchens all out of food?"

"I've requested for it to be sent up to your suite, Tuan."

He gives me a confused look but nods. "You took your time about it."

"I had to make arrangements for your tea with Che Carla."

His eyebrows shoot up even further and his voice is bemused when he says. "I suppose I should get ready then."

The minute the suite door is locked behind us, he turns on me. "What in Maha? Che Carla? *Why* are we having tea with Che Carla?"

"You are having tea with Che Carla. I am going to be confined in the room with Tok Ibrahim so that you're not hindered in any way."

"Why would I—Tok Ibrahim? I thought you were going to catch him on the way to the kitchens?" He narrows his eyes at me. "Oh no, you couldn't find a way to talk to him, could you?"

"He didn't want to talk in the corridors! And obviously we couldn't just chat it out in the kitchens! I did the best I could on the spur of the moment."

"But Che Carla!" His eyes are wide, and his breath comes out in short, sharp bursts.

"Is his mistress. Owner. It was the only thing I could think of to give him an excuse to come and look for us."

"I don't even—I've never even spoken to Che Carla in my life. This is ridiculous—"

"You can fake something, Yos. Say you've watched her from a distance or something and you'd like to know her better. You are, after all, inviting her for tea."

"Do you even know who she is?"

We're interrupted by a soft knock on the door.

Yosua freezes. "I—"

"It won't be her yet. I said eleven. It's probably Tok Ibrahim coming to confirm the appointment."

"Confirm…Right. Answer the door, then."

Tok Ibrahim doesn't enter when I ask him to. "My mistress, Che Carla Tuah is delighted to accept your master's invitation and will be here at eleven." He glides off down the corridor before I can catch him.

Yosua grimaces. "So, we have to go through with this."

"Sorry."

"You're not," he says flatly.

I grin at him. "Not really. Now, go get ready. The kitchens are sending up the food and drinks soon and you'll want to be all fresh and handsome before she arrives."

Adrenaline rushes through me. Yosua scowls but goes to get ready. I spruce up the living area, plumping up pillows and rearranging rugs and throws until it looks neat and inviting. I don't know if it works. It's not as if I've entertained any young ladies in my suite before. Besides, Yosua would have been the one setting the scene.

Yosua jumps at every sound in the corridor. I'm beginning to wonder who this Che Carla is that he's so anxious. I have no idea who she is, whether she's young and beautiful or old and nosy. She can't be all that bad—Tok Ibrahim doesn't look as haggard as some of the others and he has fewer bruises than I do. I press at the large purpling on my wrist; I can't remember what I'd done to earn that.

The food and drinks are arranged on the low table in the living room and Yosua has rearranged all the pillows into something more aesthetically pleasing than my attempt when there's a firm rap on the door. Yosua throws me a miserable glance before he leans back in his chair in an attempt at nonchalance, plasters a smile on his face, and nods at me.

Che Carla is not at all what I expected. She's a little old lady around Nek Ramalan's age. Maybe older. She comes up to about my chest. Maybe that's why I've never noticed her, hidden behind all the taller people around her. I let her in. Tok Ibrahim trails behind her in perfect form.

"Che Carla, a pleasure. Thank you for accepting my invitation," Yosua says, a blinding smile on his face. He gets up to greet her.

"Tuanku," she murmurs with a dip of her head, "to what do I owe this pleasure?"

"Some advice," he says. "And perhaps a favour."

He leads her to the chair then frowns as Tok Ibrahim moves to kneel at her feet.

"If we could dismiss them for some privacy…?"

She laughs. "What for? You're not courting me, surely."

He chuckles along with her. "No, no. But surely they shouldn't be privy to some of the, uh, political matters I want to ask your advice about."

Che Carla gives him a flat stare, before nodding. "I see."

"Mikal," Yosua says, waving us away.

"Yes, Tuan." I lead the way to the room. Tok Ibrahim follows without a word.

"What was so urgent that you needed this subterfuge to talk to me?" Tok Ibrahim asks once the door is closed behind us.

"There is an Impian spy called Rahsia in Bayangan. She's planning to rescue Ayahanda."

He quirks an eyebrow. "And?"

"She will break us out of the castle. We need to get the word out to the rest of the Mahans to be prepared."

He snorts. "And how are you going to do that? Stage a dozen or more bizarre meetings like this? You'll not get through them in a week."

"No, I thought—"

"You thought what? That everyone's owner is as kind and understanding as yours?"

"But you managed—"

"I managed because my mistress has been trying to gain an audience with the Raja Muda for weeks, but he has been obtuse enough not to understand her hints. She believes that one of her latest veiled comments has finally gotten through to his thick head."

"Hints? What hints and comments?"

"O Kudus, the pair of you fools deserve each other. You live in a warren rife with politics and underhanded scheming yet manage to be utterly unaware of everything that's happening!"

"Well, it's not as if I've ever had a chance to learn all these things, have I?" I lash out. My anger burns in me, unfulfilled rage at everything that has happened. "If Ayahanda and the Majlis had bothered to teach me instead of always pushing me away, don't you think I would be better equipped to understand?"

"If you had shown an interest in learning instead of always trying to throw your weight around, maybe we would have. But you were more interested in showing off and bossing your boy around. You were clearly unfit to rule."

"I was a fifteen-year-old child seeking for approval." More than ever, I wish for Strength so that I can tear him apart with my bare hands.

"At fifteen, your father was leading *armies*."

I don't need another reminder of what a failure I am compared to my father. Not now when it is *his* failure as sultan and defender of our faith that has landed us here.

"So, what, did that mean you could just push me aside? Were you trying to oust me and get someone else appointed Raja Muda?" His face hardens and suddenly everything seems so clear. "O Kudus, you were, weren't you? That was what the public match was about. To prove to the people that I wasn't chosen by Kudus so that Ayahanda would appoint someone else as Raja Muda."

"Your father was a failure. You were weak. It was evident that your line had failed. With a new sultan, new blood on the throne, Terang would have been able to break out of its slump."

"And who would you have suggested for that role?"

He smiles. "Who else better than his right-hand man?"

"You?" It's not such a stretch. Tok Ibrahim may only be a few years younger than Ayahanda, but he's fitter, stronger. Even though the Amok Strength bolstered him, Ayahanda aged very quickly after the death of Ibunda. Tok Ibrahim's son was older than me by a year or two. Who else on the Majlis was in on this? All of them? Including Tok Yaakub? I don't believe it.

Tok Yaakub would never have betrayed us. Yet he was the one who wanted to kill Ayahanda...to let the power flow to me. I take a deep breath. Now is not the time to worry about this. It's dead and gone. I don't know how long Yosua can keep Che Carla occupied. I'll figure this out later and they will pay for it.

"Anyway, what's past is past. We need to make plans for the future, unless you plan on being enslaved here forever. Help me understand what's happening now. Please."

He glares at me. His shoulders slump. "I take it Rahsia came with the one they executed?"

"Yes, Mahmud. They were working together with Garett and Marla to help us escape."

"Garett?" He frowns.

"Yes."

"That's certainly unexpected. I presume this means that your servant is in on this as well?"

Unexpected indeed that the Bayangan should be faithful to his pledge to the Sultan where the Mahan is not. "Yes, Yosua is part of this."

"Tell me what has been planned."

"Two days. We have two days to spread the word and prepare. A small force from Impian is expected to arrive on the second day to aid us. Rahsia aims to have them attack at the end of the dayshift, when Ayahanda and the rest of the field slaves are being escorted back to their quarters. Once that happens, we have no idea how Permaisuri Layla will react. She might decide to slaughter us all in return. But if we can make our break at the same time…"

Tok Ibrahim purses his lips. "Tell them to wait."

"What? Why? The Impian army arrives in two days and we no longer have a paderi to inform them of any change of plans. They can't risk waiting around for too long lest they be discovered."

"Don't be stupid. Send a messenger to meet them at the meeting point and prevent them from entering the city. Garett can go since no one will be checking on his movements. Tell them to hold off for five days."

"Why?"

"Because in four days, Temenggung Jeffett will be leading the Bayangan army towards Suci. The military presence here will be much reduced, and the crossing of the straits will be easier without the Bayangan navy haunting the waters. Everything in the city will be disrupted with the movement of the army, and Permaisuri Layla will likely be distracted as well.

"The day after the army leaves, the new schedules will still be a mess. Their guard will be down, so discipline might be more lax. Any disturbances and delays in transit will be excused due to the adjustment period, so no one will notice that Baginda Paduka and the other Mahans have escaped until it's too late.

"With Kudus' blessings, whoever is left in charge will try to cover up instead of reporting to Permaisuri Layla straightaway. By the time she's informed, it will be too late to recall Temenggung Jeffett and the army. Even better, if the second wave happens before she is informed, we'll be able to escape with minimal loss of Mahan life. We need to be quick and decisive."

I can see why Ayahanda relies on Tok Ibrahim so much. "How do you know this?"

"Because some of us know how to spend our time usefully instead of playing the fool."

"What?"

He presses his lips into a thin line. "I'll try to spread the word. If your master would deign to attend the permaisuri's war meetings, you would already have this information."

"He can just drop in at meetings?"

"He is the *Raja Muda*, you fool. Have you not gotten it into your thick skull that they do things differently here? Permaisuri Layla has given him the right to attend any and all meetings. No one will question his presence. Yet he doesn't. Can you tell me why?"

I don't know how to answer him. He doesn't wait for my reply.

"Because he's too enamoured of you. *You* take up all his time! You *waste* his time by being petty and acting out like the child you are. You whined that we kept you out of the Majlis, yet now that you're in a prime position to learn every secret this castle holds, what do you do? Throw tantrums so that your master has to keep disciplining you over and over again."

"What do you want me to do, Tok?"

"Grow up. Use your eyes and ears and that stupid excuse you have for a brain. Make him attend the meetings instead of gallivanting about with that crowd of youths he calls—" He breaks off and looks up towards the door suddenly. "Remember, Mikal, your *master* has privileged access to everything in this castle, and you with him. Use it."

He snaps his mouth shut and settles into a demure pose just as the door swings open.

Yosua stands there, a quizzical look on his face. I give him a quick nod before dropping my gaze.

We follow him out of the room. Che Carla is standing by the door and Tok Ibrahim hurries over to her side.

"Did you have a good chat, boy?" she asks.

"Yes, Mem," Tok Ibrahim answers.

"Thank you for your advice, Che Carla," Yosua says as we approach. He flicks a finger and I hurry to open the door.

"No worries, my dear. If you have any further questions, do send your boy to me."

Yosua dips his head. "Of course."

Tok Ibrahim shoots me a glare as they leave.

"Well?" Yosua asks. "You must have learnt something after putting me through that torture."

I relay to him all that Tok Ibrahim has told me.

He looks thoughtful. "We should bring your news to Ayah right away." He moves towards the door, turning back when he realises I'm not following him.

"Why rush? The meeting won't be until after dinner tonight. It would make sense for us to verify this news."

He looks at me with questions in his eyes.

I try to act nonchalant, but I can't. "I don't know how much I trust Tok Ibrahim," I admit.

"Surely he wouldn't be doing anything against Maha!"

"He was trying to get himself appointed as the next sultan! How do you know he hasn't made a deal with the Bayangans to put himself on the throne?"

"Why would they do that?" Yosua frowns.

"I don't know. Maybe they wouldn't. But he's proven himself able and willing to betray the throne."

"But not willing enough to kill the sultan."

Maybe I'm being too paranoid. My brain is bursting with too many things, too much information crowding without the time to process and figure out what is really going on. Tok Ibrahim's disdain hurts, but he's right. I was not prepared, I am not ready for this.

But whose fault is it?

"You're right. We should try to verify all of this," Yosua says. "Come, let's go hunt down some information."

CHAPTER 19

I spend the rest of the day following Yosua around, putting my training to good use. I keep my head down and my mouth shut. Captain Karett hovers nearby and leers at me, but as long as I keep my purpose in mind and focus my eyes on Yosua, he has nothing to accuse me of. It helps that Yosua keeps me somewhat distracted from him by providing mini commentaries with his hands.

I'm not fluent in the hand language of the dancers, but I know enough to follow some of his more sarcastic reactions. When he senses I'm getting restless, he often taps for me to wait. There are some gestures that flow right over my head and I can only guess at what he means, but it isn't important. He's only doing it to help me focus on him.

Meals here are a far cry from the communal affairs that Ayahanda hosted back in Maha. Decorum and adat ruled the day, each one knowing their place and rank. We waited on Ayahanda's grace to start eating, yet the atmosphere was communal. There was the

197

sense of friends and family gathering to eat together and share lives.

It's both more and less formal here. A big fanfare is made when the Permaisuri enters the dining hall, everyone rising to their feet and only sitting again when she does. And yet there are less rules—the hall is fraught with tensions and competition, each person jostling for position, to get seats next to whichever merchant or high-ranking person is in favour for the day. Only two seats are permanently reserved at the high table—Permaisuri Layla's and Temenggung Jeffett's—and many a quarrel has been started by those vying for their favour.

Yosua sometimes avoids the high table, but this evening, he sends me to reserve him a seat there. The merchants give him right of way.

"I think we should do it," Permaisuri Layla says to Temenggung Jeffett as I approach with a laden tray.

The Temenggung makes a disgruntled noise.

Her attention flicks to me for a second. "He needs the training somewhere."

"No. He's not ready," he replies. "He's hardly even interested."

I try not to tense, though the fear fills me that they're thinking of sending me away. *What have I done wrong now?* My mind skims through my recent behaviour, but can't identify anything specific. I can feel their eyes on me as I lay out Yosua's cutlery, followed by an overflowing plate of food, then slip down to kneel by the chair, wondering where Yosua has disappeared to. I don't dare look to see if she's still looking at me.

"Besides, who will watch over him?" Temenggung Jeffett says. "If you want to do it, at least wait until I'm back from the Suci campaign."

I freeze where I am. Tok Ibrahim had been telling the truth. I must have made a sound because the permaisuri notices.

"Yes, that's right, boy," she says. "I'm not quite done with Terang yet. We'll destroy Suci within the next month, followed by Impian. Nothing personal."

Yosua comes up then, hearing the end of her sentence. "Are you leading the campaign, Uncle Jeffett?" he asks, all innocence.

"Yes. We'll be leaving in less than a week."

"That's quite soon."

"I have a proposition for you," Permaisuri Layla says.

"Layla, we haven't decided," Temenggung Jeffett interjects.

She glares at him. "I have decided. You haven't agreed. Do you obey your permaisuri or not?"

He stares her down until she spits out, "Fine. We'll discuss this further when you return."

"Aunt Layla? What's this about?" Yosua asks.

"Don't worry about it, Yosett. I'll let you know when the time is right. I just have to get this old grump to agree with me." She smiles fondly at the man who raised her.

He shakes his head. "I'm getting too old for his."

They talk about general things for a while, Yosua making his questions sound as innocuous as he can.

I watch the servants circulating the dining hall. Back in Maha, I'd never paid much attention to them, except when they were serving me or when I wanted to request something from them. They'd always seemed very poised and collected. I'm not sure anymore. Here, the servants keep their heads down and scurry everywhere, as if there is a demon on their backs constantly chasing them. I hate it.

I spot Che Carla in the crowd, Tok Ibrahim close behind. Tok Ibrahim whispers something to a nearby slave. There's no reaction, but later on, I track that slave whispering to someone else. I hope this is it. The word is getting out.

It's the word 'Maha' that draws my attention back to the conversation.

Temenggung Jeffett has left and Permaisuri Layla is leaning forward, speaking to Yosua in quiet tones. I try to eavesdrop, but it's too soft for me to catch anything other than a few words. But those words make my stomach twist.

"...need a ruler...a province...trial ground... throne of Maha...as Raja Muda..."

Is she giving Yosua my throne? How dare she? She has no right!

Yosua's face is blank as he nods at various intervals. His hands are also silent.

"I'll think about it," he replies. He glances at me and I hurriedly look away. Maybe he's just stalling for time. I *hope* he's just stalling for time.

"Please do. I'll work your uncle around to agreeing to it."

"If I go—"

"When, you mean?" she says with a smile.

He doesn't press the issue, just continues, "—who will go with me? What do I do if I need advice?"

"Oh, I'm sure there are many in Bayangan who would love to go as part of your retinue. You just have to ask. All the second sons who don't have a chance to inherit will be vying for your favour in hopes that you grant them new land. Carla has been dropping hints about her grandnephews in the Majlis diRaja. Azett as the older boy is expected to take over her role, but Azman might do."

"But they wouldn't have experience either."

It's all I can do to keep my face blank. I train my eyes on his feet, wishing that I could burn through them with the heat of my gaze.

"Good point," Permaisuri Layla agrees.

"Are there any in your court that you would be willing to spare, if only for a few months until I get my bearings?"

No, Yosua. You can't. You can't seriously be thinking about this.

I sneak a glance up, but his face is still blank and his hands lie flat on his thighs.

What are you thinking, Yos? What aren't you telling me? No, the right question is why won't *you tell me?*

Permaisuri Layla's smile is shark-like. "We can discuss your options. But not today. I have many things to arrange before Jeffett leaves for Suci."

"When exactly does he leave?"

"The plan is to set out in four days, though it may yet be delayed depending on the status of our supplies."

"Ah, I'll not keep you then." He rises, as does the permaisuri, so I get to my feet as well.

Yosua gives his aunt a hug.

"How's your little pet behaving?" she asks as she pulls away.

"Better these past few days," Yosua says.

She comes up to me and pulls my head up to look at her. I glare right into her eyes.

"Still fiery, I see. No matter," she pats my cheek, "I'll look forward to breaking you even more." She shoves me aside as she turns back to Yosua. "Let me know as soon as you decide. Either way, I expect you to start taking up more of your duties."

"Of course, Aunt Layla," Yosua replies as she walks off. "Come, Mikal."

I hurry off after my tight-lipped master, feeling very unsettled.

 og

"Bastard. You're planning to take it, aren't you?" The rage that blazes forth from me is unexpected. Frightening, even to myself.

Yosua had waited until we were back in his suite before confirming that his aunt has offered him Maha as his princedom.

Deny it, Yosua. Prove that everything you said before is true.

"Look, it's a temporary…I don't…" He massages the bridge of his nose. "Fine, yes, I plan to accept—"

"You'd take my throne from me and laugh as I grovel at your feet. You want to break me like Layla has done my father?" I'd expected it, but having Yosua admit it to my face enrages me even further.

"It makes *sense*, Mikal. This is our chance!"

"The throne of Maha will not be taken by infidels. It will not be occupied by Bayangans. The world will end before Kudus allows that to happen!" I raise my fists, rushing at him.

"Mikal!" Yosua grabs me, pinning me to the wall.

I'm momentarily stunned. When had I become so used to backing down and cowering that I just *let* Yosua throw me around? I thrash in his grip. He's stronger than I remember, his recent training with the parang starting to show. *When did I become so weak?*

"That is not what I intend to do! Listen to me, Mikal," he whispers fiercely as he forces me on my knees. "This is how we get back to Maha. You will be restored to your throne. But for now, you must stop. Stop this before you endanger everything."

But I can't stop. Some spirit has taken over, all the fear and the anger and the bitterness welling up in an overwhelming flood that threatens to drown everything in sight.

"Stop it or I will have the guards throw you in the cells tonight!"

"You'd like that, wouldn't you? Would it help you to get into character as you wrest Maha from me? What are you going to tell Garett and Rahsia?"

"The truth."

"That you're a two-faced traitor?"

"Mikal!"

"Because if you accept this from Layla, you are. You'll be undermining everything we've been working for." *You've betrayed me once. I can't let you betray me again.*

"It is the best and safest cover to get you back to Maha, where you can *conveniently* raise an army without her knowing. We don't even have to smuggle you out."

"You believe she will send me with you?"

"Of course she will, silly!"

"Why would she do something as stupid as that?"

"Because that's the way things are done here. Haven't you been listening? Don't you pay attention to the things going on in Bayangan? Ibu, Che Carla, and Tok Ibrahim have all confirmed at different times that they will allow even *you* into the war meetings just because you are my slave. They don't see you as a person. They think they have you under control so they don't care what you hear because they think you can't do anything about it."

"But if she sends me back with you—"

He snorts. "It's her grand plan of humiliation. Show you off as a slave to emphasise to whoever's left in Maha that she and Bayangan are mightier than Maha and its royal family."

"That's not how—"

"It's how the Bayangans think. How *she* thinks, anyway. She'll send you back with me, and once we're there, out from under her thumb, we'll be able to get aid from the rest of Terang to overthrow her rule in Maha."

"And your precious Aunt Layla is just going to accept that without sending her army over to smash down the rebellion?"

"You heard her—the army will be busy in Suci."

"You say that like it's a good thing!"

"No, it's not. But it takes eyes off us, Mikal. Don't you see? This is Kudus' plan. This is Him opening a way for us to return to Maha without dying."

"Don't be ridiculous. Kudus' plan would never involve putting you on the throne."

Even if Yosua's right, the plan is weak. We would still be surrounded by Bayangans—the advisors and guards that Permaisuri Layla is sure to send. Who's to say we won't be watched by her spies? If she's testing Yosua's capabilities at ruling, someone will report his every move back to her. Besides, he's got a taste of power now. I hardly think he's just going to sit back and give Maha back to me no matter what he says. He'll rally Terang to overthrow her rule in Maha, but who's to say he won't claim Maha's throne for his own in return? It's not like we can go back to what we used to be.

Yosua grabs my arm. "Come on."

"What?"

"If we are going to make it for the meeting at Ayah's tonight, we need to leave now."

The journey to Garett's is silent. If I open my mouth, I'm liable to scream at Yosua, so I clamp it shut. He just looks at me and sighs, constantly sighs until I want to punch him.

We're almost at Garett's house when I ask, "What are you going to tell them?"

"Everything. Why? What do you want to keep secret? Rahsia's going to know anyway."

"She said she doesn't read minds without permission."

"She also said you project like you're screaming."

That shuts me up. I need to learn how to quiet my mind. Rahsia says she can teach me—this 'shielding' is something she says anyone can learn whether they have Impian's mindreading powers or not—but when and where will she be able to do that here? No, it's one of the things that will have to wait until we're out of this place. She'll just have to put up with me until then.

"What's wrong?" Rahsia asks the minute we close the door behind us.

Yosua shoots me an I-told-you-so scowl. We gather around the kitchen table and, between Yosua and I, tell them all that has transpired today.

Garett rubs at his temples. "I'll meet the Impian army. They should have a paderi with them who will be able to warn Suci."

"I doubt Suci will have the manpower to defend themselves," Marla says.

"They can evacuate the outlying areas and pull back into the Temple compound. They should be able to defend the Temple." Garett doesn't look like he believes his own assurances.

"There aren't enough soldiers in Suci, are there?" I hazard a guess.

He looks at Rahsia, who stares at her hands.

"It doesn't matter," she says. "Nek has been expecting it. We'll warn them, and Tun Ikhlas and Nek will have to decide what to do. They should already have plans in place." She shakes herself and then looks around at us. "Yes, we'll do as Garett says. The Impianans will have to lay low and wait. I agree that if we delay until the Bayangan army leaves, we will have a better chance of escape. It also gives us more time to prepare and spread the word."

"If we wait for my appointment, I can bring a larger group back to Maha right under Aunt Layla's nose," Yosua insists.

"You are not accepting that post!" The table shakes with the strength of my rage.

"It's the safest way, Mikal!"

"You don't even know when that will be. It could be next week, or next month, but what if it's next year? It will be much too late then."

"The way she talks about it, it will be within the month. If she can persuade Uncle Jeffett, we'll leave with the army this week so that they can escort us to Maha."

I scoff. "Jeffett hasn't agreed, and it's unlikely that he'll change his mind in a mere matter of *days*. He could manage to veto it, or change all the terms, and then we would have missed our chance here and now."

Garett splits us apart. "We should take a vote," he suggests.

"No one is going to support Yosua's stupid plan."

"Mikal, calm down." Marla lays a hand on my trembling arm. "What are our options here?"

Rahsia sighs and lists the options.

Her preferred option, of course, is to stick with the original plan and rescue Ayahanda and those with him in the fields first—even if they delay for a few days to let the Bayangan army leave—before hitting the castle. It puts all the remaining Mahans, especially those based in the castle, at risk. I remind them about Layla's threat, but both Garett and Rahsia vote for this.

The second option is Yosua's suggestion that we use the subterfuge of his political appointment to get us to Maha. This means leaving Ayahanda behind until a later date, but also means that if Yosua is smart about choosing his retinue, a high number of Mahans, including Tok Ibrahim, will be able to return to Maha without bloodshed. It's the least risky, except for the timing. What's the point of waiting until Suci falls to launch a rebellion? Yosua, Marla, and Ali vote for this.

I don't like either choice so have abstained so far. If it comes down to it, I would rather vote for the first option. To my surprise, Hakim and Iskandar haven't voted either. They're deep in a whispered conversation.

"Hakim? Why did you not vote?" Rahsia asks.

"We think that Raja Muda Mikal's safety should be prioritised over that of Baginda Paduka. However, we cannot agree that Yosua should accept this role, even as a political appointee to rule over Maha."

"What do you suggest then?" Garett snaps.

"To reverse the order of the release. The first wave should be those in the castle, followed by those outside, which includes the Sultan."

I smile at Hakim, wondering what has changed his mind since he had been so skeptical of me the first time we met.

"And I assume the three of you will vote for that?" Rahsia tries to confirm.

I nod, as does Hakim and Iskandar. This leaves Rahsia and Garett's plan on the losing end. Whichever way, there's no majority. We're stuck at another impasse.

Try as she might, Rahsia can't stop the bickering. I don't envy her position as leader of this fractious group. The most vocal in the argument are Garett, Yosua, and Hakim. I sit back and listen, still trying to piece together everything in my head. As much as I've been trying to understand, it still feels as if something is missing. There's some key item I'm either misunderstanding or don't have enough information about.

Or Bayangan's mindset is so different from ours that I cannot even begin to comprehend it from the outside.

Rahsia raps on the table, calling us to attention. "As I see it, the biggest challenge here is Yosua's acceptance of the appointment. Between our suggestion and Hakim's, it's a mere matter of timing—which I believe we can come to a suitable compromise on when we work out the details."

Yes, that's it. "Mahans will never accept Yosua's rule," I say.

"Why don't you believe me? When have I been untrue to you?" Yosua's voice is quiet and not a little hurt.

"How do I know that all of this hasn't been going to your head?" I should trust him. He's been a brother to me. He's saved me many times, and has pulled me out of despondency over and over again. I don't know why I can't. The bridge between us has been damaged ever since Maha's fall and there's this wall I cannot breach.

"Will you let me help?" Rahsia asks. "One of the roles a Justice plays is to resolve disputes and to step in as arbitrator. In a matter like this, when intentions are important, a Justice can, if allowed, search the memories of the people involved. It won't solve everything—we cannot read hearts or intentions. All we can see are the memories of actual events building up to the final result or decision. We won't know your interpretation of events, only what actions and reactions you have taken in response to it and extrapolate from there."

"But you also read thoughts," I blurt. "Isn't that intentions and interpretation of events?"

"I cannot read past thoughts, only current ones. Thoughts aren't stored like memories. Only what's absorbed by the physical senses can be accessed in a memory, not your thoughts and feelings about them on that day."

Yosua studies me then fixes his gaze on Rahsia. "I have nothing to hide."

I want to be as open as he is, but I don't want her to see all the things that have happened to me. Yet if I don't let her, it will seem as if I have something to hide. "Will everyone see it or only you?"

Rahsia smiles. "A Justice never reveals what she has seen to anyone else, unless she is given permission by the person involved, or if it is requested by the Secretkeeper as part of a court action."

"Fine. Do it."

CHAPTER 20

Rahsia's touch on my mind is like fingers skimming through a sheaf of papers. It doesn't hurt, but it's uncomfortable. I get glimmers of the memories she sees, for as she riffles through, I recall the events as well. She works backwards until she reaches the night Maha fell. She pauses there, as if considering if she should continue, then withdraws. I assume this means she's absorbed all the memories she needs. She sits for a moment with her eyes closed. Does she watch them like a play, or does she experience them in the moment?

There's no emotion on her face, but her body stiffens and I know she's reached my torture. What must she think of me now? That I am poor and broken and unfit to be sultan. That I give in too easily to my own pain and to the pain of others. That I cannot hold my ground and my convictions, learning to grovel and beg in such a short span of time. I'm not whole, no matter how much clarity I have in this moment. Maybe she will side with Yosua after all. They don't need a broken puppet like me on the throne.

When she opens her eyes again, she doesn't say anything, just looks at me with sorrow. Then she reaches for Yosua's memories.

At the end of it, she looks at the both of us and says, "I cannot find any duplicity in either of you."

Has she nothing to say about my actions? Yet it's better this way.

"But he did betray us," I insist, to stop myself from blurting out what I'm really thinking: *But I'm still not good enough for this.*

She turns to me as she says, "He did, but it doesn't appear to be intentional or premeditated."

"You said you can't read intentions."

"I can't. But I can tell when someone is being honest and earnest in their actions, and there was nothing leading up to it or after it that shows it was done on purpose. Yosua here acted out of good faith, even if his actions ended up betraying us all."

"You don't know that," I argue. I know I need to trust him, I know I've been able to trust him before. But now? After all he's done? It's going to take more than a Justice's judgement of his honesty and earnesty.

What do I even know of this Justice Rahsia anyway?

Yosua doesn't defend himself. He looks away, hands gripping his thighs.

"Have all your actions been pure, Tuanku?" Rahsia turns the question on me.

"Why are you doing this?" I ask.

She appears confused. "To help you and your father."

It's not her I want to question. She's from Impian, here under the orders of the Uskup Agung. She believes Yosua is truthful when he says he's innocent. But now that the issue of trust has arisen once again, I am on edge. Who can I really trust? This unknown woman from Impian that no one knows anything about? The friend and confidant who has betrayed me one too many times, whether intentionally or not? The woman who is like a mother to me? Or the enigmatic man who is both my father's greatest nemesis and yet his most devoted servant? What about Kudus, who speaks in riddles?

I trust Kudus, I *do*. But I don't quite understand what He's saying.

It's Garett I look at when I ask, "And what would you require of us once we return to Maha? Do you intend to use us for your own purposes? To rule on your behalf and issue your commands?"

"No!" Garett exclaims. "We only seek to return you to what is yours, to what Kudus intends."

"And to enrich yourselves when we reward you for your service, is that right?" I press.

Whilst Garett has always been kind to me, he has no cause to love my father. If anything, he has a stronger reason to hate Ayahanda for what he did to them, the same way I hate Permaisuri Layla and Temenggung Jeffett for all they are doing to us. To me.

"No." Garett's eyes blaze. "I do this for honour, for the honour of my family name which has pledged to serve yours. Do not take my honour lightly, nor disparage it for your own faithlessness."

I study his face, the fire in his eyes, the worry on his brow, the anger on his lips. Yosua's posture and gaze echoes Garett's.

"I swore myself to you, Tuanku, and I'll swear it again if you need me to," Yosua says.

Their intensity burns me. I want to withdraw, to shrink away, but I can't. Not if I'm to prove my worth.

Marla breaks the stand-off, reaching out and laying a warm hand on my arm.

"We do this because we love you, Mikal ayell Simson, Raja Muda of Maha. Because you do not deserve to be here, treated as you are, expecting only the worst from the hands of others. Kudus has a purpose for you, and it is not here."

Tears slip out of the corner of my eyes, a burning warmth that flushes my cheeks. I can't hold it back. I've been wound up for too long. Everything is just too much. Too overwhelming.

"Hush now, don't cry." Marla wraps me in her arms, just like she used to when I was small and afraid.

I should be strong. Stronger than this. Show the world my courage and bravery, my strength and my will. But the tears keep falling. My defences have fallen; there is no rebuilding the walls. I blubber like a child, burying my face in the crook of her neck, breathing in the scent of *mother* and *home*. When it all subsides, I look up.

"Thank you." The words don't sound right in my mouth but it's the best I can do. I must look a sight, and I wish they hadn't seen me this way. This open, this broken. Yosua comes alongside and puts an arm around me too.

Brothers.

"Remember this, Mikal," Rahsia says. "You are chosen of Kudus, you and your line. Nothing man does can come between that. Only you can make or destroy your legacy. Your father has fallen away from the faith—if he had listened to Kudus and to the priests, this tragedy would not have happened. Or even if it still happened, he would have overcome it with the Amok Strength that Kudus grants to your blood. What is done is done. What has happened has already happened. What we do now is seek the face of Kudus and see how He can and will restore your line, if you stay true to Him."

I will stay true. I vow it.

Garett nods in agreement.

Hakim clears his throat. We all turn to look at him.

"This is all very nice and good, but it doesn't solve the problem of what our plans are going to be."

"We get Ayahanda out first," I say. I remind myself that Rahsia cannot read my intentions. "The Secretkeeper's vision called for his repentance."

I quote the lines, knowing they are fresh in Rahsia's mind if she had seen me reading the scroll.

"'*Repent, O Sultan, and you may yet be saved. Maha depends on your faithfulness, Terang on your loyalty in the night. When vision fails you, call upon Kudus, Maha Esa, and He will incline His ear to you in your desperation. Listen carefully, O Strength of Maha. The Amok Strength will fall upon you in your time of greatest need.*'

"If his repentance and renewal will return Kudus' Amok Strength to us, then that is what we must pursue."

Things are aligning. The Bayangan army will leave, the Impian army will arrive, and we will fight for our freedom and our city. Ayahanda will repent, Kudus will forgive, and our Strength will return. I feel it in the depths of my heart, squishing the niggling *what if you're wrong* down. I keep my true plans guarded, refusing to think of them now, so that Rahsia cannot overhear. I *know* I'm right, but I'm too tired to argue with her.

"But what about—" Yosua starts to protest.

"We'll keep that as a last resort."

"You still don't trust me," he says.

I do. I *should*. Haven't I just acknowledged him as brother? But Maha's throne is not something I will willingly give away even on a temporary basis. Once given, even the most honest of men may be reluctant to give it back—and I'll not put Yosua in that position if I can help it. But explaining all my reasons will take too long and it's late. We need to disperse soon if we are to continue avoiding detection. I fumble with the hand signals I remember. The open left hand, palm down, *wait*. Two hands clenched on each other, *trust*. He squints at me but doesn't comment.

"So, we'll send a messenger with the news of the Bayangan army's movements as well as our updated plan," Rahsia summarises.

"What *is* our updated plan?" Hakim asks. He's a man who likes clear direction, always keeping us on track. If he survives until we regain Maha, I will make sure Ayahanda rewards him.

"The fields first for Baginda Paduka's sake, then the castle," Garett says, looking at me. "And last of all, the city, for whoever remains."

"Is it possible to do both fields and castle at the same time?" I ask, though my hope is slim.

Rahsia hesitates. "It depends on how many soldiers Terang has sent, and how equipped and skilled they are."

"So we won't know until they arrive."

"We need to prioritise, Tuanku, and you've agreed that Baginda Paduka is our main priority," she says.

"Yes." I don't elaborate. There's nothing to elaborate.

Three days to freedom. I start counting down in my head.

CHAPTER 21

Uskup Agung Ikhlas asks them to leave.

Garett went out to meet the Impianans as planned and told them of our change of plans and the reasons why. Their paderi does his fancy thing to talk to Uskup Agung Ikhlas and *he asks them to leave.*

The safety of Suci, the Uskup Agung argues, is the greatest priority right now. Although the vision foretells the attack, he says he cannot bear to see the holy city fall. The city must not fall, even though the prophecy says it will. He wants the entire force that Impian has sent to make for Suci as quickly as possible to stand against the Bayangan army. Does he think Suci will stand protected by untrained Impianans where Maha, the Strength of Terang, has failed?

And if Bayangan destroys Suci and the Impianans with them, what then? Who will we have left to defend any of us? Terang will be utterly lost.

Did I understand you wrong, Kudus?

It's only Garett's family, Rahsia, and me in his house right now. Hakim and his men dare not shirk too often lest their masters realise their absence. Rahsia rails against Uskup Agung Ikhlas, but she cannot do anything. Not now, not anymore, now that they have left. They did not have a paderi to spare to replace Mahmud so we are still cut off from them.

"I should have been there," she grumbles as she paces Marla's kitchen. "I could have made Nek see sense!"

"Why were you not?" Yosua asks.

"Don't question me, Yosua," she spits, before shaking her head. "I was trying to scope out the mood in the fields, to see if the other slaves would work with or against us. I did not think the Impian army nor the Uskup Agung to be among those I needed to wrangle."

"What did you find?" I ask.

"Not enough. Only half of those I managed to skim still have thoughts of escape in their minds. The others have lost hope. I cannot predict how they will react when the opportunity is given to them. But there are too many I have yet to cover, and far too many soldiers to avoid. If the Bayangan army leaving reduces their guard I'd be grateful. Otherwise, it will be difficult without the Impian army behind us."

"Could you not have convinced even some to stay? Those of the army who were of Mahan origin?" Marla asks.

"I tried," Garett answers. He sits at the table, head in his hands. "I have no power of persuasion over the Uskup Agung and the priesthood. Without Rahsia or Mahmud there to vouch for me, they looked at me with suspicion."

There is a heavy, drawn out silence until I ask, "What does this mean for our plans? Do we move on? Do we stall? What?"

Garett and Rahsia exchange long glances.

"We continue," she says, "Baginda Paduka first." She glares at me as if challenging me to say otherwise.

"Fine." I keep my thoughts and plans as close to my heart as I can, so that she cannot overhear them, I hope. It's not as if I can still push for the simultaneous attack I'd been hoping for.

It doesn't matter. The numbers don't matter. If Kudus is with me, we will still prevail. He's said it in His Firman, confirmed it in the vision. I just have to keep trusting Him.

"We will lose many good men this way. Too many men," Garett mumbles.

"Didn't we expect to anyway?" Rahsia says mulishly.

"Not *this* many. It doesn't mean I have to like it."

"Is there any update on the status in Maha?" I ask. The Temple in Maha is the nearest place that Ayahanda can perform his ablutions and sacrifice in order to reinstate his vows. They have to be ready when we are, so that he can be purified as soon as he arrives. We need that Strength if any of this is going to work at all. It's the weak spot in our plans, but there's no other way. Still, Kudus has promised it.

Yosua frowns at me.

"They've cleaned up the Temple, and Uskup Daud is waiting along with a couple of paderi," Garett says. "That, at least, Uskup Agung Ikhlas assured me. There are still Bayangan soldiers in Maha, though not many. It has been easy to evade them."

Uskup Daud! Hope wells up in me. All is not lost if Uskup Daud is there. He, at least, has yet to break my trust. The last interactions between Uskup Daud and Ayahanda were less than cordial, but I'm sure they can move beyond that.

Tok Yaakub warned me before not to trust in the priests. I hadn't believed him then, but now I do. Even the Uskup Agung, the highest authority of religion in Terang, will use information to his own benefit, for the sake of his own city, instead of for the benefit of the entire sultanate. Even despite their own visions.

Can he not see that releasing Ayahanda and restoring his Amok Strength is the only way to prevail against Bayangan? It doesn't matter that there is no one ready *now* to defend the holy city. Once we are free and restored to power, our Mahan soldiers will be able to overtake the Bayangans and slaughter all of them before they even reach Suci. We'll be able to regather our scattered people, retake Maha, and hold it against anything they have left to send against us. We'll shatter them so utterly they'll take another forty years to rebuild.

I never thought I'd see the day where my faith in the Temple itself would be broken, but broken it is. Men are indeed faithless, despite what they preach.

ை

Yosua confronts me when we get back to his suite. "What are you planning?"

"What makes you think I'm planning something?" I lift my hands up, palms open, innocently.

"You had that look in your eye. The one you get when you're trying to hide something. I know you, Mikal. What is it?"

"If I tell you, you have to promise not to go running to your father or to Rahsia about it."

He bites his lip as he stares at me.

"Promise me, Yosua. If you don't, I'll find ways to work around you, even if it kills me to do it."

"Please, Mikal, don't get yourself into trouble now that we're so near escape."

I can't hold back my snort of laugher. "So near escape? Near death, you mean. Haven't you been listening? Rahsia's plan means death for me."

"But you agreed to it! You supported her plan!"

"In theory."

"What do you mean in *theory*? Wait, are you going behind their backs?"

"Once Permaisuri Layla hears that Ayahanda has escaped, or has *tried* to escape, I'll be the one put to the sword. I don't intend to be here when that happens."

"How—"

"I'm preparing my own escape, Yosua, and you're not going to block me."

His cheek twitches, jaw grinding. "If it will mean your death, then I will."

"Staying here will mean my death. Leaving gives me a better chance of staying alive." He continues biting his lip, so I press on. "You were the one who argued that your aunt will kill all the slaves in the castle once she found out that Ayahanda and those out there had rebelled."

"Yes, but—"

"So that means that I need to *not* be here when that happens."

"What about all the other—"

"It's too risky for me to break them all out. We'll have to rely on Rahsia's second wave to do that. It's selfish, and I'm sorry, but there's no other way. I'll take Tok Ibrahim, and one or two who can fight. But that's it. Any more and they'll notice too quickly."

"I don't understand." His hands are trembling as they grip the back of the chair. The pallor of his face isn't just his normal fairer skin, or the way he's been hiding inside, away from the sun.

"You don't *want* to understand," I retort. He's terrified, but so am I. This isn't about him and his safety. It's not even about my own safety any longer. This is about revolution and death. Maybe I won't live to see past the next three days, but I need to get out of here. Terang needs her Sultan and her Sultan's strength, and both Ayahanda and I need to be purified by the Temple if we are ever to be free of these shadows.

He looks away. "Why won't you just wait, Mikal? Wait until I'm sent and you with me?"

"I don't think it will happen." It's not a lie. "Permaisuri Layla offers you the post now, but she can change her mind at any time. Temenggung Jeffett might win her over and veto the plan. I won't trust in that promise until it happens."

"So, you're just going to run away now and leave me alone."

I hesitate. "You've got it good here, Yosua. Why would you want to come back with me?"

"Oh, I don't know, because I swore my loyalty to you, *Tuanku*?"

"Still…You don't…There's nothing in it for you."

He drops to his knees, taking my hand and kissing it. "As I said before, my fealty is to you. Not to Maha like Ayah swore, but to you, until you release me. Also…I choose to because you're my friend."

My lips curl up in a smile. It's weird to say it that way, but they do. It's not something I can control, not right now, not when my heart is bursting with gladness that Yosua still counts me as his friend. Not when I'm so astounded and amazed by his continued loyalty despite everything.

"Does this mean you'll help me?"

His face drops. "I don't agree with—I think your plan is too risky, but I'll…help you in whatever way I can."

"Thank you."

We decide on a list of supplies that I'll need, but the first problem is coming up with an excuse that's not going to raise any suspicions. I don't think anyone will question him about it, but we need to be prepared in case someone notices what I'm doing.

"Oh, just say I want to follow Uncle Jeffett out to the port when they leave for Suci," Yosua grumbles. "It will get you nearer to the straits anyway."

"That's brilliant, Yos."

"Don't thank me when they kill you."

"I thought you're supposed to be the optimistic one."

"No, I'm the realistic one, and you're the one stuck in some fantasy."

"Yos."

"Sorry, I'm just…"

I lay a hand on his shoulder. "It's all right. You'll be fine."

"It's not *me* I'm worried about."

"I'll be fine, Yos. Kudus is with me."

He looks set to argue, but then he shakes his head and shrugs. "If you believe so."

I do believe so. Kudus hasn't *said* anything else yet, hasn't clarified any part of the prophecy, but He hasn't stopped me either. I have to believe that this plan, this route is what I'm supposed to be doing. It's part of Kudus' plan. If I don't believe it, I have nothing else to hold on to. I ignore the doubts in my heart that I am rushing things, maybe if I waited...

No more waiting. We've been waiting for rescue for far too long and all they've done is let us down. Terang has failed us so it's now my time to take the future into my hands.

"If you asked my father for help—"

"No, Yos," I cut him off. "He's made it clear that he sides with Rahsia. They don't see me as important, Yos, so what makes you think Garett will actually try to help me?"

"Hakim does."

"Hakim follows Rahsia."

"He stood up for you."

"Yos, we can't keep arguing this point. The decision has been made. We won't go against it. They will free Ayahanda and get him back to Maha, where Uskup Daud will perform the purification rituals. With the return of his Amok Strength, the remaining soldiers here will regain their Strength too and be able to break out of their chains. I plan to be there by my father's side when that happens, to save Maha together."

And maybe then he'll finally approve of me.

I hope to be the Raja Muda and right-hand man he's always wanted me to be. To be the son worthy of his blood and of his gift. That he won't be disappointed in me any longer. They'll have rescued him, but I'll have rescued myself.

I hope that's enough. To prove my worth.

O Kudus, Maha Esa...

I push aside the niggling doubts that remain and press Yosua to continue with the plan.

It's easier than I expected. No one questions me when I request things in Yosua's name. They just look over the lists I hand to them, squint at Yosua's scrawl and seal at the bottom, then nod in approval. There are so many orders and requests coming in from the army that they don't have time to question it. The hardest part is to keep my face downcast, or at least neutral, so that no one can suspect I'm up to something.

"What's this then?"

Captain Karett's question startles me so I almost drop all the packages I'm carrying. It's at least my third trip from the stores to the suite. I hadn't realised that he was nearby.

I don't need to pretend when I stammer, "Tuan's requests." I offer up the current list of items with shaky fingers.

He snatches it from me impatiently. "A tent? Bedrolls? What are you up to?"

"Nothing, Captain. I'm just following orders."

His face reeks of distrust, but he can't argue with Yosua's seal and signature. "We'll see about that. Come along."

He strides towards our suite. I hurry behind him.

"Tuan is not…he's in a meeting, Captain."

"Is that so?" He knocks anyway, throwing the door open when there's no reply. "Hmph."

"May I—"

"No. What meeting is he in?"

"With Temenggung Jeffett, Captain."

The captain's eyebrows shoot upwards. "Interesting."

He drags me with him before I can put down the packages. By the time we find Yosua and his uncle in the Temenggung's office, my arms are strained from lugging the heavy packages up and down the stairs.

Temenggung Jeffett looks down his nose at me and then at the Captain. "Well?"

I drop the packages and hurry to prostrate myself.

"I wanted to verify these strange orders, Tok Jeffett, in case he's managed to forge Tuanku Yosett's signature."

Temenggung Jeffett scans the list and laughs. Fear grips me.

"You have no idea how to plan for a camp do you, nephew?"

"No? I've never…is there something wrong, Uncle?" Yosua's voice sounds tense.

"Look, you're only going to be at the port for one night while we load up the ship. You don't need half of these things. These rations will last you a month."

He runs through the list, striking off various items until he gets to the bottom. "Two bedrolls? Who—oh, you're bringing him along? He doesn't need a bedroll."

"But the ground is *hard*," Yosua grumbles.

"And you're still too soft on him. No wonder Captain Karett thinks he's trying to run away." He chuckles again. "I see why Layla wants to train you. There's a lot you have to learn, and it's easier while in a post but…not until I'm back from this campaign. We'll ease you into it, eh?"

"Sure, Uncle."

"Thank you, Captain, but all this is in order," Temenggung Jeffett addresses the captain.

"What do I do with the extra stuff? Should it be returned?"

"Keep it. The stores are going to be annoyed if you return things at this point. Messes up their records.

There will be other campaigns, other camps and trips you'll need them for. They'll keep." He dismisses the captain and me with a wave of his hand, turning back to Yosua.

Captain Karett hauls me to my feet. I scramble to pick up the scattered packages to bring them back to Yosua's suite. He follows me all the way there. I can feel his eyes on my every move, his constant scrutiny jangling my already-strained nerves. I keep reminding myself that as long as I keep my head down, he can't stop me for anything else.

I heave a sigh of relief when I've gotten everything into the suite. The captain doesn't make any move to come in with me, so I give him as shallow a bow as I dare and close the door in his face. It takes a long while before I can breathe properly. I survey the piles of items with awe then spend the next few hours splitting the goods into four portions.

"I hope you're happy," Yosua grumbles when he returns. "I was just subjected to an hour-long lecture on not pampering slaves and how I'm too soft on you."

"Thank you."

He just shrugs.

CHAPTER 22

The second problem is how to get Tok Ibrahim out with me. I don't really want to, but there is no one better to ask. Of the Majlis, he's the only one I know who is still alive. Tok Yaakub and Tok Rizal are dead. I haven't seen Tok Benyamin since that first day in the cells, nor have I seen any of the three shahbandars in the castle. If there is one person that I can save who *will* be able to make a difference, it's the former Bendahara, no matter how much I distrust him now.

I have a day left to figure out how to meet Tok Ibrahim and to convince him to come with me. There's space for one more—but I do not see anyone that I can ask, or that I even know will be eager to join us and not report us to their masters.

Yosua has no brilliant ideas this time.

I try to catch Tok Ibrahim's eye when I see him in the dining hall during lunch. He pretends he doesn't see me. I'm left confounded. Surely he must know I have updates for him, after that last meeting!

Yosua kicks me to stop fidgeting and I stew where I am. It doesn't matter, I tell myself. Having Tok

Ibrahim along is a bonus. I can make it back on my own. The others will still save him. Eventually.

I'm heading to pick up the laundry after that, when I'm suddenly dragged into a corner.

"We should have taught you stealth," Tok Ibrahim whispers in my ear, a hand clamped over my mouth. "Your education is entirely lacking." He lets go of me.

"Not quite my fault, is it?"

"This evening, my mistress is sending me on an errand into the city."

"Ah. Perhaps I will meet you on the journey?"

"I leave at four."

He disappears and I continue on to the laundry room somewhat in a daze.

Yosua plans on attending a war meeting that afternoon so he writes a message for me to deliver to Garett as an excuse for me to leave the castle. It's the perfect cover for me to ask for more updates anyway, though I doubt there are any. We're all just waiting for the Bayangan army to leave.

I wait until I see Tok Ibrahim crossing the courtyard from the window in our suite before I set out. This way, if anyone asks, I met him while on my own errand.

The road is deserted at this time of day. Tok Ibrahim slows, but doesn't stop, when I call out to him.

"Took you long enough," he grunts. "What news?"

I tell him all that has happened, including Suci's recalling of the Impian force. He listens without reaction.

"But?" he asks. "You looked entirely too excited for this to be it."

"Tomorrow. When the army leaves, I'm leaving too."

He raises a brow in question.

"I have supplies for three. Yosua will be going with the army as far as the port. In the bustle of the army leaving, we'll slip out and head off on our own. If you can join us."

"Three? You, me, Yosua?"

"No. You, me, and one more person if you have anyone in mind. Yosua will be going with the army."

"To rat us out?"

"To *confuse* them. Right now, Jeffett is under the impression I'll be going with them because, as you know, poor Raja Muda Yosett can't be separated from his little slave. But Yos will change his mind at the last minute and decide to go alone. Those in the castle will think I'm with them, the army will think Yos has finally left me behind. No one will look for me for at least three days when Yos arrives back at the castle without me."

He's quiet for a while, thinking it over. "Do you have weapons?"

"Two knives."

"Better than nothing."

"You'll have to source uniforms in your size. I have one in my size, but I don't think you'll fit." He's much taller than both Yosua and me.

"That's not hard to get."

"Does this mean you're in?"

A few minutes pass before he answers, "I'll think about it."

We're coming up to the city. The roads are getting busier, and every time we see someone approaching, we have to stop our conversation. We give the patrols a wide berth, keeping our heads down as we pass.

"We don't have much time. Terang needs you, Tok Ibrahim. Ayahanda will need your help. If you stay…" I'm not sure how to end the sentence, how to convince him. *If you stay, Layla will kill you? If you stay…*

"I'll be there." Then he slips away into the city and I continue on towards Garett's house.

It's hard not to act excited when everything is falling into place. A few passing Bayangans give me queer looks and I keep my head down to avoid questions. But Kudus is smiling on me today. Nothing untoward happens. No one stops me.

Garett reads Yosua's message with a questioning frown. "What does he want with—" He turns to Marla.

She reads the message and shrugs.

"What does it say?" I ask. I hadn't bothered to read it, had been too busy going over our plans again and again.

"He just wants this old bag he left here months ago," Garett says. "Do you even know where it is, Marla?"

Marla and I end up digging through a pile boxes before we find the bag. I stiffen at the sight of it. It's the same bag Yos carried the night of our failed escape. It has to be. What did he want with it now? I take it from Marla, stifling my urge to open it and dig through its contents. It can't be still full of my stuff from Maha. No, the scroll and the Firman are already in our suite. This must just be some other junk.

Garett has no updates. They're all just waiting until the Bayangan army leaves. I confirm that the army is planning to set out tomorrow morning, and Yosua and I with them.

Garett is surprised by that. "What does he hope to accomplish?"

Oops. I wince. "To gain his uncle's favour? Jeffett is pleased that Yosua is showing an interest in state affairs."

"Jeffett is not so easily appeased," Garett growls.

"Yosua *has* been attending the war councils. He's at one now."

"Then why are you here?"

"He thought this was important! I don't know."

We stare at the bag. Garett makes as if to tear it from me and discover what's inside. I almost want him to, but Marla stops him.

"Our son is entitled to his privacy," she says, gripping her husband's arm.

"What if he puts us all at risk?"

"Don't you trust him?"

The older man nods.

"Then trust him one more time."

The guilt eats me as I take my leave, slinging the bag across my shoulder. Garett shouldn't trust us. Marla shouldn't trust us, shouldn't trust me! What's in the bag is probably not important, some random thing that had come to Yosua's mind in his haste to produce an excuse. Yet…my curiosity burns within me as I return to the Bayangan castle for what I hope is the last time.

There is reverence in his eyes as Yosua takes the bag from me.

"How was the meeting?" I ask, to divert my own curiosity.

"All is going according to plan. We muster at ten tomorrow." He bites his lip and his grip tightens on the handles of the bag. With a big exhale, he opens the clasp. Out tumbles some clothes—the clothes he'd packed for me.

"What are you—"

He holds up a hand to stop me, then keeps digging, strewing old belongings I'd never thought to see again on the ground. They're like ghosts from years past, even if it has only been months. Finally, he finds what he's looking for. He grinds his teeth a little, trying to make up his mind, then he pulls it out.

It's my keris. I gape at it. I'd thought it left behind in the palace, fallen where I dropped it in my tussle with Captain Karett's men.

"You should have this back. Take this with you." Yosua holds the keris up to me balanced on both open palms, an offering to a superior.

"You kept it?"

"I went back to look for it. I couldn't let…it didn't feel right to leave it behind."

I take the blade from him, unsheathing it. It feels right in my hand, like a part of me that I'd lost has now been restored. I do not deserve Yosua's love, nor his respect, nor his loyalty, but he has granted all of them to me so freely. The words *thank you* are not enough. I embrace him, pulling him to me and holding him tight. It occurs to me that tomorrow may be the last time I see him, whether things go well or ill.

"How was *your* meeting?" He turns the question back on me as he pulls away.

"Tok Ibrahim will come. He sounded reluctant…but he said he'd be there."

Later that evening, while Yosua hides himself in his room in prayer, I go through my forms. I need both the mental focus as well as the practice. I've been practicing a little in the past few days, but I feel like I've lost a lot in the preceding dark months. This one session won't fix everything, but it will at least give me some comfort. The return of my keris gives me hope too. One more weapon, one more way to defend myself, even without the Amok Strength. I resync myself with its balance, letting my body flow with it once again. I miss Tok Yaakub more than ever, hearing his instructions in my ears.

O Kudus, Maha Esa, berkatilah hamba-Mu dengan kuasa ajaib-Mu.

There's a strange crackle in the air, a change in the atmosphere. A presence greater than any other enfolds me. My fingers tighten around the hilt of my keris, knuckles whitening with the strain.

This is right. This is it. A sign from Kudus, finally. But no voice accompanies it, nothing other than this strange magnetic feeling. Is this how Ayahanda felt with the Amok Strength? I feel—not exactly powerful—but like there is a person with me. A presence. Then He speaks.

Soon, He says. **Soon, my child, but not yet. Have patience. Keep the faith. Your time will come.**

I'm confused, because I do not have much time left. Tomorrow Tok Ibrahim and I will leave this place behind. In two days, we will rally the remaining Mahans in our city, and with the help of Uskup Daud, will call the rest of Terang to arms. When Ayahanda reaches us and is sanctified again, our new army will be standing ready for the infilling of his power. And we will go to war.

By next week, Bayangan will be no more.

CHAPTER 23

The army musters at ten sharp. Yosua is down in the courtyard with his pack. I'm there to assist him. He mounts a horse, looking uncomfortable and unsettled. He's had riding classes since we arrived, but he's never ridden anywhere on his own yet. I've only ever watched; it was beneath my dignity to ride on horseback—Mahan royalty ride on elephants and slaves don't ride anything. He looks for a groom for help.

"Maybe you should take the groom along," I whisper.

"Don't be silly," he hisses back.

The courtyard is a teeming mass of bodies. As soon as I'm sure I've been seen by enough people, and Yosua is settled with his horse and his equipment, I slip away.

There's no time for goodbyes. We've said all we needed to last night. In my drab slave's garb, it's easy enough to weave in and out of the crowd until I'm by the store room where I hid my things early this morning. Tok Ibrahim is supposed to meet me here, but I don't see him anywhere.

I peer around the store room. Satisfied that it's empty, I duck behind the equipment and change into Yosua's spare uniform. He's altered it to fit me, also removing the insignia and rank badges so I'll appear to be a new recruit. A rap on the door, one short, two long, and Tok Ibrahim slips in with another man behind him. I peek out from my hiding place, waiting until the door shuts before waving them over.

Tok Ibrahim introduces the man as Jamal, one of the captains in our army. Jamal produces a small lockpick and in the dim light, he picks the locks that keep the collars around our necks. It's a relief to have the weight off my neck and shoulders. I've become so used to it that I suddenly feel so much lighter.

I drag out the three packs I've prepared. With our uniforms and army-issued packs, we look just like the soldiers milling about outside. I'm glad for the cap they wear, because that means I've been able to wrap my hair tightly into a bun and hide it under the cap. It's a little wobbly, but nothing a few pins can't help secure.

The ex-Bendahara runs an eye over us and nods. "We'll pass."

Outside, there's the sound of talking. I lean against the door and press my ear against the wood to listen.

Permaisuri Layla. She's giving a rousing speech about winning more honour and glory for Bayangan. I try to suppress my grimace. Her speech ends with loud cheering followed by shouts and orders. I look at the other two men. They nod back at me. It's time.

We slip into the milling crowd. It's not difficult falling into line with the other soldiers. They keep their eyes ahead on their captains for orders, not questioning our presence. Although I've heard the numbers Yosua has been bringing back and I've seen some of their drills from my vantage point in Yosua's suite, the sheer number of bodies around us is overwhelming.

"Hold on," Tok Ibrahim says in a soothing voice. "Stay calm."

I take several deep breaths and nod back at him. Yosua is somewhere up ahead. I can't see him or hear his voice. I focus on imitating Tok Ibrahim beside me, marching to the beat of the enemy soldiers, the drum beat that knells the death of everything I love.

We will get through this.

We fall into a rhythm. The lines are orderly as we leave the castle, four abreast. Tok Ibrahim is on my right, Jamal on my left. There's an unknown soldier at the end of the line, on the far right. One or two passing captains spare us a glance, but nothing more than that. And then we're out of the city, leaving Bayangan behind us. I can't believe it's been this easy so far.

Don't question Kudus' blessings. You still need to get away from the army unobserved and across the straits.

When we stop three hours later, the three of us keep to ourselves, trying to stay inconspicuous. I guzzle down the water they've passed around whilst Tok Ibrahim surveys the countryside. If we can find some way to sneak away, even here, we'll take it. But we're too far from the line of trees and there's no way to cause a distraction. We'll have to wait for another stop, or until we break for camp tonight. This is the riskiest part of our plan.

With the large number of new recruits, it's unlikely a random soldier will know who we are, but there is a high chance that those stationed in the castle will recognise us, especially me. Jamal keeps an eye on the captains, telling me to duck when one of them comes too close.

"Psst," a voice says.

The three of us jump. We'd been so busy watching the higher ups we didn't notice the young recruit who'd wandered over to us. He's the one at the end of our line.

"Are you new?" he asks me.

"Yeah. Is it that obvious?" I reply.

"Half of us are new too." He squints at me. "You look too young to be a recruit."

"Hey, I'm eighteen," I protest.

Tok Ibrahim snorts and the soldier glances at him before turning back to me.

He doesn't look like he believes me. "You've got to fix your pack," he says instead. "Your straps are all wrong. You could be disciplined for that."

He bends down and adjusts the positioning of the straps until it looks like all the others around us.

"Thanks. I...I didn't know," I say.

"Saw them looking. No worries. Gotta stick together, huh."

I nod, wishing he'd just go away.

"Reb," he introduces himself.

"Mik..." I blurt then stop. I doubt he'll recognise my name, but it's not a common one in Bayangan so it'll stand out. Reb doesn't say anything though, just accepts it and nods to himself.

I can feel Tok Ibrahim rolling his eyes.

"These your friends?"

I shrug. "I guess."

Jamal leans over and shakes the boy's hand, introducing himself as 'Mal'. Tok Ibrahim doesn't bother.

"Don't mind him. He's crotchety. Off in the head from all the deaths," Jamal says.

Reb chuckles. "Do you think we'll see a lot of dead people?"

Tok Ibrahim fixes him with a glare. "You're going to *cause* a lot of dead people," he says before getting up and walking away.

Jamal just shrugs. There are some shouted orders and we scramble to our feet, grabbing our packs and hoisting them back on our shoulders. We shuffle back into the column. One chance of escape gone. Reb stays in our line. This is going to be difficult.

We stop twice more before we reach the camping ground near the old port. Both times we look for a chance to slip away, but both times, Reb sticks close to us, covering our silence with pointless conversation. Tok Ibrahim's growing irritation is written on his every move and my desperation increases with it. Jamal entertains Reb, keeping him occupied. At any rate, we're never near enough to cover to try to break away without anyone else seeing us.

It's evening when we reach the campsite, the sun just starting to set. There's organised chaos as everyone breaks away to their assigned duties. No one has noticed us so far, but it's only a matter of time. I can hardly believe we've been lucky for so long. We need to go now. We head towards the encampments nearest the cover of trees, and make as if we're about to set up our tents. When no one's looking, I shove my pack off into the underbrush.

The coast looks clear when Reb appears again. Jamal and Tok Ibrahim exchange several hasty whispers.

Kudus, please, make him go away.

Tok Ibrahim beckons to me and I hasten to him, trying to shake off my unwanted follower. Reb follows me doggedly until Jamal intercepts him.

"Where are they going?" I can hear Reb say in clear tones.

"Firewood," Jamal says flippantly. He steers the boy away with a grip on his shoulder.

"Go," Tok Ibrahim mutters.

I head off towards the bushes, snagging my bag on the way, and run into the cover of the trees. Moments later, Tok Ibrahim is beside me.

"What's Jamal going to do?" I ask as we head deeper into the forest.

"He'll find a way to shake him off or kill him."

I wince. Death is inevitable, I know, but Reb is an innocent. He doesn't have any blood on his hands. *Yet.* I remind myself that he's part of the army heading to destroy my holy city. He's no longer innocent once he signed up for the army.

The light wanes as the sun sets. Jamal doesn't return. Tok Ibrahim starts cursing to himself.

"He'll come back," I say. I push aside my own doubts. Someone has to have faith. Someone has to believe this will work.

We eat cold food from our packs, wrapping ourselves in blankets for protection from the swarms of mosquitoes. It only makes us sweat more, attracting even more bugs. The noise from the camp dies down as they start to turn in for the night. We should start moving, but we keep holding out for Jamal to reappear.

I'm about to fall asleep when I hear rustling in the underbrush. Tok Ibrahim grips my arm, holding a finger over his lips in warning. We wait in the dark, hoping the noise will go away. The animal—or person—gets nearer.

"Tok? Tuanku?" Jamal whispers.

I let out a breath I didn't know I was holding.

"Jamal," Tok Ibrahim says. "Thank Kudus. What happened?"

"Couldn't shake Reb. Was ordered to help with unloading and loading. They're loading the ships tonight. Probably going to make an early start tomorrow, so we should get out of here now. Finished my assigned batch and tried to sneak off, but Reb was still following me. I led him into the forest and knocked him out."

"Where is he now?"

"Left him tied up by the edge of the trees."

"What if they see him?" Tok Ibrahim sounds irritated.

"They won't see him in the dark. He's hidden in the bushes. They might find him in the morning, but we'll be long gone by then."

"Couldn't you have just killed him?"

"What has he done to us?"

"Almost exposed us, that's what."

"Do you want to go back and do the job?"

"It's fine, it's done," I interrupt. I'm glad Reb isn't dead. Less bloodshed on my conscience. "We need to focus on finding the boats."

The Impian army left behind several boats for our use—well, technically for Rahsia's use. We'll take one and leave the rest. The problem is, I don't know exactly where they're hidden. I only have a verbal map from

Garett, who described their meeting point as 'several kilometres to the left of the camping grounds, near the inlet'. That is a large swath of beach to search. I don't know how far away the inlet is.

"We should just steal a boat from the port," Jamal grumbles.

"How do you propose to sneak in with the entire army there?" Tok Ibrahim says.

"We *are* in their uniform."

"But we don't have any orders to show."

"Should've gotten Yos to write us orders," I say.

"Too late."

We pick up our bags and start heading towards the beach. For a long while, there's no sound about us except for the crunch of leaves and sticks under our feet.

Then Jamal says, "The port is nearer. If I remember the maps correctly, the inlet is quite far from here."

"We're not changing our plans now," Tok Ibrahim insists. "We're not equipped to fight our way past the army and steal a boat."

"We don't have to fight our way in. We just march in as if we're under orders and by the time they think to stop us, we'll be on the boat and far away."

"Wishful—"

He's cut off by the sound of alarm from the campsite. Shouts escalate, someone's blowing a horn.

"Kudus! They must've found Reb," Jamal swears.

"You fool!" Tok Ibrahim snarls.

"Why would they be—"

"Headcounts!" The realisation hits me. "We forgot the nightly headcounts. His supervisor would have reported him missing."

"The *port*," Jamal snarls.

"They're on alert now," Tok Ibrahim growls back.

They both turn to me. I have to decide. I can't decide. Jamal's right, it's nearer, we can be on a boat in twenty minutes if we run there now. Who knows when or even *if* we'll find the Impianan boats? But Tok Ibrahim's also right; we can't just run right into the arms of our enemies, even if it's nearer. And they're searching for us now. Reb can recognise us. He knows there are three of us. He knows in which direction we went.

They're staring at me and I have to think fast.

O Kudus, help me make the right decision.

There's no voice from heaven, no lights, no presence, nothing.

Where have You gone now? Kudus, please, what do I do? You're supposed to be with me.

Tok Ibrahim shakes me.

"Stick to the plan," I gasp out. Jamal looks furious, but he nods.

We start running.

CHAPTER 24

We abandon all stealth, running helter-skelter down the beach as fast as our feet can take us. The noise from the camp starts to fade away, and a moment of relief falls over me, but all too soon, a new sound catches up with us.

Pounding feet and yelling voices. I veer back towards the tree line, banking on the uneven terrain and the poor visibility to help me. I weave between the trees until I find one that seems large enough to hide me. Stepping behind it, I try to listen. They've mostly followed Tok Ibrahim and Jamal. At least, the sound of their pursuit seems to flow in that direction.

There's rustling heading in my general direction though—at least a few soldiers must have seen me split off. I glance upwards and decide to try to climb. I'm too tired to keep running. It was a wrong decision to come here. We have no way of finding the boats like this—Jamal was right. If we'd headed towards the port, we'd have taken them by surprise and might even be on our way away by now.

Stupid.

I hoist myself upwards and clamber as high as I can. Two soldiers pass by a few metres away. If they look up, they might see me, but they don't. Kudus is with me. Soon, they're out of sight. It's quiet again. Do I go back? Do I head for the inlet? I don't know what has happened to Tok Ibrahim or Jamal. I haven't heard any cheers of celebration, so I'm hoping that means they haven't been caught.

I slip down out of my hiding place in the tree and head back in our original direction. I need to find the inlet and get on a boat out of here. Except I must have been turned around after climbing down the tree. After blundering about in the darkness for ages, I find myself back near the camp. It's bustling, full of movement. How can they still be looking for us after so long? Why have they not gone to sleep?

Stupid.

I don't know what to do next. To head back will take too long, time I do not have. I may even run into the returning soldiers after having evaded them for so long. But to press on ahead, where I can see masses of Bayangan soldiers just waiting, would be sheer stupidity. If I can find a place to wait until they're gone before I head back towards the Impianan boats? But there is no place here to hide. I can't stay, I can't go. I want to claw my eyes out.

It takes me a while to realise that the soldiers aren't looking for me. They're getting onto the ships. Why hadn't Yosua told me they were going to leave in the middle of the night? Have they changed their plans? Ship after ship sails away until the campground is deserted. Almost deserted. All that milling around in the evening hadn't been to set up camp, but several tents have been erected—Yosua and his honour guard,

I suppose. It's tempting to run back to Yosua for shelter, to pretend all of this hasn't happened.

Maybe that's the smarter plan.

I eye the port. It's quiet enough now. One soldier patrols the perimeter, but it's a contracted circle around the few remaining tents. He doesn't seem to be looking very far out, ignoring the port altogether.

Yosua and temporary safety, or the port and a way home?

It's hardly a choice. I wait until his back is turned and dash across the open ground. It's farther than I judged and again, it's only by Kudus' favour that no one sees me. The guard doesn't turn around, doesn't hear my panting and my heavy footfalls. It has to be a sign that this wretched disaster of a plan is still somehow according to His will.

The dilapidated port feels even more haunted than the first time I saw it. Back then, confused and in chains, I hadn't had time to look around me, crushed as I was between so many other captives. But now, I stand in a vast, empty building that gazes up at the slowly-brightening sky. The crumbling walls echo my falling hopes, held together by frail vines of faith. If I snip one, will this whole building crash down on me?

There's nothing here I can use, not even a measly sampan. What the Bayangans could not use, they have sunk. Broken shells of countless small boats rest on the bottom of the straits, flitting in and out of view behind the stirred silt of the seabed and shoals of silver fish.

I sneak out the same way I came in. The inlet, with the hidden boats, is my only remaining hope. Assuming the boats are still there, still hidden. What if they've been discovered? I push my doubts out of my mind—now is not the time for doubts. I must believe that Kudus is with me, that Kudus shines upon my mad, ridiculous plans. It's either that or break down and give up.

O Kudus, O Kudus. What do I do?

The trek towards the inlet feels longer than before. So much time wasted retracing steps, going backwards and forwards, but it has kept me out of the enemy's hands so I cannot complain. I must not complain. I *must* hold on to the fact that Kudus has allowed this to happen, therefore, it is His will. If only He will speak again! If only He will speak to me as clearly as He did back in Yosua's suite. What use is asking for guidance if He only shrouds it in riddles? The Secretkeeper's vision is a roadmap that can't be used, not without a key of understanding, which so far has only come after the fact. I hate prophecies.

There's no sign of the soldiers who'd been chasing us, nor of Tok Ibrahim or Jamal. I hope they got away. Maybe even now, they are sailing away to freedom.

The sun is beginning to rise. I leave the beach and walk along the tree line, hoping it makes me in some ways less noticeable. I'm too tired for stealth, and there doesn't seem to be any living creature on the ground.

The breeze is warm, balmy. The smell of salt lingers in my nostrils, stickiness gathering on my exposed limbs. My clothes are dishevelled and encrusted in mud. No one would take me for a soldier now. I realise as the wind whips my hair about that I've lost my cap somewhere along the way and my hair is escaping from its bun. I really just want a bath.

Birds call in the distance, welcoming the new day. Their cries sound so normal, so commonplace, as if I'm not an escaped slave running for his life. As if I am once again Putera Mikal, walking the beach, looking out for Tok Rizal's warships on the horizon, Maha's flag flying high. The seas are restless, devoid of human presence, even though I know the Bayangan ships are out there just beyond my sight.

"There!"

I freeze at the sudden yell. There are shapes in the distance, rushing towards me.

"On your knees, now!"

I've nowhere to run. I have no *energy* to run. Deep breaths. Steady. Evaluate.

O Kudus Maha Esa, berkatilah hamba-Mu dengan kuasa ajaib-Mu.

I drop my pack, draw my keris, bend my knees, keep my back against a tree. At least they cannot stab me from behind. Whatever strength Kudus gives me, it's not going to be enough anyway, not against these many soldiers. Ten? Fifteen of them? Still, I can pray and hope for deliverance.

The first one comes at me and I slash him across the face. He reels backwards, blood spurting everywhere. They come in pairs, hemming me in even as I slash wildly. I look for a way to escape, for a way to slip through, but there are too many of them crowding around me. No space to use any of Tok Yaakub's fancy tricks. With each slash and parry, I'm drawn away from the meagre protection of the trees. There are too many of them, forming an impenetrable circle all about me. If I kill one, another just takes his place.

I manage to kill two. There's blood everywhere, more blood than I've ever seen in my life. It's the first time I've killed anyone and I am sick to my stomach. My hands shake. How does Ayahanda handle it? How does any soldier handle this?

"Drop your keris!"

I run at the sergeant issuing the orders. My keris no longer glints in the sun. It's stained and slippery, it slips from my fingers as they grab me.

O Kudus, please. This once. Your will. Your strength. My time of need. You promised! You promised!

But He is silent once again. I don't understand. I *don't* understand.

My breath rushes out of my body as I'm slammed to the ground and held there. Breathe. Cannot breathe. Short, shallow. Don't panic. My breaths are sharp, painful, shattered glass and smashed hopes. The tingling in my limbs is not of power and strength, but of uselessness and shame. My wrists are shackled behind my back, pulled so tight I fear they will break.

"Did you really think you could escape?" Captain Karett is an apparition in the dawn light, a ghost. He's not supposed to be here. He's supposed to be on a ship, sailing to Suci, where I will not see him until I have earned my Strength. "Come see what you have done."

They drag me forwards towards the inlet we've been seeking for so long. Three men are held kneeling in a row, each held by two soldiers. Tok Ibrahim, Jamal, Reb.

No.

They push me to my knees facing them. I gape, confused, at Reb. Why is he there? What has he done wrong? Is he not one of theirs? He who has plagued us and delayed us? It's his fault we wasted so much time trying to cover our tracks! It was his unwanted presence that betrayed us to them!

Reb cries out his innocence, saying he only wanted to stop us, that he knew there was something wrong with us, though he did not know what.

Captain Karett stands over him, his arms folded across his chest. "Did you not conspire with them to help them escape? We saw you with them all throughout the day."

Had they recognised us even then? No, he must be lying. The captain is cruel but he is prompt in his punishments. He would not have waited so long. If he had known I was there before, he would have dragged me before Temenggung Jeffett in the encampment right away, if only to gloat that he had been correct in his suspicions. There's no glory to be gained in this ambush.

"No, sir! I...I was only trying to be friendly! I didn't want a fellow recruit to get into trouble!"

"So you helped him escape?"

Reb shakes his head so hard, I wonder it doesn't fly off. "No, no! Then I stuck around because, well, I don't know! I felt something was wrong and I wanted to find out what it was!"

"Didn't you think to inform your superiors?"

He hangs his head. "Please Captain, I thought—"

"Obviously you can't think. And now you've helped these criminals escape."

"Captain, no! They haven't escaped! They knocked me out but I told you all about them! I led you to them!"

"Only because smarter heads than yours have salvaged the situation."

Captain Karett signals to the soldiers behind him. Reb is still pleading his innocence when his head drops to the ground, his body falling a few seconds after it.

Bile surges in my throat. I turn to retch, but the arms that hold me are hard and unyielding. The thick, smelly liquid drips down my lips and onto my clothes. Captain Karett spares me an amused smile.

He doesn't bother interrogating Jamal or Tok Ibrahim, just flicks his finger and their heads tumble to the ground in unison. More bile, until I'm dry heaving, nothing left to expel.

"Look what you've done, Mikal." He clicks his tongue in disappointment. "What a waste of life. I knew something was wrong the moment I saw that requisition form. Temenggung Jeffett has a blind spot for his nephew, but with this as proof, even Permaisuri Layla won't defend him."

I should keep my mouth shut. "It wasn't his fault."

"Did I say it was his fault?"

"He didn't know. He wasn't involved in this at all." *Keep on digging your grave, why don't you.*

The captain leans over me. "I find that very hard to believe, when his signature is all over everything."

"I—I forged—"

"Don't lie, Mikal. It does not become you. Remember, I was there when our dear Raja Muda Yosett claimed all these provisions was for his *camp*." He kicks at our packs. "No, he is definitely complicit."

I look at Reb's body. His death is my fault. Tok Ibrahim's and Jamal's deaths are my fault. They would not be here, dead, if I hadn't asked them to come with me. Whether they find him guilty or not, Yos is going to be punished, and it's all my fault. Tomorrow, Rahsia and Garett are going to lead Ayahanda right back into the arms of these soldiers, and it will be all my fault.

You failure.

"Take him back to the castle and throw him in the dungeons. I'll deal with that traitor Yosett myself," Captain Karett orders.

I'm hauled to my feet.

"No! It's not Yosua's fault! I made him do it! I forced him—"

The blow to my cheek stings. I taste blood on my lips, in my mouth.

"That's for Permaisuri Layla to decide." He surveys the inlet, looking at the boats pulled up high on the shore. "Destroy all of them."

The soldiers use their parangs to smash a hole in each boat. Each pound of their parang is a nail in my heart, the sealing of my own coffin. There will be no escape tomorrow, no proud Sultan Simson and his gallant Mahans sailing away to safety.

I will not rise from this, even if they try to resurrect me.

CHAPTER 25

We leave the bodies behind on the shore. I utter a prayer for them under my breath, begging for forgiveness. This has been a foolhardy plan right from the beginning and I knew it. I knew it then, know it now. The only excuse I have is the one Ayahanda has always used, weak as it may be: *I prayed about it and Kudus didn't strike me dead.*

I wish He had. It is evident He hates me, when everything I set my hands to fails. Why did I ever think this would be different?

Not for the first time, I admit to myself it's a pitiful excuse. If we expected Kudus to strike us dead every time we made a stupid decision, there'd be no one left alive in Terang.

The entire company is silent. There's no camaraderie or excitement as there was when the army set off yesterday. The men in Captain Karett's company are solemn and professional. Their grips on my arms are bruising, holding me upright as I stumble. I have not slept for a day. The physical weariness of marching all day and running all night is beginning to

257

catch up to me, but the emotional weariness of death and fear and failure is overwhelming my soul.

I cannot remember much of the journey back to Bayangan, just the growing feeling of dread the nearer we get. They must have fed and watered me at some point, or maybe they didn't and I am too shocked to register hunger or thirst.

Why, Kudus? Why did this happen? You were supposed to help me escape! You promised to set Maha free!

We pass by Garett's house on the way back into the city and I cannot help but look at it. Something flickers in the window, the twitching of a curtain. Rahsia, maybe? I pray it is not Marla. She should not have to see me like this.

The boats are destroyed. Do not proceed. Do not proceed! I think as hard and as loudly as I can, hoping Rahsia will somehow catch it. If she's there, if she's not too far away. It if even works this way.

I'm sorry. I'm sorry. Our plans are ruined. Tok Ibrahim is dead. His body lies on the beach. The Impianan boats are destroyed and there is nothing left in the port. I tried to escape. Permaisuri Layla will kill me and Yosua with me. I am sorry I am sorry I am sorry Garett forgive me Marla forgive me. It is my fault we are undone.

I land on my knees in the throne room. The permaisuri is livid, her face red and her eyes hard, her voice sharp and her teeth biting. Captain Karett is talking over my head and I don't know what he is saying. I cannot listen, I cannot concentrate. Rahsia is not near enough to overhear my thoughts, but all I can think on is the loop in my head that is begging for forgiveness.

"Bring him to me!" Permaisuri Layla's shout is loud enough to pierce through the fog.

Am I not already here? I look up, only to have my face pushed down into the ground again.

"I gave you many chances, boy. I even considered sending you back to Maha with my nephew and this is how you repay me? By corrupting him as well?"

No no no no, I'm sorry, it's my fault. Don't harm him.

But the words won't form, stuck in my throat. All that comes out is a whine.

"Get your hands off me! You will not disrespect my person. I am your Raja Muda!" Yosua's voice rings out from the corridor. He storms in, the door slamming shut behind him.

"What's going on, Aunt Layla?"

"That's what I would like to know." Her voice is steely, dangerous. "Can you tell me why we found him far from the city?"

A sharp intake of breath. "Mikal? What? Why is— oh Kudus."

I flinch.

"So you *do* know about his escape attempt. Aided him, maybe?"

"I don't—I don't know anything. I've been looking for him ever since my return."

"Have you? Really?"

"I—"

"Don't lie, Yosett. If you had been looking for him, the castle would be in an uproar. I know how you are with your little pet. That you kept so, so quiet since your return means you knew he was gone. You helped him escape."

Yosua stammers through several excuses, each one sounding flimsier than the last. I want to tell him to shut up, to stop implicating himself, but I can't. Not with my face being ground to the floor, hands trapped behind me. I try to form a warning, but I cannot think with my hands, not like he can. He stutters to a stop and takes a deep breath.

"The truth this time, Yosett."

The tap of Permaisuri Layla's nails on the wooden armrests are driving me crazy. It's the only sound in this room, except for my harsh, panicked breathing.

"Yes, I sent him away. It is within my rights to do with him as I will. He is *mine*."

Yosua steps beside me. The pressure on my head reduces, the foot holding it there shoved off. There is a hand in my hair, pulling me to sit up. Yosua's hand. It's almost calming, grounding.

There is sharp irritation in the permaisuri's voice when she says, "You have aided in the escape attempt of a political prisoner."

"Is that what he is? I thought you said he was my slave." Why does he sound so calm?

Permaisuri Layla makes an impatient sound. "Don't play the fool with me, Yosett. You know why he is here. I am permaisuri of this land and my word is law."

"Even the permaisuri of this land cannot come between master and slave. Or have I not learnt well enough the lessons you have been trying to teach me? On how I should treat my property? You invoke often the way of the merchant and the right of masters. Would you come between me and mine now? Our affairs are our own."

"Not when it involves treason."

All around the room, I can hear a collective gasp.

"It is not treason to send my own slave away on errands." I can hear the strain in his voice, feel the quiver of his hand on my head.

"It is when he is a political prisoner gifted to you of my own goodwill *and* if his intent is to stir up unrest and rally an army to attack Bayangan. What errand would you send him on all the way to Maha? I will give you three days, Yosett, to plan your defence. Think very carefully what you will say during your trial. Three days, only because you are my nephew and the Raja Muda. Any other traitor would have been executed on the spot. You'll be confined to your rooms until the trial."

"What happens to Mikal?"

Her smile is sharp, predatory. "I promised him pain should he try to escape. Him and his father and all his former subjects. Karett, there is to be a public whipping tomorrow morning. Bring Simson and select five Mahans. I don't care who they are. Forty lashes for Mikal, twenty each for the rest of them. You, Yosett, will watch."

"No!" The cry escapes me before I can stop it. The subsequent blow sends me back to the ground.

"I warned you, Mikal. I told you this would happen."

"It's not their fault, Tuanku, don't punish them. They have nothing to do with it! Please."

She ignores my blubbering. "After the whipping, I want both Simson and Mikal held in the dungeons until the trial." She dismisses us.

Yosua is immediately surrounded by soldiers. They don't touch him. He looks as if he wants to approach me, then his face hardens and he turns on his heel and leaves the room, the soldiers forming a cage around him.

"Come on," Captain Karett mutters with a kick.

I'm grabbed by the arms again and half-hauled, half-dragged to the dungeons.

○3

Another sleepless night. I toss and turn on the cold floor, unable to find a place to rest, a comfortable enough position to afford me sleep. I feel like I won't be able to find sleep until I am dead. It's almost a relief when the light changes, signalling that morning has come.

The stares are unbearable when I'm dragged up to the courtyard. The five selected Mahans huddle together, confused but silent. Three men, two women. I don't recognise them. I fix their faces in my mind, promising to compensate them in whatever way possible if we ever get out of here. They obey meekly when told to strip and are tied up at the whipping posts.

Ayahanda is led in by two guards. He is scrawnier than I can imagine, his ribs in sharp relief, a strange bump in his belly. He seems confused, disoriented. The fuzz on his head is all white, stringy, thin and greasy, but reaching down past his ears. The sockets of his eyes are still raw, red scabs.

Yosua is there, but I can't bear to look at him. He is under guard, two soldiers at his side at any time.

I'm sorry.

Captain Karett reads out the charges. *My* charges. And the punishment. The gathered slaves glare at me, the judgement and anger in their gazes like a physical weight pressing against me. I clench my teeth in defiance. I did it for them. Judge me all they want, I did it for their benefit so that we could win free of this place, of this torment. Then the fire goes out. I did it for them, but now I am doing it *to* them, subjecting them to this punishment because I have failed them once again.

I beg for mercy, but Captain Karett is made of rock. All his men are stone.

"I promised you this would happen, and I keep my promises," Permaisuri Layla says.

I hadn't realised she'd come to watch, but why wouldn't she? Why shouldn't she relish the pain and terror she is causing? This is not a faceless punishment for wayward slaves she does not know. This is part of her revenge on her hereditary enemy.

Ayahanda turns his face towards her with a whimper. His movements are hesitant, the lack of sight stealing the rest of his confidence and strength. My heart twists within me.

All my fault.

"Punish me alone," I beg of her, grovelling at her feet. "It was my fault, not Yosua's, not my father's, not any of the other Mahans. I beg you, take out your wrath on me alone."

If Captain Karett is a rock, Permaisuri Layla is a granite mountain. Why would she be moved for me when she will not be moved for her own nephew?

"Why do you act as if I'm meting out cruel and unusual punishment when I am merely doing what your father did to my people? Why do you think my brother has always been so docile? Do you think he truly loved you and longed to serve your father? No." Permaisuri Layla grips Ayahanda's hair and pulls his head up so she can inspect his face. "You bought my brother's obedience with the blood of my people. I will do the same with the blood of yours."

She shoves him away and sneers at me. "Your father has made this bed. Now don't complain that you have to lie in it."

I don't fight the orders to strip. I'm too weary to fight. They tie me to the post, arms stretched high, balancing on my toes. Then Captain Karett starts. There's a difference to the way he aims his blows. Before, he was minimising injury, promising to Yos as he did that I would not come to harm. Today, he is maximising it, not holding back his strength, laying stroke upon stroke to draw blood. It's not long until I'm a writhing, screaming, bleeding mess. I lose consciousness a few times, but they splash water on my face, shaking me awake again before they continue.

I'm made to watch as they whip Ayahanda next, then the five of my people. For each stroke they receive, I beg for forgiveness. I don't deserve it, but I beg anyway, hoping my contrition will move someone, anyone. It doesn't make any difference. Even the heavens are silent, Kudus turning His face away from my pleas.

My fault.

Yosua is pale. He is pale and haggard and he looks at me with deep sorrow in his eyes. I look away. I cannot bear his scrutiny nor his judgement. He is in the very predicament he has been trying to avoid all this while because I persuaded him that it was safe, that it would be fine, that it would work. He should never have had any faith in me. Why did he? He has been telling me ever since I was twelve that none of my plans ever made sense and that was why he was there to help me. I've always known he's the better strategist. I should have listened to him. Taken the easy way out.

Let him sit on his play throne while I rallied the remnants.

The last stroke falls. The only sounds in this courtyard are their sobs and my regret. I shiver despite the warm air, each soft caress of the breeze like a blow on my bloodied back. It smells of piss and iron and salt.

Captain Karett dismisses the crowd. They disperse slowly, silently. No one says a word. No one dares. The Permaisuri nods her approval and sends Yosua back to his suite like a scolded child. He doesn't spare me another glance, just leaves without a word, without a *sign*. He must hate me so.

My eyes are drawn to the window I've looked out of hundreds of times in these past few months, watching the punishments in terror, wishing I could just walk out past the gates without repercussions.

The five who have taken my punishment are sent back to work, bloodied and naked, as an example to those who would still think of escape.

Permaisuri Layla picks her way past the splashes of blood, looking with distaste at the mess she has created, leaving us kneeling in the courtyard to bake under the hot sun, scrutinised by the flies that buzz around us.

CHAPTER 26

Evening comes as a blessed relief. They release us from the posts and let us put on our soiled clothes. The clothes are still wet and sticky, reeking of blood and urine. The cloth scratches uncomfortably against my skin. I am still grateful for it.

We're given food and water then taken down to the dungeons. It is a tiny comfort that they lock us in the same cell.

"Ayahanda."

"Mikal?" His voice is soft, broken.

"I'm sorry."

"What for?"

"This is all my fault. I was impatient. I wanted to prove myself to you, to Kudus. I should have stayed and waited, trusted more. If I had, you would be free right now."

He told me to wait. He told me to have patience. I didn't listen. My guilt overwhelms me.

Ayahanda holds me close as I whisper to him all the things that have happened. The spies from Terang, Garett's advocacy, their plans for his rescue, my plans for escape. Tok Ibrahim's death. How I have single-handedly destroyed all the months of planning because of my foolhardiness.

"Garett?" he asks. "Garett has aided you in all this? For my freedom?"

"Yes. He's the one who has pulled us altogether. He alone stands steadfast for you."

"Why would he? After all I've done…Kudus knows he hates me. He should hate me."

Kudus knows that it is us Mahans, who profess to be His followers, who have betrayed our faith, whilst it is the Bayangans, led by Garett and Yosua, grafted into it by force and circumstance who have remained steadfast. I tell Ayahanda of Yosua's faithful keeping of Jemaah. He spares me a small smile.

"Don't blame yourself, Mikal. I have blamed myself for a very long time and it has yet to prove useful."

"I should have known. I mean, I have always known I don't have Kudus' favour. He would never have granted me His Strength. I don't know why I keep trying." I do know why I keep trying. I keep trying to prove Him wrong, to prove myself worthy. It is a waste of effort.

"Don't be silly, Mikal. You're my son. Whatever you think, you're wrong. Kudus will grant you this. He's promised it. If there's one thing we can hold on to, it's that Kudus never fails to fulfil His promises. You just have to wait."

Anger is a double-edged keris piercing my heart, sharpening my tongue. "For what? Until I die? We have two days, Ayahanda. Two days until she either maims me or kills me. I would prefer death." How *dare* he talk about the promises of Kudus when he was the one who first left the faith? How hypocritical of him to speak this way when *he* was the one who refused to listen to the warnings!

"Is it such a hardship to see me thus?"

"No, Ayahanda, I…I don't mean—"

"You would rather die whole than live maimed?"

"I don't have your strength. I can't. I'm weak. I've always been weak, not like you."

Ayahanda is silent. His bony arms around my shoulders are so frail I fear I would break them just by leaning wrongly. There's no warmth in his touch, not half enough.

"For a time, I thought Kudus listened," I find myself saying. "I thought I heard His voice speaking to me. Maybe I was just hallucinating, just a way to keep myself from falling deeper into despair. But it felt so real! It was like you described, a voice, a presence, an infilling. But there never was any power. There never was any Strength. Always this hollow promise just out of my reach. Maybe I desired it so much I made it all up in my mind.

"I don't know what I've done wrong, Ayahanda. Maybe I was born wrong. Kudus has never listened to me. As a child, I prayed for Ibunda, but she did not recover. As a youth, I prayed for Strength, but I never received it. I sought Him in the Temple, I prayed until my knees were sore and my throat dry. I memorised His Firman fervently, storing them in my head and in my heart. I did everything the priests asked me to. If you were to ask any of the uskups who have served in Maha, they would tell you that my religion was faultless, my practice was diligent, my sacrifices the sweet incense required. But it was never enough. *I* was never enough."

Bitterness is the churning in my guts, the bile on my tongue, the pain of always being overlooked. Anger and bitterness, the two sharp edges of my keris, cutting into me an ever-widening wound. I could bleed dry on bitterness alone, but anger keeps the blood flowing, until I am all empty inside, scraped and hollowed out like a tempurung.

"I have kept all my vows. All my life, I have kept them. From the moment you taught them to me, even until now. No razor has yet to touch a hair on my head—Yosua refused to let them cut it, despite their fear that I would inherit the Strength. They did not have to fear that! No alcohol has passed these lips. I have been righteous in all my ways, even here. But still it is not enough.

"Kudus doesn't love me, despite his promises. If He did, if He ever did, why would He never turn his face towards me? Why would He never comfort me or provide His guidance? Why would He never grant me the only thing I ever wanted of Him? Why is He always against me?

"Now I pray for deliverance and yet again He is silent. Yet again he foils all my plans. If it weren't for me, you would be free now. Kudus has forsaken us all because of me. Because He cannot ever grant me one good thing."

The weeping, when it starts, is a deluge, a thunderstorm that sweeps in in seconds and pours for hours. It blinds me, obscuring my view, twisting what my eyes can see behind the veil of wind and water. It is hard and destructive, pummelling everything in sight, leaving in its wake the devastating landslide of my self-esteem and worth.

Ayahanda is still silent. What is there to say? He just sits beside me until the storm calms, skin against skin, until the rumbling thunder of my woe subsides and the lightning flashes of my anger burn out.

"Do you think yourself the only one who has felt abandoned by Kudus?" Ayahanda finally says in the deepest silence of the night. "Ikhlas and Ramalan sought to invoke Bintang's life, hoping that by bringing her memory to my mind, I would turn back to Him, I would somehow find faith again. Did they not realise she was the reason I lost all faith?"

He is silent for so long I wonder if he has fallen asleep. I shift where I sit. I want to pace, but they've put chains on our feet and our hands, tying us to this spot. It is a mercy they leave us so close. I find comfort in Ayahanda's presence, leaning into his embrace. The lamps have burnt themselves out, leaving us in pitch blackness. In the deep dark of the dungeon, I am as blind as he.

"I prayed long and hard for Bintang's life," he continues. "She was my true north star, the one who kept me anchored. I could not imagine living without her by my side. At the end, when she was too weak to even get out of bed, she told me to marry again. She gave me her blessing.

"I told her I couldn't. How could I bear to marry someone else when she was the only woman I'd ever loved? Yet she insisted you needed a mother, and that Terang needed a Permaisuri. What woman could take her place? How could I crown any other person Permaisuri in her place?"

Yet after a decade, he had made that choice. He made the decision that undid us all.

"For three years, all of Terang prayed for her health, for her recovery. Kudus never answered. In all those years, Kudus was silent. Not a word came out of the Temple. The priests promised she would get better, that Kudus was hearing our prayers, that He would answer. We had to have more faith, less doubt. Our fears were hindering our prayers. Our lack of faith was what kept her ill. We held more vigils, more prayers, sacrificed more, lit more candles and incense. The doctors did everything they could, but it wasn't enough.

"Do you know what her last words were to me?"

Ayahanda doesn't wait for my answer. He groans and says, "'The ways of Kudus are true and just, yet inscrutable to His followers. Will you trust Him?' She trusted Kudus even as He betrayed her to death. She died the next day, still trusting.

"I couldn't. Something broke in me that day. I could not trust Kudus after that. Could not find a way or a reason to believe. Not after all the empty platitudes dished out by the Temple, not after the way my eyes opened to how they only served themselves. They would always ask for more—more gold, more sacrifice, more offerings—as a price for the Temple's blessings, to enrich themselves, but they gave little in return. And when we did not receive what we asked for, what we were beseeching Kudus for, they turned it back on us and blamed us for our lack of faith.

"Yet it is the Temple herself and her priests that have created this lack of faith."

"We are not so different then, to have come to the same conclusion." Before all of this happened, I would have condemned him for his lack of faith. I *had* condemned him for it, wondering how he could be so callous towards his vows. Now his lack comforts me that I am not alone in my faithlessness, that my bitterness is not something new, not something I have to face alone. Maybe I am my father's son. Maybe faithlessness is passed down through our genes, each generation adding a little more, and I am the culmination of it all.

His hands search out mine, grasping them tight. It's not the firm grasp I've always known. His hands are worn, calloused. Not the calluses of the keris, the nimble dexterity he used to maintain, but the broken blisters of hard work with hoe and hammer, of hardened scars from beatings and whippings.

"I know you blame me."

"Ayahanda! I don't—"

"Hush. All of Terang blames me, I know. My lack of faith, my disobedience, my anger at the Temple. A sultan owns up to his mistakes, and this *was* my mistake. I am to blame. Even without the warning of the priests, I should have been more cautious. Bintang still held my heart—and I could never marry anyone else for love, but if the Bayangan permaisuri wanted me, why was that a bad thing? I was blinded by my own pride, thinking that *I* could broker peace, *I* could do the thing my forefathers could not, by negotiating a permanent treaty with Bayangan."

"Your intentions were right—"

"Yes, but my ways were wrong. Even Garett himself asked me if I knew what I was doing."

"Garett? But he—"

"I did not forget who he was, as Yaakub used to accuse me. Garett came to me before Layla returned for the wedding. He told me of their relationship and that he felt that they were not true to their word. He cautioned me against the treaty, saying they had lost all honour, consumed by revenge. I did not believe him. I thought he was jealous that his sister had taken his throne and was seeking to undermine her authority. What could he know of her intentions from meeting her once when we had been corresponding for the past year? When she was so sweet to me in our time together, promising a brighter future? I should have listened."

"How did she betray you? What happened that night, Ayahanda?" It's the one piece of the story no one has discovered—how someone could have snuck in close enough to Ayahanda to be able to cut his hair.

Ayahanda weeps. "I let her in. She was to be my wife! I trusted her. She came to me in the middle of the night, whispering sweet words of love in my ear. I was intoxicated by lust. What was one night early in the face of eternity? And then, when we were sated, when *I* was sated, mind dulled and bleary, she asked me, 'Is it true? Is it true that your mighty strength lies in these beautiful locks of yours?'

"She ran her fingers through my hair and I told her yes. I couldn't lie. Why would I lie? I told her yes, my vows, my Strength, my honour, were all bound in the hair none but my wife has seen since my youth. None but my wife, and now her, my bride. She smiled at me, kissed me, and bid me sleep.

"I laid my head in her lap and when I awoke, it was all gone."

CHAPTER 27

We fall sleep in each other's arms, drawing warmth from each other, drained by our confessions, and the pain of our wounds. In the morning, I help him eat and drink, putting the meagre provisions we are given in his hands. We try to relieve ourselves as far away as our chains allow us so that we are not sleeping in our own filth.

We don't speak. What is there left to say?

What is faith but a vapour? It is the hopes and dreams you place in hands other than your own, whether those hands belong to another human or some being that claims to be god. I believe in Kudus; I cannot dispute His presence. I have felt that ineffable presence too many times for me to deny His existence. I have heard His voice too recently to be able to say He does not exist, not unless I were to accept that I have lost my mind. I am not mad. I do not believe that I have voices speaking to me in my head. What else can it be, other than Kudus or the spirits?

Yet who knows if Kudus is nothing but an illusion, a hallucination we make up in the darkest hours of our existence, if only for the purpose of helping us stay alive for one more day? My days are ending and whether this spirit is of my own conjuring or not will not matter for much longer. Tomorrow seals my fate. Our fates. Whatever Layla does to me she will do to Ayahanda too. I am sure of that. And I am sure that he will not survive it, not as weak as he is now. It is a hard day to face the fact that Kudus has deserted us.

The hardest thing to deny is the wealth of evidence of the Amok Strength that Kudus himself has granted my family. Spirits and voices can be dismissed as illusions, periods of hallucination, tricks of the mind or of the tongue. There is no way I can look at history and say He does not exist or that He did not grant this power, this miraculous, magical, otherworldly power to my ancestors, nay to my very own father. The thousands of soldiers in Maha who have been granted a portion of this Strength can also attest to how real it is, even if I haven't personally experienced it. It's not something that I have created out of my imagination. It's written in our very histories.

The question is why He will not give it to me. Why could He not love me enough to grant me the one wish of my heart? The very wish that would also protect the sultanate He claims as His own. I still cannot find any fault in my actions.

Without Kudus, there is no Terang. There is no reason for Maha, Suci, and Impian to stand as one. We share a history, a belief, that has held us together as one nation for generations. Our cultures have evolved together until none can tell which began as Mahan, or which Sucian, or which Impianan.

Without Kudus, there is no need for war between Terang and Bayangan. For Bayangan disbelieves the evidence of Kudus, rejects the gifts and miraculous deeds they have seen with their eyes and felt with their bodies. The Amok Strength that fills our soldiers, the Mindreading Powers that guide our Justices to the truth, the Perantaraan Gift that connects us via the priesthood.

The fault, therefore, if there is any, must lie in me. It lies in the fact that, even from a young age, I have been unable to fully believe in His love for me. In my inability to accept Him as the kind, loving, merciful God the priests make Him out to be. This failure is rooted in the same core as my father's faithlessness: the loss of Ibunda. We are a broken family, rotten from the roots, unable to heal. And this brokenness has cost us. Has cost more than *us*. It has cost every single one of our people who have relied on us for strength and guidance.

Why had He let her die? Why did He not love her enough to let her live? Why did He not love *us* enough to let her live? Why did He not love Terang enough to save us from ourselves? If she had lived, none of this would have happened.

The ways of Kudus are true and just.

What is true in His denial of me? What vow have I broken that Kudus would not honour His own word? Yet if the basis of faith is broken, my vows are invalid no matter how faithfully I have kept them. They do not hold because I have never had true faith in them. My faith is then useless, like a rudderless ship tossed by the winds.

Is Kudus just then to deny me? Would I fulfil a covenant to one who has not upheld his side of the bargain? Only if I were a fool. Kudus is not a fool, therefore He is just. There is no other conclusion. I cannot see any other conclusion.

I am not made for this twisting and turning of words, for this intrigue of the courts and temple, for the need to say one thing and mean another. I do not know how to veil my talk, to shroud my meaning in lies and half-truths. Oh, if Yosua were here to talk me out of this, to tell me straight to my face that I am turning over stones to seek blame where there is none. He's the one who has always been confident of his faith, always sure of what he believed in and why. I'm always the one floundering to find a balance between my faith and doubt.

Yet inscrutable to His followers.

Who can understand Kudus? Who can even understand their fellow man? I cannot even understand myself. I cannot understand my lack of faith in the middle of all the evidence. Why can't I just believe as my ancestors have? Why can't I trust the evidence of my forefathers, the evidence of the many who surround me? Why must my wretched heart insist He is faithless because *I* am faithless?

Will you trust Him?

"You must kill me," Ayahanda murmurs. He speaks so quietly I almost miss it.

"What?"

"I have been considering all you have told me." He turns his face towards me. In the gloom, the scabs of his eyes haunt me. "The only way I can redeem myself is through death. You must kill me."

"No, Ayahanda! No!" It comes out fiercer than I thought it would.

Ibunda's death was a wound that has never healed, a wound I never knew needed healing. I was too young to know her, but her absence has been a gaping hole in my life. Ayahanda's death will be a blow I will never recover from, especially if it is by my hand. No matter how distant he has always been, he is still my father. He is still my strength. He is still my Sultan. I cannot lose him.

"It has to happen, whether through your hand or through another's. Only by my death will you inherit."

"That cannot be true. No, Ayahanda, that cannot be true. You earned your Strength whilst your father still had his."

I refuse to let it be true. The Amok Strength is supposed to fall upon him in his time of greatest need. I once thought the Secretkeeper was referring to me in her prophecy, but she wasn't. I have had great need. Each time, I beseeched Kudus, thinking it to be my greatest need, but He has never deigned to listen. What other greatest need is there? Will Kudus wait until the deathblow has fallen before He listens? No, she was only always referring to Ayahanda.

I hate prophecies. They are riddles that can only be solved after the fact. They are of no use before the events happen.

Ayahanda shakes his head. "What I had as a youth was the overflow of my father's blessing, the same way our soldiers receive a measure of my Strength according to their faith and abilities. Only when my father died did I gain the Amok Strength in my own right. I have lost my right to the Strength, so even now you cannot have it, no matter how worthy you are, because it still resides in me."

"I know. I know all that. That's why you needed to escape. To be sanctified again at the Temple. Your hair is growing. You can reconsecrate yourself, renew your vows. And then we will all be saved." Why does he not understand?

He grips my shoulders, fingers digging into my flesh. "If you can find a way for me to escape and be reconsecrated before you are killed tomorrow, then I will accept your interpretation. But there is no way out. There is no escape, not now. You're the only one left who is worthy. You need to kill me now so that you can inherit. It is the only way."

I scramble backwards in horror. "No! I cannot kill you. No, please, don't ask this of me."

Ayahanda purses his lips. "Then we both die tomorrow."

He turns away, facing the wall.

"Ayahanda…Ayahanda, please." He doesn't respond.

Will you trust Me?

Now He speaks. Now, at the end of all things. Isn't it a little too late? Isn't this cutting it a little too close?

Why should I trust You? You weren't there when Ibunda died. You weren't there when I needed You, when I was growing up and trying so hard to please You, trying so hard to please Ayahanda. You weren't there when Ayahanda humiliated me in front of both the court and the Bayangan delegation. You weren't there when Maha fell, when my best friend betrayed me. You weren't there when I begged You for Strength, for a sign, for anything, when I disappointed my father's closest friends and the people. My people who were relying on me—all saw my failure. You weren't there when Tok Yaakub died. You weren't there when they beat me and broke me. You weren't there when they killed Mahmud and blinded Ayahanda. You weren't there when I was terrified in the forest, running for my life. Tok Ibrahim died because of me, because I was stupid enough to think that You would guide me and help me escape. You were never there for me.

Will you trust Me?

I cannot. I cannot trust an invisible Kudus who doesn't care about me, who lets me fail again and again, who makes my humiliation complete because He withholds His gifts at His whims. I cannot trust a silent God who toys with me in my desperation, who turns a deaf ear to my cries and speaks in nothing but riddles. I cannot trust a petty god, who promises but doesn't deliver, who turns my smallest fault against me, who hides his face from those who seek him, although he says that he will be found. I—

Will you trust ME?

Yet what is faith, except hope in desperation? I am desperate. There is nothing left to cling to, nothing left to rely on. I have no strength, no energy. All I am has been drained from me and I am a hollow husk tossed on the waves, the endless, restless waves. I am ashes in the wind. Dust. Tomorrow I face my death, and if faith will keep me standing, then so be it.

A faith that cannot stand in the absence of evidence is worthless. A faith that cannot stand in the presence of evidence even more so. I have had both presence and absence all through my years, and yet I could not find my faith. Instead, I have relied on the faith of those around me, on the blessings that have poured my way because of the faith of others, because of the goodwill of Kudus, because of the prayers others have prayed. Now, at the end of all things, I need to believe. I need to believe for *myself*.

I need to have faith because if I don't, everything I've built my life upon will crumble.

Yes. I will trust You. Though I know not how.

The tears, when they come again, are not a thunderstorm. The storm has passed, destruction has run its course. In this rain, there is healing. A gentle, steady drizzle, the cleansing rains that bring new life. This is the rain of little things, of green grass pushing past the barrier of the brown soil, of flowers turning their faces to the light of the sun, of grey skies gradually brightening, of gentle winds and peace.

Ayahanda has his arms around me again, the missing embrace of a father now presenting itself a final time. His touch is both the comfort of presence and the pain of my flayed back. If we could undo the past, would he hug me more often? Spend more time with me? Would I have sought him out more, trying to find refuge in the Strength of Maha instead of pulling away in pain at his rejection? It is too late. We have been estranged by our own pride. We cannot undo the past and I cannot see any future. All I have now is his silent, brooding present. I will make the most of it.

"When vision fails you, call upon Kudus Maha Esa and He will incline His ear to you in your desperation." The Secretkeeper's prophecy falls from my lips. My vision has failed. Maybe now He will listen.

Ayahanda stiffens. "What is that? Say that again?"

I recite the Secretkeeper's prophecy from memory, the words of the scroll still burnt into my mind. I do not know if he has ever heard them. Uskup Daud had entrusted the scroll to me and I had been too afraid to bring it to my father. What if I had...? Would things have turned out differently?

"O Kudus, Maha Esa…" he starts and I join him in finishing the one phrase seared into our very beings.

"Oh to see clearly," Ayahanda says, "to see with clarity the vision set before us."

"What do you mean?"

"Tell it to me again."

I repeat the words. They no longer hold any meaning for me. Meaningless, meaningless riddles. Yet I said I would trust. So I will. I will believe that this makes sense somehow, that tomorrow, maybe, when I see the end of all things, Kudus will finally do something on my behalf.

O Kudus, help me believe.

"Maha has fallen, the city has burnt. Suci will fall." Ayahanda falters, his voice breaking, lowering into a hoarse whisper. "My vision has failed, so now I must call upon the Almighty one final time. And you—you must survive to fulfil the Covenant of Salt. It falls to you to redeem Terang. I am sorry."

"Ayahanda?"

"Sleep, Mikal, sleep now. Tomorrow you will need all your strength."

"Tomorrow? Why do I need strength to die?"

"Tomorrow I will do the one thing I have refused to do ever since your Ibunda died. Tomorrow I will beseech Kudus again. I will beg for His forgiveness until He listens to me. Isn't that what you want?"

I cannot decipher the strange blend of bitterness and resignation in Ayahanda's voice. He turns away from me and curls into himself.

I pretend I do not hear his soft cries. He pretends he does not hear mine.

CHAPTER 28

The grand Court House looks different from below, sitting bowed and broken in the same cell Mahmud had stood so defiantly in a week ago. The dais is high and imposing, the ornate throne an impressive yet oppressive display. The executioner stands over the bloody bench on the right, sharpening his tools. I shudder at the sight, remembering Mahmud's head rolling, Ayahanda's screams. The second throne is empty. Yosua won't be sitting there, not today.

The hall starts to fill. The merchants strut in and take their seats near the front, their slaves kneeling at their feet with wide, frightened eyes. Do they know what this trial is about? Are they informed beforehand or are they just herded in to watch? The common citizens crowd in next, filling the place with uneasy murmurs. They snatch what seats are empty, even if the rich merchants scowl at them. Most stand, pressing close to each other so that they can keep gossiping. It is speech that sustains them.

Garett pushes his way to the front, sending another merchant scrambling at the look on his face.

Marla grips his shoulder, whispering in his ear. I spy Rahsia taking a place as far forward as she can, her eyes widening when she catches sight of Ayahanda. There is surprise on her face. Surprise and desperation. And resolve. She does not know then.

There is only one guard at each entrance, not like the last trial, when the soldiers lined the walls as a show of force. Hakim, Iskandar, and Ali stand at separate entrances. What are they planning? Rahsia's eyes flick to me, a disappointed scowl.

Ayahanda kneels next to me, mumbling under his breath. Sweat collects on his brow. He prostrates himself and I wonder if he is all right. If he is in his right mind. Can Rahsia hear his thoughts from where she stands? Or is she just upset at this turn of events?

The last of the soldiers march in with the remaining inhabitants of this accursed city—the slaves. They shuffle in, heads bowed, chained to each other to prevent escape. The soldiers order them to their knees as they lock the chains to hoops in the wall.

Then Yosua walks in, still under guard, his hands manacled before him. He is led to stand beside our cage, hands resting on the bar that separates the people from the Permaisuri. Despite the dark circles under his eyes, he is calm, resigned. He gives me a weak smile. I turn away, hanging my head.

Permaisuri Layla enters last, sparkling in all her finery. Her dress is the deep dark blue of Bayangan's flag, lined with jewels that glint in the light. Who is she trying to impress? Ayahanda has no eyes to see her, I hate her too much to care how pretty her dress is. Maybe Yosua will be persuaded by this, visual evidence of what he is going to lose by supporting me.

Behind me, the citizens rise then sit again at her gesture.

"You are gathered here today for the trial of Raja Muda Yosett Regis Baya. He has been arrested for treason, for attempting to aid the escape of our prisoner Mikal ayell Simson, former putera of Maha. We have also found in his possession items of the outlawed religion of Maha."

She gestures at the table set up before her. Candles and incense sticks are laid out beside the Secretkeeper's scroll. Yosua's precious Firman has been ripped apart, pages fluttering. My keris lies next to it.

"What is your defence?"

Yosua looks her in the eyes. "None."

"None? You have nothing to say for yourself?"

"What is there to say when you have already decided my guilt?"

Permaisuri Layla sneers. "Do not make a mockery of this trial."

"I do not, Tuanku."

"So you admit your guilt."

Yosua closes his eyes briefly, then answers, "Yes."

Her eyes glisten. "I am not unmerciful, nephew. If you will renounce your title and your faith, I would give you pardon and your life."

"You may have my title. I have no use for it now. Bestow it on whomever you wish."

"And your faith?"

"My faith is mine. You may not agree with it, Aunt, but I have made my choice."

"You would die for this fake god of yours?"

"Is He fake? If He were fake, you would not quake in fear of Him."

"Be reasonable. I do not wish for you to die. I'm sure your parents do not wish for you to die either." She gestures behind us.

Yosua turns and notices his parents for the first time. He swallows hard, then turns back to the permaisuri. "Neither do I."

"Then give up your faith! Renounce your god and I will allow you to live."

"And what kind of living would that be?"

"You would die for him?"

Yosua's hands flex around the bar. Knuckles white, jaw set, eyebrows drawn close together. "Even unto death," he whispers.

Even unto death. It pierces my heart, secures me in place.

The permaisuri leans forward, a frown on her face. It's not what she expected. She wanted him repentant and compliant, moulding himself to her will. After all these months, does she not know that Yosua can be as stubborn as an ass? That he can dig his heels in and not budge for months? It's so ludicrous I cannot hold back a sharp bark of amusement.

Permaisuri Layla turns her attention to me. I stand under her scrutiny, gripping the bars for strength. Mahmud's image flashes before my eyes. If only I had half his defiance!

"You I will not pardon," she says. "If he dies, you die with him. Yet if he lives, so will you. It would be in your best interest to convince him to stay alive."

I look at my best friend and betrayer, my confidant and my master, my brother and my enemy. He stares back, jaw set. His faith has ever been stronger than mine, his decisions firmer and wiser. He would have made a good Raja Muda if circumstances had been different, if he had been in my place. We call ourselves righteous, but Garett and Yosua have always been more honourable, more faithful than Ayahanda and I have been.

My throat is dry. I swallow hard. I'd made my decision last night, but everything is different in the light. It isn't any easier.

Why do I need strength to die?

My own words come back to taunt me. I do. I need strength to die, if I am dying for a faith I'm holding on to by the barest tips of my fingers. The faith I am desperately trying to cling on to, but which keeps slipping out of my grasp, just as the Amok Strength keeps eluding me. I do not need that Strength now. Have I ever? All I've ever needed was Kudus.

Ever-loyal, ever-faithful Yosua ayell Garett is right, and the best I can do is follow his lead in this.

"Even unto death," I echo.

Yosua smiles.

"Come, come. Be rational. What can this foreign god do? You are here, bound before me. Would you not rather live? Why do you seek the bosom of death?"

"What kind of life would that be?" Yosua asks again, his eyes still on me, holding me to his resolve.

She takes his question as a sign of his wavering. "I would give you everything you would ever want or need. You'll live like the prince you are, lacking for nothing. You'll be the son I've never had."

"I would be kept hostage in the castle, never leaving it."

"Whatever you desire will be brought to you."

"And Mikal?"

She hesitates. "He would be there with you, if you wish it. I will take his tongue so he can no longer fill your ears with lies, but he would otherwise be yours to do with as you will."

Yosua laughs. "And you think that enough?"

I flinch at the smack of her palm on wood.

"I am offering you your life, you fool," she snarls. "Do you not realise how great a boon it is? I could have killed you on the spot but I refrained. I refrained because I am a sentimental fool to put family above my own laws." She waves her soldiers over.

Yosua tenses, fingers tightening against the bar.

"Take the slave Mikal. Kill him first."

O Kudus, O Kudus, I am not prepared for this. My breath hitches. The cage door opens and they pull me from it.

"No."

It's the first word Ayahanda has said aloud since Permaisuri Layla entered the hall. I'd forgotten he was there, huddled on his knees in the corner of the cage. He stands now, arms outstretched, feeling for the bars that surround him.

"No," he repeats. "He will not die."

"The beast speaks," Permaisuri Layla sneers. "I thought it had died there. I'll slay you next, don't worry."

Ayahanda faces her, gripping the bars before him, his arms trembling. Is he afraid for me? Afraid of my death? Of his coming death? But I look at his face as the soldiers pull me away and it is not fear. It is anger. It is his rage. It is the face of the Amok that has made the Bayangans quake in their boots for decades. Something jolts in my heart. A tingling. A buzzing. Around me, I see the Mahan slaves look up, almost as one.

Permaisuri Layla doesn't notice. Her ire is on Ayahanda. "I do not fear you. You can do nothing more to me."

Ayahanda ignores her. He raises his face and his hands, begins the litany. "O Kudus, Maha Esa, berkatilah hamba-Mu dengan kuasa ajaib-Mu."

A dozen voices repeat it after him, like reflex. Immediately after comes the sound of pain as a dozen masters beat their slaves.

The permaisuri looks amused. "Your god won't listen to you, not now that you've broken all your vows. You're impure, and if there is one thing I know about your *god*, it's that he doesn't listen to those who aren't holy enough for him."

Ayahanda just keeps his hands up as he repeats the litany, more voices joining in. Until I join in. He turns at the sound of my voice and nods at me.

"You who listen to the broken, hear my pleas now. I have fallen far away, I have spurned Your Firman and Your call. Now You have chastised me, You have brought me to realise the error of my ways. You who are ever-gracious, ever-merciful, ever-forgiving, I pray, forgive me now. Forgive me my wandering, my fear, my doubt, my anger, my bitterness. Take it. Take it all!" His voice is a broken roar, hoarse, earnest.

"O Kudus…"

He doesn't complete it, but every single Mahan in the hall takes up the cry, "Maha Esa, berkatilah hamba-Mu dengan kuasa ajaib-Mu!"

The sound is sweet in my ears even amidst the background of slaps and fists and choking. It is the sound of faith rising.

"Kill him!" Layla screams from the dais.

Ayahanda grips the bars and pulls. A hush falls. The Bayangan soldiers pull me away, dragging me towards the executioner's block. A creak first, then they snap. The iron bars snap apart in his hands.

"Kill him now!" Layla screams again. The soldiers raise their parangs. They rush at me.

"Run, Mikal. Run!" Ayahanda roars.

I swipe the soldiers away in my haste to reach Ayahanda.

"Ayahanda!"

"Get out of this building. Garett, take him and your son and go!" Ayahanda stumbles forward, still reaching blindly with the twisted off bar in his hands to find his way, to test his way.

"Baginda—" Garett shouts.

"Get them out now!"

Then Ayahanda is lost in the chaos as all around the hall, the Mahan slaves break their chains. The merchants scream in terror, trying to stampede out but the way is blocked by both the hapless Bayangan soldiers and by *us*.

Yosua still stands there, gaping as Ayahanda surges towards the pillars that hold this building up. Garett grabs Yosua by the shoulders pulling him away.

"Come, boys," Garett orders, and I follow. He struggles with the crowd and I step before him, pushing the people aside easily with the Strength that flows from Ayahanda, and before him from Kudus. I can feel the lines of energy that unite us, that connect all the Mahan soldiers. I know who is strong, who is weak, who is tired and flagging, who has rage to spare.

It is too much to process all at once, this bewildering power I have been searching for for so long, that has come so belatedly. I feel a new connection and I stop in my tracks.

Yosua stares at his hands. The chains around them have snapped, and he pulls the remaining cuffs off, breaking them apart like tearing paper.

"Mikal! Yosua! Go!" Garett pushes us out the nearest door. He has no Amok Strength, but we obey the press of his hands in our daze. He stops in the doorway.

"Ayah?" Yosua asks.

Garett turns back.

Most of the Mahans have exited the building, taking the place of the guards to keep the Bayangans inside. I cannot see where Layla has gone. There is fighting in the hall, whether Mahans against Bayangans, or Bayangans amongst themselves I cannot tell.

Ayahanda stands at the main pillars that hold up the ceiling of the Court House. He lays both palms upon one, then turns towards us. Two Mahans take the pillar opposite him, mirroring his stance.

Ayahanda raises his head and calls, "Is Mikal safe?"

"Baginda Paduka, they are outside," Garett replies, "I will come—"

"Sultan Mikal, keep the faith." Ayahanda pushes. Beside him, the soldiers strain.

"No, Baginda Paduka!" Garett tries to run in, but Yosua is too quick for him. He grabs his father by the waist and drags him away from the building.

Ayahanda strains against the pillars, muttering under his breath. Bayangan soldiers converge about them, parangs drawn. The building itself creaks. The ground shakes and rumbles.

"Mikal! Move!" Yosua shouts.

I dash away as the building collapses in a great cloud, burying my father and everyone in it.

CHAPTER 29

I know the exact moment Ayahanda dies. All the lines of power disappear, the Strength that has been holding me upright gone in a blink. My knees and palms hit the dirt, pain flaring. Yosua is saying something, somewhere. Garett and Marla buzz like flies but Rahsia is silent. I can feel her watching me, feel the bent of her thoughts upon mine.

Our people falter, all turning as one to the rubble of the building before me. We are bereft, adrift, rudderless. Sultanless.

Ayahanda.

The loss is gutting.

O Kudus, he's gone. It's gone.

There is panic and slaughter all around me, words caught in a jumble of noise.

Garett shakes me by the shoulders. "Tuanku, the soldiers are coming. The Bayangan soldiers are coming to slaughter us all."

I am the only one left.

Call upon Me.

I can hear the marching, the running feet, Layla screaming orders. The clash of metal, the dying cries of my fellow countrymen. Layla is still alive. Ayahanda is dead but Layla lives.

She is mine to kill.

I can grieve later.

I rise to my feet, lift my hands, speak the words, weak at first, but steadying as I go. "O Kudus, Maha Esa, berkatilah hamba-Mu dengan kuasa ajaib-Mu!"

The men look at me, falling to their knees. They repeat the lines after me. It is a chant. An echo. A unifying force.

My feet tingle, a warmth blossoms in my heart. Fire descends, heat flowing down from the crown of my head to the tips of my toes. Light bursts into being all around me. The Amok Strength surges into me, a jolt of lightning, the lines of them drawn—no longer to the dead man in the rubble before me—but to my heart.

See your light has dawned.

I reach, exploring the lines, the power. The Presence. Oh, that overwhelming presence. He engulfs me, He is before me and behind, beside me and all around. These lines of power are His, the Strength we harbour an outpouring of Him. It is everything Ayahanda has ever described and more, so much *more*.

Raise your keris in my Name.

There are twenty men…and Yosua. How have we lost so many people? Yosua's presence tugs at me, foreign and yet familiar. I open my eyes and look at him.

Yos opens his grip and presents to me the one thing he'd grabbed before we ran. My keris.

Raise your keris…

"How...?"

Yos shrugs in reply.

I take up my keris and raise it to the heavens. "For Kudus! For Maha!"

For Ayahanda.

The fight is sharp, furious. They outnumber us more than twice over, but we are empowered by Kudus, fuelled by our rage and grief.

It's almost too easy to fall into the forms, shunting pain aside to focus on the enemy before me. No holding back, no mercy, just giving in to the rage. They're not people, they're targets, puppets set up to be cut down. For a moment, it feels like silat practice, me against Tok Yaakub, but this time, I manage to defeat him. I finally defeat all the targets he sends my way. Then my focus hones in on Layla, the woman who has brought my life crashing down around me. I want her to pay. I need for her to pay.

We circle each other, careful steps over rubble and sand. My heart is tight within me. I have fought—and defeated—the others, but they are ordinary soldiers. What if nothing has changed? What if I am as weak as ever, despite all this? Unskilled against what the permaisuri of Bayangan would have trained for?

The queasiness that surfaced on the beach threatens me again. I push it aside. I've killed too many now, there is too much blood on my hands for regret.

She attacks, parang slashing. Her reach is longer, her techniques more practised, but the Strength of Kudus sustains me. I do not tire.

Or maybe I tire but I do not feel it. This light in my veins sustains me, feeding me strength and fire. We are surrounded by bodies, men I have killed, men she has killed. So much death, so much blood. She lunges and I twist, catching her hand with mine. Her parang skitters away. She rushes towards it but I intercept, throwing her to the ground. There we tussle.

I have never won hand-to-hand back home, never managed to defeat any of the Mahans I sparred with. I've always lost no matter how good my technique, not matter how focused, because of this Amok Strength they had...but I too now hold. I gather it around me as a shield.

Time itself slows. Her right arm rises, I raise my own to block her. She grabs instead, twisting, but her strength is like a child's compared to mine. Her chest heaves with the strain as she pushes against me with all her might. It's a mere flex of my arm to throw her to the ground the way Tok Yaakub used to flip me over and over again. She lands on her back, hands scrabbling and nails scratching uselessly at my forearms.

A strange reversal. I remember Tok Yaakub's hand on my chest, Ayahanda's thumbs against my neck. But this time I win. This time, I'm the one kneeling over the disarmed enemy, keeping her pinned with my body, my keris pressed against her throat.

"Go ahead. Kill me. You've already lost." She spits in my face.

"What have I lost? *You've* lost. It's my keris at your throat."

"You may kill me now, but even your precious prophecies say I've won. Maha has fallen, Suci is falling. Terang is destroyed. I have fulfilled what I set out to do."

"Suci will not fall." *It cannot. Not now. We've won.*

Our soldiers standing watch in Suci should also have received their portion of Strength. Yet, how many of them are still in Suci, I do not know. Rahsia said before that most of them left to defend what remains of Maha.

"No?" she mocks. "Even now, my army is at their gates, burning and slaughtering. You cannot stop it. You have failed."

She can't know that for sure, unless she has Suci's gift herself. "We will rebuild."

"At what cost?"

"If you're trying to make me spare you, it won't work." But my hands are trembling again. No, she doesn't have the full picture. The prophecy speaks of our salvation, of His Strength that has come through in the end. At the cost of Ayahanda's life.

"It doesn't matter if I live or die. Jeffett will return to avenge me. And now we know your weakness, Maha will fall again and Jeffett will kill you—"

I cannot listen to this anymore. I press the blade into her neck, and watch as the blood wells up, as the life fades out of her eyes. I want to look away, but I can't. I need to face my deeds, need to face the end of my enemy.

I have won. *We* have won. I don't know what to feel. I don't feel victorious. I don't feel like rejoicing. Instead, I feel sick again, turning away as my stomach heaves. But there is nothing to throw up. There's nothing in me. I am hollowed out, empty.

O Kudus, forgive me.

Be still. Be still and know that I am God.

So much death. So much blood. This is not what I thought it would be.

Vengeance is Mine. It is no longer yours to pursue. Rest.

Is this what You gave us this power for? For death and destruction? For blood and guts? Where is the glory in this? Where is the holiness? Where is the love and the mercy, the peace and the righteousness? This is not what I expected.

No, this is not what the Strength is for. This is the result of its misuse. I bestowed my gifts on Terang for protection and defence. It is not for gain, nor war. Not for the useless loss of life.

But all we have done is protect ourselves! To free ourselves from Bayangan's grip. Surely that is right. Surely that is what You will for us.

It shouldn't have come to this at all. Your father let the enemy into the gates and you have borne the brunt of his decisions. Yet I waited patiently for him to return, and he has. I have called you, and you have sought Me. The past is gone and forgotten. Now is the time to rebuild.

I am caught up in the clouds, a bird in the air, looking down on the lands that now belong to me. No, the lands I rule on behalf of Kudus. They are not mine. I see Maha in ruins and Suci aflame. Impian depletes itself as it tries in vain to sustain its sister cities. Everywhere I look, there is destruction and despair. Bayangan smoulders.

Now we start anew. Fulfil the Covenant.

The Presence disappears, and I am on my knees again, covered in mud, drenched with blood.

"Tuanku? Tuanku, are you all right?" Garett shakes me by the shoulders. "Mikal, can you hear me?"

I'm back in Bayangan, knees still pressed on Layla's corpse. I scramble away, my keris clanging to the ground. My ears are filled with the sound of weeping, my nose with the stench of death. The sun beats down, unheeding of our sorrow, of the devastation that has swept this land. How can the sky be so cheerfully blue? Why does it not weep with us? But this brightness itself is like the flare of our anger. Strong, relentless, unforgiving.

"Tuanku?"

My eyes focus on Garett and he sighs in relief. The Strength seeps away. I let it go. I do not need it any longer.

"She's dead. She's really dead." It doesn't seem real, somehow. As if after all these months, it should have taken her longer to die. As if there should have been a bigger show of her defeat. Some fanfare. Thunder! Lightning! An earthquake! Not this.

"Yes, she's dead. It's over."

He holds out his hand. I grab on to it, using it as a crutch as I stumble to my feet.

Permaisuri Layla is dead and most of the merchants and soldiers with her. There are fewer bodies than I expected. The Bayangans surrendered once news of Layla's death spread. Hakim's men watch over them with blades drawn. There are many wounded, both Mahan and Bayangan, whether from the battle or from the collapse of the building, I cannot tell.

One by one, the Mahans drop to one knee before me, pressing their palms together in front of their foreheads. Garett and Yosua do the same.

"Tuanku, we pledge our lives and our keris to you, as we did to your father. May you reign long in Maha!" they pledge in one voice.

I stand frozen. "Do not pledge to me yet. Do not pledge to me until we have regained Maha, until I have proven myself worthy of you. Do not pledge until the Temple has given her blessing," I whisper.

Garett bows his head. "Still, we will follow you until then."

I gesture for them to rise.

"What are your orders?" Hakim asks.

I'm glad he is alive. One more familiar face in this disorienting state.

What are my orders? I do not know. Do I order them to be executed? Do I perpetuate this cycle of war and death? No, Kudus has spoken. This is not what he has given us our Strength for.

The Bayangans huddle together, watching us with fear. There are few of us left, but we have prevailed. Their own soldiers have surrendered and are being rounded up by Hakim, on their knees with their hands bound behind their backs. The rest are citizens, not warriors, lost without a leader. They're not prepared for this. I've trained for this all my life, and I'm not prepared either. I've never had a class on 'what to do when you defeat the enemy in their land'. Neither have I had a class on 'what to do when you are captured by the enemy'. I have still somehow survived both.

"Tend to their wounds then send them home." It's what I would have wanted in their position.

"Tuanku?" Hakim sounds incredulous.

"There will be no retribution. I'm done with death."

Garett smiles. He smiles and it's like the ground falls away.

∽

Ayahanda is dead.

I should be rejoicing at our victory like my people around me, but I am numb. Morning seems so far away, yet it's still only mid-afternoon. Yosua stays with me, standing amidst the rubble, even as the others bustle about their business.

Garett makes his rounds to the Bayangans, offering them what comfort he can, assuring them there will be no further slaughter. They do not believe him. They cast wary glances all about them and shy away from all the Mahans, even the women. As quickly as they can, they flee. I hope they go home. I hope they find refuge in their houses until they realise we will not displace them or loot them of their belongings.

"Make sure they know that," I tell Garett, even as I tell Hakim to make sure that we don't.

Hakim deals with the Bayangan soldiers, sending them away under the guard of his men. At Rahsia's urging, Yosua and I follow her as we go through the city, checking that all the Mahans are freed. We don't find many—most of those in the castle and the city were present for the trial this morning. The last to be released are the field slaves. The last people who knew and tended to Ayahanda. My eyes are drawn back to the rubble. Ayahanda still lies buried there. But the sun is setting. And my energy is flagging. My strength flees, and hunger and thirst and pain take its place.

I want to go home, but Maha is too far to reach tonight. We need to find ships to take us back over the straits to our home. Ships. Wagons. Not that we have much to carry but our dead. We need to find the bodies, prepare them for burial. We need to contact Suci somehow, or Impian. We need to rout out the rest of the Bayangan soldiers, need to make sure that they know who is now in charge. Make sure they don't start another retaliatory war, embroil us in another pointless battle. Too many things to do and I am paralysed with indecision.

"We should tend to your wounds, Tuanku," Yosua says quietly beside me.

Now he says it, I'm suddenly aware of the constant pulse of pain. "Where can we go? Is there a place that can hold all of us?"

"The castle?"

I almost protest—I do not want to see the inside of the castle, do not want to scurry around like a wretch, do not want to remember—but I let it slide. He's right. The castle has the supplies we need. I need to leave behind the past and stride in like the conquering sultan I'm supposed to be.

There are hundreds of us, all displaced. I direct everyone to the castle. There has always been more than enough space there, too many empty rooms to count. With half the nobility and merchants dead under the Court House, there will be even more place for us. The dead will not mind.

I limp my way back, leaning heavily on Yosua. Now that the Amok Strength has subsided, I feel all my wounds, from the barely-healed lashes I received two days ago to the countless nicks and stabs I sustained in my battle against Permaisuri Layla. I don't know how I hold myself together, except by the grace of Kudus.

The castle is subdued. The servants gather in the courtyard, rounded up by one of the men—Hakim probably. What remains of the country's leaders are a handful of frightened nobles. I don't have the energy to deal with them today, but it seems like I need to.

What would Ayahanda do?

I scoff at my own stupid question. Ayahanda would have either killed them or locked them up. That's not how this is supposed to go.

What would Garett do?

He's standing beside me. When I turn to him, he murmurs that I should say something to put them at ease.

I take a deep breath. They are his people. Of course he feels tender towards them. I feel nothing towards them except contempt. Did they care about us when their army came and did the same to us? Did they care when we were dragged here in chains and stuffed into their crowded dungeons? These are the same people who abused me, who laughed at and taunted me in my distress. Their crying hits me hard. I haven't finished crying yet myself. Maybe in this I can understand them, can soothe them.

"There will be no retribution," I repeat what I'd told the soldiers earlier. "Go back to your beds, to your homes. Your permaisuri is dead and Garett—" I pause, looking at Yosua. He's the Raja Muda after all. Wouldn't that make him their next Sultan? "Raja Muda Yosett will stand in her place until we find a solution that fits both Terang and Bayangan."

CHAPTER 30

I hesitate in the doorway of Yosua's suite. I can't stay here. There are rooms aplenty, still rooms empty even after we've filled them with all the displaced Mahans. Should I still sleep on my pallet, or should he sleep on it instead? No, I take the empty suite beside his. Still, after I have washed away the grime of the past week, Yosua sits by my bedside tending to my wounds.

"You don't have to do this, not anymore," I say.

"This is the nature of our relationship, Tuanku," he replies. "Do not deny what I was meant to do."

"Surely your life's purpose isn't to serve me. You're the Raja Muda of Bayangan, after all."

"The exact nature may change, but I have pledged my life to yours. This is all I can do in the moment—making sure that your wounds are tended to."

I send him away, telling him he is no longer my servant. He isn't. Neither am I his. I don't know what we are.

When I wake, I throw myself into business. A steady trickle of people come and go from the room

I've commandeered for myself. Yosua is not one of them.

Hakim reports, telling me all he has done—the confinement of the soldiers to the barracks, the clearing out of the dungeons, releasing both Bayangan and Mahan prisoners. He's also set what Mahan soldiers he has to patrol the city, both to keep an eye out and to keep the peace. He is capable, and I will ask Ayah—no, *I* will reward him.

"Tuanku," he says, pausing a little.

"Yes?"

"I wish to send out two crews today. One to search the port and the inlet, to find if there are any ships to be salvaged. If we can salvage any, we can send messengers to Maha for assistance."

"Yes, yes. Do that." I tell him of what I'd seen in the port as well as the destruction of the boats the Impianans had left for us.

"We'll do what we can." He lists some names, saying that they are skilled woodworkers.

I agree, then ask, "And the second crew?"

He shifts uncomfortably. "We need to clear the rubble of the Court House. The bodies—"

"I will come with you." They will dig up Ayahanda's body and I want to be there when they do. I need to be there.

Hakim nods. "I will send someone for you when the crew is ready to go."

"Thanks, Hakim."

He bows and kisses my hand, steps three steps backwards and then leaves.

Garett comes in next, after a hesitant knock on the door. He comes in and falls to his knees like a supplicant. "Ampun, Tuanku."

"Garett, please." I rush to him and pull him to his feet. "You've known me since I was a baby. Don't."

"Things change," he says. "I didn't want to presume."

"How can I help you?"

He tells me what he's done. He's talked to the soldiers, wrested from them their loyalty and their word. He's spoken to the nobles and the merchants alike, those who know him, those he remembers.

"They won't oppose you," he says. "You don't need to keep them locked up."

"I'm not—" I start, before remembering that Hakim has posted guards on the doors of the barracks. "I'll tell Hakim to let them return to their homes. Unarmed."

Garett nods. "And the others?"

"They're free to leave. Or to stay. Whichever they prefer. Don't they normally keep residence in the castle?" Another detail I should already know after being here for months. I am not ready for this. Why couldn't Ayahanda have survived?

"They are uncomfortable staying here in the castle. But they are also afraid they will be attacked if they leave for their homes in the city or their estates."

I shrug. "Hakim has ordered the men to keep the peace. If they do not provoke a fight, neither will we."

"I will tell them that." He clears his throat. "Tuanku, I don't know if this is the best time to bring it up, but…"

Garett trails off for so long that I have to look at him. I don't realise until I do that I've been avoiding his gaze all this time. He looks slightly embarrassed, looking away.

"What is it?"

"We won't be returning to Maha when you go. Marla and I have decided to stay. Bayangan is our home and…well, it's good to be home."

"Oh." Why had I expected Garett to return with me when I all but commanded Yosua to stay? I didn't even ask Yosua if he wanted to stay, despite the fact that he'd once sworn to return with me to Maha.

"I thought I should tell you first so that you can prepare. When you return, you'll need to appoint a new Majlis. Be careful whom you choose."

Of course. There are none left in Ayahanda's Majlis who are alive, none who can guide me. A new beginning. A fresh start. Garett will not be there to advise me. Neither will Yos. I will be all alone.

I will be with you. I am always with you.

There is that. "Thank you, Garett. You have done so much for Ayahanda and me. More than you needed. More than we can ever thank you for." I clasp his hand.

"It is an honour. Should you need anything, do not hesitate to ask. I will do all I can to assist you while you are here."

A knock on the door interrupts us.

"Yes?" I call.

It opens and one of Hakim's men salutes. "Tuanku, the crew will be heading out to the Court House now. Will you be accompanying us?"

I nod at him. "Give me a moment. I will meet you at the gates."

The man salutes again and withdraws.

"Come with me?" I ask Garett. "We're dealing with the bodies. And Ayahanda's…"

He comes with me. The walk into the city is solemn. The crew talk amongst themselves, but Garett and I keep to ourselves. Once there, the men set to work moving the heavy stones whilst the women deal with the bodies. The Bayangan dead are piled to one side to be claimed by their kin. Gradually, the Bayangans come to join us as we work, claiming their dead.

There's a short discussion amongst the crew. No one knows what to do with the bodies. Some want to bury them, to hold a funeral, some want to hold on and to bring the bodies home to Maha for burial. Who knows if they still have kin living at home? They come to me for a decision. I tell them to ask the nearest kin they can find to decide. The unclaimed bodies will be buried here. We will hold vigil for them.

Ayahanda's body is brought to the castle, where it is cleaned and treated. I don't want him buried here in foreign soil. We keep his body in the cold rooms. It won't last long, not in this heat. We've temporarily stopped the decay, delayed it, but we need to bury him as soon as we can, before he starts to rot.

I sit by his body until evening, when we congregate in my room—Garett and Marla, Rahsia, Yosua, Hakim, Iskandar, and Ali. It feels a little like our former clandestine meetings in Garett's house. Sometimes I look around to see if Captain Karett will appear out of nowhere to reprimand me. He can't any longer. He's dead. I saw his corpse.

"The crew just sent word that they managed to find a few sampans that can be repaired, Tuanku," Hakim reports. "They'll start work tomorrow morning, but it may take a while to ensure they can carry passengers."

"So quick! But it takes nearly a day to get there. How did they send word so fast?"

Hakim smiles. "We used the horses in the stables, Tuanku."

"Ah. The sampans—how many people can they carry?" I ask. "Can all of us return?"

"They're small and unsafe. I'm not convinced they will be able to carry much weight, even after repairs." He does some mental calculations. "Not more than three per sampan. It would take a long time to get everyone home using those. I want to send some men over, see if we can commandeer ships from the Mahan port. Bring a paderi back so we can finally communicate with Suci and Impian."

"Do it."

"I'll relay the message. If all goes well, they will return with the ships in two to three days."

"Fine." Is being in power like this? Discussing plans and hoping I'm not messing things up? Letting others make the plans and saying yes even if I don't know what I'm doing?

"What are your plans for Bayangan?" Garett asks.

I shrug. "I said that Yosua would take Layla's place, and I meant it. Unless, there's something in Bayangan's rules of succession that doesn't allow it? Or..." I hesitate, turning to Yosua, "unless you don't want to?"

"As you said, I am the Raja Muda of Bayangan. How can I leave?"

I cannot read his face or his voice. I know he's meant to be here, that this is *his* place. This is where he can make a difference, instead of returning to Maha with me and doing what—reducing himself to my servant again? I don't want that for him. I wouldn't wish that on anyone else. Whatever laws Ayahanda had written about the Bayangan servitude, I'm going to

312

remove them forever. No one should suffer the way they did. The way we did here.

"And what about Jeffett?" Garett asks. "He's going to return with the army. We need to prepare for that."

I'd forgotten about Jeffett. *How could I so quickly forget about the destruction of Suci? Will he return demanding vengeance again?* "How do you stand with Jeffett? Will he listen to you? Either of you?"

"I doubt he'll listen to me," Yosua says.

"He'll be difficult," Garett says. "We used to be friends, but since—we fell out when we met in Maha. He couldn't accept all the compromises I've made."

"I'll talk to him," Marla interjects. "I can deal with my brother."

Yosua clears his throat. "You said something about finding solution that fits both Terang and Bayangan. What do you mean by that? Are we now subject to Terang?"

"No. Other than maintaining cordial relations with Terang, Bayangan is wholly in your hands." *Bayangan is not mine. I don't wish to absorb it into Terang. I don't think they would wish for that either.*

And how can he truly be Sultan here, independent of you and Terang, if he is still sworn to your service?

"I release you from your vows, Yosua ayell Garett. Be free."

He raises his eyebrows in surprise.

"I thank you for your loyal service. You have been more than enough and I—and all of Maha—are indebted to you. But Bayangan needs you now, and you cannot serve her if you are bound to me."

He inclines his head.

"You asked about the rule of succession," Garett says. "Layla may have appointed Yosua as her Raja Muda, but there is a pool of eligible families that the Raja can be chosen from. They'll have to fulfil certain criteria to be considered for the post."

"So Yosua doesn't automatically succeed her?"

"No. With the trial, the Majlis DiRaja might not see him as a suitable replacement. Or the families might want to put forward their own candidates, ones they see as more Bayangan. We'll have to wait for their decision."

"What about Jeffett? Does he have any claim to the throne?" If they elect Jeffett, who's going to stop him from retaliating against us?

"Jeffett *is* from an eligible family. But if he had wanted to rule, he would have kept the throne instead of handing it over to Layla," Garett says after a long pause. "After all, he was regent for more than a decade until she came of age. I suspect he won't fight for it, unless the people push him. And…as I said, they don't want war any more than you do—which is what Jeffett would agitate for."

"What if they reject Yosua? Who else is eligible?"

Garett shakes his head. "I don't know. One of the Tuahs, maybe."

"What about you?"

"I've refused it before. And I'll refuse it again."

"But Ayahanda is no longer alive. You're free of your vows."

Garett hesitates. "I'm sure they'll agree that Yosua is the best candidate for the job. But if it comes to that…We'll see."

"I won't let it come to war," Yosua assures me.

A slight weight lifts off my shoulders. Maybe true peace is in our reach then, if Bayangan doesn't want war and neither do we. And if Yosua remains in charge, we will have a sympathetic ear.

Rahsia has been unusually quiet.

"Do you have anything to add, Rahsia?" I ask.

She shrugs with a smile. "My duty here is done. It ended when you killed Layla."

That, at least, is good news. I stifle a yawn, suddenly tired beyond belief. It has been a long day.

Marla looks at me curiously. "Tuanku, when was the last time you ate?"

I frown. Why does it matter? But now that she asks, I don't know. I don't recall. Yesterday? Or the day before.

She shakes her head. "This meeting is over. You cannot do anymore without proper nourishment and rest."

"But—"

"There's nothing more you can do now. Decisions can wait until tomorrow."

Wasn't that what I said yesterday?

She steers me out of the room and leads me to the kitchens. It feels like old times, sitting in the kitchen with Marla bustling about, bullying the staff good-naturedly for food. She tuts at their offerings and commandeers a stove. Yosua wanders over, sits beside me, saying nothing. Soon, Garett is there too. They hem me in. Hold me together.

The fragrance of the chickpea curry bubbling on the stove releases a bout of longing so strong that I cannot hold on any longer. It is home, family, love, the large dinners Ayahanda hosted, but also the tiny room in the servant's quarters that sheltered me as a child.

We have won the war, but I have lost my world. I have gained my Strength, but at the cost of my only family. I'm swarmed with so many decisions, so many lives in my hands, and I don't know what to do with it. Marla engulfs me in a hug, the way she did when Ibunda died. I am five again, hiding in her arms, because Ayahanda isn't there for me. Ayahanda isn't here any longer, will never be here for me again.

"Release, child," she says. "You need to grieve."

"I've grieved. Yesterday. Today. I sat by—"

She shushes me. "One day? You think that's enough?"

"There are things to do—"

"That can wait. No matter what you decide, nothing can happen until we make contact with Suci, or you find a way to cross the straits. Let it rest. Give yourself time and space. Once you return to Maha, you will no longer have time nor solitude enough to grieve."

Grief and sorrow overflow and I cannot stop the tears, cannot stop the weeping. My heart keeps breaking over and over again and Yosua jokes that I will be now known henceforth as Sultan Mikal, the Saltwater Sultan, Fountain of Tears. I want to laugh with him but my mouth won't cooperate, my lungs won't issue that breath.

I am broken. I keep breaking.

Marla holds me until there are no more tears, until I pull myself together. I wash my face, the cold water soothing my frayed edges. The curry has gone cold, the roti hardened. But it is the best thing I have eaten in months. I'm suddenly hungry again, the stone that sat in my stomach washed out with the tears and I can now eat. We sit there until late, all the other servants leaving once their chores are completed. We don't speak much. I cannot find any words to say.

Life, apparently, continues on quietly.

CHAPTER 31

The heartache doesn't go away, but with a full night's sleep and a belly full of food, I feel much better the next day. Marla makes sure that I have breakfast. With the morning also comes incredible news. A rider gallops up to the castle after I'm done eating and reports that a ship has arrived from Maha, bearing both soldiers and priests.

"Why are they here? How did they know to come?" I ask.

"They didn't say, Tuanku. I didn't have the chance to ask, either. I was told to report this to you as quickly as possible so I left while they were still disembarking."

"Thank you. This is great news."

"They must have felt the Strength returning," Garett muses.

"Shouldn't they have gone to defend Suci then?"

"Their loyalty is to Maha and the Sultan. They wouldn't go there without orders."

"As if Uskup Agung Ikhlas couldn't order them otherwise!" They shouldn't be here, but I am glad they

319

are. I ask Marla to check that there are enough rooms in the castle to house the newcomers.

"Don't worry about it," she says. "We'll get it all sorted."

That leaves me nothing to do except to pace and wait until they arrive. I end up sitting by Ayahanda's side until Hakim comes looking for me.

Uskup Daud waits for me in my room. He rises as I enter. His gaze flickers behind me for a moment as if looking for someone else, then he bows at the waist. "Tuanku."

"Uskup Daud." I hold out my hand and he steps forward to kiss it.

There's some shuffling around the room as I sit down and gesture for him to take a seat. Hakim and Garett array themselves behind me, standing as if they are either my advisors or my bodyguards, I cannot tell which. Yosua sits on my right.

"If I may ask as to the health of your father—"

"He's dead," I blurt, then wince at how rude it sounds.

"Ampun, Tuanku. My condolences. I assumed…"

"I'm sorry. I didn't mean to sound so rude. I'm still dealing with the loss."

"Did it happen in battle?"

"No. Before. He gave his life for Maha." It is all I can bear saying now. Later, maybe I'll be able to tell the full story, or one of the others will. Or I will write up an official announcement. Document it for history. "I didn't expect to see you here so soon. I thought we'd have to build a raft to get to Maha to fetch you here."

The uskup smiles at my attempt at levity. "Your people were doing a fine job patching up the boats on the beach when I arrived. Tuanku, the Amok Strength inexplicably returned to Maha yesterday morning. The people we had took the opportunity to defeat what remained of the Bayangan occupiers. We have reclaimed Maha as our own."

I nod. "What of Suci?"

Uskup Daud sighs heavily. "It was too late for us to send aid to Suci. The city was razed yesterday. There were few fatalities. Uskup Agung Ikhlas and Nek Ramalan managed to evacuate the people in time, but the Suci Temple records are in ruins. There was no point sending men there at this juncture as the Bayangan army has finished looting and is preparing to return. We decided that to come and assist you, as well as to defend you when the Bayangan army returns, would be our best course of action.

"I contacted Uskup Agung Ikhlas on the way here and he has been apprised of our actions."

"He agreed?" I wouldn't have expected him to, not the way he left us in the lurch when he heard the Bayangan army was heading his way.

Uskup Daud's lips quirk upwards. "He could not disagree when we were already on the ship. Furthermore, he has too much to do to deal with the needs of his own people than to worry about us. Impian is sending aid to them. Maha doesn't have much in the way of aid to send them. We have been receiving aid from Impian ourselves."

"Yes." I remember the depletion that faces Impian. They may not face actual war and bloodshed, but they will be impacted all the same. "This war has cost all of us too much."

"But it is over."

I think he means it as a statement, but the tail end of the sentence still raises itself like a question mark so I answer, "Yes, it is over."

I tell him of our plans, half-formed as they are. Yosua will act as our liaison, with Garett advising him until the Bayangans elect their own leader. Jeffett will hopefully be convinced to keep the peace. The rest of us will return to Maha as soon as we have enough ships to carry us and our dead.

Uskup Daud nods. "I will contact the paderi in Maha and ask them to send ships. They should be able to be at the port by tomorrow, if your people are ready to leave."

"Have we enough ships? Weren't all our ships destroyed or taken by Bayangan?"

Uskup Daud smiles. "Laksamana Rizal managed to escape with part of the fleet. He has been hard at work cutting down the Bayangan navy and reclaiming our ships these past few months."

"Tok Rizal is alive?"

He confirms it with a nod. I can scarcely believe it. I'd been so sure that everyone was dead.

"How is Maha? Did many survive…?" Maybe if Tok Rizal lives, so do others.

The uskup is more hesitant with his reply. "Thousands were slaughtered by the Bayangans, but many more managed to flee the city. Our refugees are still scattered, either in Suci or Impian, but they have slowly been returning to Maha. More might return now after the sacking of Suci."

I'd been afraid that all we had left was the mere hundreds here in Bayangan. We will be able to rebuild then. All is not lost.

Sanctify yourself, Mikal of Maha. O firstborn of Terang, you must consecrate yourself. The Covenant of Salt must be pledged anew. Return and perform your penance before Me that Terang might be fully restored.

I sit with my head bowed. I'm still not used to that voice in my head, not sure how I should respond, if I should tell Uskup Daud about it, if people notice when Kudus speaks to me. But Uskup Daud should know this—the prophecy he'd given me had mentioned the Covenant.

"Tuanku?" he asks.

"We have many arrangements to make, Uskup. For the ships to take us back, for Ayahanda's burial, the selection of a new Majlis," I say. "And the Covenant. But for now, you must be tired after your long journey. Come, let us sup together."

❣

It takes us two days to organise the people, to arrange the horses and the wagons, to ensure no one is left behind, none forgotten. Last night, we buried the unclaimed bodies of our fallen countrymen in an empty field that Yosua granted to us. Uskup Daud performed the rites and spoke the prayers over them.

Now, standing by the ships, I realise there is much more I would like to say to Yos, to find some sort of closure between us. A distance has been growing between us, one I don't know how to broach, not when I don't quite know what I am to him or who he's supposed to be to me. Maybe it's not quite important. There is one thing though…

"The other day…the Strength…"

He looks at me sharply. I don't know how to complete my question. I just remember my surprise at tracing the lines of power and finding one leading back to him.

"I felt it," he says quietly.

"How?" I muse. "The Temple has always said it is a birthright of Maha."

"And I am Bayangan, so how can it be?" There's a faint tinge of familiar hurt in his voice.

"You've always said you were more Mahan than Bayangan," I remind him. "You were born there, after all. Grew up there. Maybe that's it."

"I know, but I've been told all my life that all I can be is Bayangan because of my blood. No Mahan would accept me as one of them. Maybe now I'll be able to find out the truth. Discover who I'm supposed to be. Maybe one day..." he says, fingers twisting the hem of his shirt. He stares up at the mast of the ship. "When I've discovered—when I truly know who I am, maybe then I will return to Maha."

"I would like that. That you'd come."

We stand in silence, watching as the ships are being loaded. The sailors call amongst themselves as they prepare to sail. Time is running out.

"Yosua," I say, just as he blurts, "Mikal."

He gestures for me to continue.

"I'm sorry for how I've treated you all this time. You've been a friend—more than a friend, a brother— yet for most of my life I've treated you callously, as if you were just a servant. Like you were my slave. I'm sorry. I know just saying sorry doesn't change anything. It doesn't make things right, but...it still needs to be said. You've given up so much for me and I don't know how I can ever repay you."

"I don't know that it needs repaying," he says. "I've treated you badly too."

"But you only did it to keep me safe."

"I know. This is why I can't return with you."

I nod. "I hope you discover who you need to be."

Uskup Daud and Hakim call for me. We need to leave with the tide. Yosua holds out his hand and I clasp it in mine. And then I lift it to my lips and kiss the back of it.

"You'll make a great Raja of Bayangan yet," I whisper.

He gawks at me, mouth ajar as I step backwards, bow, and board the ship. He's still standing there, his parents flanking him, as we sail away.

I stand at the stern of the ship, watching until he is nothing but a speck.

CHAPTER 32

I stand at the edge of my city, weeping over the devastation Layla has caused. As she promised, almost everything has been razed to the ground, including the palace. Haphazard shelters have been raised by the returning refugees, much like the mad, disorganised patchwork of houses on the outskirts of Bayangan. Restoration work has begun under Uskup Daud with aid sent from Impian.

Today, we bury my father. I have prepared a speech, but I don't know if I can go through with it. There is too much to say about the man I called Ayahanda and others called Sultan. Did I know him well enough? No. I doubt anyone can know another completely. I regret the time we wasted pulling apart instead of together as a family. I wish, more than once, that Yosua were here to talk me through this. I hope he is doing well.

I've started wrapping my hair in a turban, no longer to be seen by others. I am no longer a boy, though I am only sixteen. We never celebrated my sixteenth birthday. It had slipped my mind while we were in Bayangan. It doesn't matter. I have many more birthdays to celebrate, I hope.

Today, I forgo the yellow of the royal family for the white of mourning. The Temple is stuffed full of people when I arrive for the funeral service. There are more than used to attend the weekly Jemaah, even though our population has been decimated. Tragedy brings us together in faith, I suppose. They want a final look at their late leader. I wish Garett could be here to say goodbye to the man he served so faithfully. He's said his goodbyes in Bayangan, so that must be enough.

Uskup Daud leads the ceremony, committing Ayahanda's spirit unto Kudus. He glosses over Ayahanda's faithlessness, emphasising instead the good things he once did for Maha. I am grateful. I need that reminder too. He calls upon me to say my eulogy.

I take a deep breath and walk up to the lectern. The last time I was in here, I had a deep sense of unease, Layla's presence a taint to the proceedings. Now, even in the midst of sorrow, I feel peace. Peace and sorrow. Maybe Kudus grieves with us too.

"My people, we gather here today to say the last rites over our late Sultan Simson, my dear Ayahanda. The events of the past few months have been tragic. Our city has been destroyed and our faith shaken to its core, but Kudus himself has brought us through it.

"Uskup Daud has said many kind and gracious words about Ayahanda, but I would be one of the first to admit that our downfall was due to Ayahanda's disobedience and lack of faith. For that, we beg your forgiveness. It is the sultan's duty to protect this city and this sultanate, and it was our failures as a family that have brought us to this state.

"Yet, in the end, Ayahanda found his faith again. In the darkest moment of my life, Ayahanda shared with me his struggles as I shared mine with him. And it was at that moment that both of us found renewed faith and strength in Kudus. It was Ayahanda, in obedience to the prophecy, who invoked the Strength and pulled down the Bayangan Court House on himself and all the ruling class within it. With his death, the Amok Strength came to me and we were able to defeat Permaisuri Layla in her own land.

"As he found his purpose and faith in his final moments of life, he also issued his final wishes to me. *Sultan Mikal, keep the faith.*"

I have to stop to compose myself, to push down the emotions that are threatening to overwhelm me. I clear my throat and press on, fixing my eyes on Uskup Daud's encouraging face.

"I have avenged Maha by defeating Layla in combat. We have set ourselves free and that is enough. Bayangan is gutted by the deaths of her leaders, by the depletion of their resources for the war Layla started. The cycle of revenge ends now. I promise you that.

"Ayahanda was a man—fallible and broken. He failed us in life but he also saved us in death. He knew what he was doing; that to save me, to save us, and to redeem himself he would have to die. He didn't flinch from his duty in death, even though he once abandoned it in life. There is nothing more I can say except that we have to accept him as he was and honour his last deed."

The Temple is silent. I look down on their bowed heads. I do not know what they think. I do not think I care. I have said what I can to honour Ayahanda.

I step forward to the raised platform where his body lies in his coffin, ready for the final burial. The thick perfume the priests have sprayed on him barely masks the stench of rot. Only the slot above his face remains clear, covered by a thin sheet of glass. I take a last look, lay a flower on the smooth wood and say a prayer. Then I walk away.

One by one, each noble and citizen follows in my footsteps, laying flowers on his coffin. As they leave, they mutter words of condolences, some with a hug, some with an awkward pat on the shoulder. I just receive it all with a grave face and a short nod. I am all cried out and there is decorum to be observed.

I stand there until my legs ache and my face and neck hurt. Then we follow the coffin out. I watch as it is lowered into the ground. Uskup Daud says more words, utters more prayers. More flowers are thrown into the gaping hole. And then they fill the hole with soil. I watch until there is nothing left to watch, until even the gravediggers have finished their work and the brown soil is flat and neat, the gravestone erect at its head.

Then I go back alone to the house I have borrowed until the palace is rebuilt.

CB

I'm tired of waiting.

Time moves too slowly and I am ever restless. I give up pacing and fall into the forms, letting the familiarity take over, letting my body move to the rhythms. I don't invoke the Strength. I have no need to. I lose myself to memories of Tok Yaakub berating me, Ayahanda looking on with an expression that is both proud and yet disappointed, Yosua hovering nearby in case I need something.

There's a soft knock and someone enters the room, but I ignore their presence. They aren't a threat.

"Tuanku?"

A boy stands by the door, watching me warily.

"Ah, it's time?" I drop my hands, straighten my back. Readjust my clothes.

"Yes, Tuanku. All is ready. They're waiting for you."

A quick check in the mirror shows that I look presentable—at least I think I do. Yosua would probably not agree. I follow the boy down the rebuilt corridors of the Mahan palace. Everything smells of new wood, new paint.

New beginnings. Garett has sent word that the Bayangans have elected him Regent, with Yosua as the Raja Muda until he comes of age next year. A training period of sorts. Jeffett has agreed to peace. He has retired to his house in the country, grieving the loss of Layla, who was a daughter to him. I wish them the best. Soon, we will sign a peace treaty.

But first, I must be crowned. There will be no regent to hold the throne until I am "old" enough—I have come into the Amok Strength and that is enough in Terang to prove my manhood and my eligibility to rule. The one thing I have chased for so long is finally in my grasp—and now I wish I could give it back to have Ayahanda alive with me again. Funny how your dreams can come true and you find that they weren't what you truly wanted.

Today, I will stand before Kudus and all of Terang, pledging my life to them. Uskup Agung Ikhlas, Nek Ramalan, and Tun Nadir themselves will be present. They travelled all the way from Suci and Impian, arriving just yesterday. The ceremony will be broadcast to the citizens in Suci and Impian by the paderi. I don't know if I am ready for this, but I have to be.

It is the Uskup Agung himself who performs the ceremony. I kneel before him as they place the crown on my head. The crown is heavier than expected, a weight I never thought I would bear this young. Ayahanda was supposed to live for many years more, until I'd had my fill of life and was ready to settle down.

I repeat the pledges, each promise sinking down like a weight on my soul.

I cannot do this!

You will, by My grace.

I am not enough for this.

No, you are not, but I will make you enough.

I stare into Uskup Agung Ikhlas' warm brown eyes as he touches my shoulders and guides me to my feet.

"Kudus is with you," he says. "Do not fear."

That I know. The peace settling in my heart is proof enough.

Uskup Agung Ikhlas anoints me with holy oil. It's heavy, a thick warmth on my face, the fragrance overwhelming in my nostrils. It burns on my skin, sanctifying me.

O Kudus, Maha Esa, help me. I am all alone. I don't have the wisdom nor the strength.

You are never alone, child. Lean on Me, rely on My strength.

I pray the only prayer I can say: *O Kudus, Maha Esa, berkatilah hamba-Mu dengan kuasa ajaib-Mu.*

The weight lifts. This burden is not mine to carry, nor mine to labour beneath. This nation, this sultanate, is not mine to protect nor to lord over. It is Kudus' and all I do is stand here as His representative, as His human face, as His hands and feet to fulfil His decrees. He is the one who holds its future, the one who gives it direction. He is the one who shoulders the weight of the promises I have made, the one who gives me strength in times of need.

There is much to do in the future to rebuild Terang. I have not forgotten His command, but for now He holds me safe here.

I don't have to go it alone.

"Behold Sultan Mikal ayell Simson, ruler over Maha, Sultan of all Terang," Uskup Agung Ikhlas announces.

Saltwater Sultan, Fountain of Tears, Yosua's teasing words come back to me and I smile. Then I take a deep, calming breath, and turn to face my people.

GLOSSARY

Adat – Customs/culture.

Ampun – Forgive (me).

Ayah/Ayahanda – Father (Informal/court language).

Baginda Paduka – His/Her Majesty. Used to refer to the ruling monarch; gender neutral.

Baju – Set of clothes, usually official/formal.

Baju kebaya – A traditional women's dress consisting of a fitted top and an ankle-length sarong.

Bendahara – Vizier, advisor to the Sultan.

Che – A title of the nobility, similar to Lord/Lady; gender neutral.

Diaken – An acolyte or assistant in the Temple.

Firman – Holy Scriptures.

Gelanggang – Training court/field.

Ibu/Ibunda – Mother (Informal/court language).

Jemaah – Religious assembly, used here to refer to both the worship service as well as the day it service is held.

Jubah paderi – Long robes, normally worn by the priesthood; an alb.

Justice – Members of the judiciary in Impian, akin to judges.

Keris – An asymmetrical dagger, usually with a wavy two-edged blade from the Malay Archipelago.

Kompang – A traditional handheld drum made of goatskin stretched over a round wooden base.

Kudus – The God of Terang.

Kuih – Bite-sized snacks or desserts that include cakes and pastries. Can be sweet or savoury.

Laksamana – Navy Chief.

Majlis – Council.

Nek – Short for Grandmother, used as a term of respect for older women.

Paderi – An ordained priest in the Temple.

Parang – A machete used across the Malay Archipelago.

Penghulu Bendahari – State Treasurer or Finance Minister.

Permaisuri – Queen.

Putera – Prince.

Raja – King (used in Bayangan).

Raja Muda – Crown Prince.

Sampan – A small wooden boat.

Samping – A type of sarong wrapped around the waist worn by men over their trousers that reaches to their knees.

Sayang – Dear/love (endearment).

Secretkeeper – The Head of the Justices, overseeing the whole judiciary system. They often have other special gifts or extraordinarily strong Mind-reading Gifts. The Secretkeeper also holds all the memories of her predecessors, in an unbroken line to the founding of Terang.

Seruling – A flute-like instrument.

Shahbandar – District Head.

Silat – A class of traditional martial arts from Southeast Asia.

Sultan –King (used in Terang); often has religious overtones.

Temenggung – Chief of Security or Army Chief.

Tempurung – Coconut husk or shell.

Tengku – Term of address for royal family-adjacent or highly honoured noble; gender neutral.

Tok – Short for Grandfather, also used as a term of respect for older men.

Tuan/Mem – Master/Mistress; also generally used as Sir/Madam.

Tuanku – Your Majesty/Your Highness. Term of address for members of the royal family; gender neutral.

Tun – An honorific, in this case used by the rulers of the city-states of Terang, including members of the Majlis in Maha.

Uskup – The head of the particular temple, a higher rank of ordained priest.

Uskup Agung – Head of religion, similar to an Archbishop.

O Kudus, Maha Esa, berkatilah hamba-Mu dengan kuasa ajaib-Mu – O God Almighty, grant Your servant Your miraculous strength.

ABOUT TERANG

Terang consists of three city-states who worship Kudus. Their rulers form the Triumvirate, which ultimately oversees the government of Terang according to the giftings of the city.

Maha – The first city-state of Terang, Maha is the seat of power where the Sultan resides. The gift of Maha is the Amok Strength, which flows from the Sultan to the members of the military. The Sultan is assisted by the Majlis Maha, which is a council of seven advisors.

Suci – Suci, also called the Holy City, is the second city-state of Terang and the seat of religion where the main Temple is located. The gift of Suci is the Perantaraan Gift that allows them to communicate via mirrors. Suci is ruled by the Uskup Agung.

Impian – The third city-state of Terang, Impian oversees the judiciary. The gift of Impian is that of Mind-reading, manifested in the women. Members of the judiciary are called Justices. They are led by the Secretkeeper, who holds the memories of all the women who held the post before her. Because of this, the identity of the Secretkeeper is held in strict confidentiality and a separate figurehead is appointed as the known ruler of Impian.

ABOUT BAYANGAN

Bayangan is located across the Mahan straits and is said to have been formed by rebels who seceded from the Terang Sultanate due to differences in belief.

The rulers of Bayangan have maintained its animosity and enmity over the years, leading to frequent wars between the two kingdoms.

ACKNOWLEDGEMENTS

Amok (or *The Weight of Strength*, as it was called then) was mostly written in London as part of my dissertation for my MA in *Creative Writing: The Novel* at Brunel University London, which means credit goes to Chevening—the *Foreign, Commonwealth and Development Office* (FCDO)—for making sure I didn't go hungry while writing; the many Malaysian Chevenors who made the journey enjoyable; and my supervisor, Dr Benjamin Zephaniah, who was super supportive and wrote many kind words about the first 15 chapters that he read.

NaNoWriMo has always been a huge part of my writing journey, and this is no different for *Amok*. This project began as a NaNoWriMo draft, cheered on by the *West London Writers*. Major portions of my early drafts were written during various write-ins at Café Nero, Harris & Hoole, Tea Darling, and the Uxbridge Library.

One of the reasons why this story exists is the Realm Makers community, who showed me what's possible in speculative fiction and faith-based fantasy.

The Iron Sharpeners critique group read early chapters through changing POVs and asked many questions. I also connected to my editor through the Realm Makers Consortium—Nadine Brandes gave me very insightful editorial feedback and made this book so much better!

I also had a group of awesome beta readers from all over the world who gave me many things to think about and helped shape this novel: Rae Graham, Gina Yap Lai Yoong, CS Wachter, Lauren Salisbury, Shona Levingston, Chew Yuin-Y, Sue Wong, Wendrie Heywood, Hamizah Adzmi, and Cathrine Bonham.

Parental support has also been crucial, without which I would still be in accounting. The ability to write and publish—whether traditionally or through independent means—is definitely one of privilege. To my parents, Albert Tan & Meng Eng: thank you for helping me make this work. Also to my siblings Deborah & David: thanks for your encouragement.

I cannot NOT mention the fact that this book has been made possible by copious amounts of tea and Nando's…but most of all, this book would not exist without God.

ABOUT THE AUTHOR

Anna Tan grew up in Malaysia, the country that is not Singapore. She is interested in Malay/Nusantara and Chinese legends and folklore in exploring the intersection of language, culture, and faith.

Anna has an MA in Creative Writing: The Novel under a Chevening scholarship & is the President of the Malaysian Writers Society. She can be found tweeting as @natzers and forgetting to update annatsp.com.

OTHER WORKS

Under Teaspoon Publishing:
Coexist
Dongeng
The Painted Hall Collection

Under MYWriters Penang (editor)
Nutmag Volume 1
Nutmag 2: Coffee or Tea?
Nutmag 3: Island Living
NutMag 4: Transitions
Home Groan: A NutMag Anthology

Anthologies edited by Anna:
Love in Penang (Fixi Novo; 2013)
Emerging Malaysian Writers 2018 (Malaysian Writers
    Society; 2018)

Short stories:
"Codes." Cyberpunk: Malaysia (Fixi Novo; 2015)
"Jentayu's Tear." Insignia Volume 4: Asian Fantasy Stories
    (BWWP Publishing; 2017)
"The Longest Mile." With Our Eyes Open (Bausse Books;
    2017)
"Beautiful Hands." Bitter Root Sweet Fruit (Word Works;
    2017)
"Operation: Rescue Pris." The Principal Girl
    (Gerakbudaya; 2019)
"Takpe." A Kind of Death (Uncommon Universes Press;
    2019)
"Batteries." 2020: An Anthology (Fixi Novo; 2020)

Lightning Source UK Ltd.
Milton Keynes UK
UKHW021834100621
385302UK00005B/201